THE GATECRASHER

MADELEINE WICKHAM

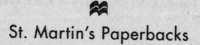

St. Martin's Paperbacks

FOR *F*REDDY

Previously published in Great Britain by Black Swan, a division of Transworld Publishers.

THE GATECRASHER

ISBN: 0-312-97864-2

Printed in the United States of America

St. Martin's Press hardcover edition / April 2000
St. Martin's Paperbacks edition / April 2001

St. Martin's Paperbacks are published by St. Martin's Press, 175 Fifth Avenue, New York, NY 10010.

10 9 8 7 6 5 4 3 2 1

Rosamunde Pilcher's Introduction to
The Gatecrasher

It is always an unexpected pleasure to be able to recommend a novel in which the heroine is experienced, beautiful and totally unscrupulous. Apart from her looks, Fleur Daxeny seems to have nothing to commend her, and yet her story holds from the start, and by the end the reader is strongly on her side.

Perhaps this is because only Richard Favour, the mega-rich widower who is Fleur's latest victim, is truly likeable. The rest of his family all have their problems and hang-ups which they take out on each other. Philippa, his plain daughter, cruelly ignored by her husband Lambert, and living in a fantasy world of romantic fiction. Lambert, whose only thought is how much money he can lay his greedy hands on. And Gillian, the homely sister-in-law, who housekeeps for Richard, unappreciated, and riddled with resentment because she has never been able to escape.

But perhaps the most manipulative of all is the late Emily Favour, a woman so cold that when she dies, Richard is painfully aware that he never truly knew her, and here lies his grief. Fleur, gatecrashing her funeral, is the charmer he has always yearned for, and the woman who brings colour and laughter back into his life.

The venue of this story is in itself something of a black joke. The Golf Club community, housed in some comfort around the fairways, and with cocktail talk concentrated on who will win the annual Ladies' Foursome, or how many strokes were taken at the fifteenth hole.

Fleur becomes embroiled in this scenario, with the intention of fleecing Richard for all she can, and then moving on, as is her custom. But events take an unexpected turn, and as she finds herself involved in Richard's family, she begins to fall in love with him.

Madeleine Wickham writes with a funny, acid pen, revealing human weaknesses, and yet, at the end of the day, treating them with a certain dry compassion. A great achievement.

Rosamunde Pilcher

Chapter One

Fleur Daxeny wrinkled her nose. She bit her lip, and put her head on one side, and gazed at her reflection silently for a few seconds. Then she gave a gurgle of laughter.

'I still can't decide,' she exclaimed. 'They're all fabulous.'

The saleswoman from Take Hat! exchanged weary glances with the nervous young hairdresser sitting on a gilt stool in the corner. The hairdresser had arrived at Fleur's hotel suite half an hour ago and had been waiting to start ever since. The saleswoman was meanwhile beginning to wonder whether she was wasting her time completely.

'I love this one with the veil,' said Fleur suddenly, reaching for a tiny creation of black satin and wispy netting. 'Isn't it elegant?'

'Very elegant,' said the saleswoman. She hurried forward just in time to catch a black silk topper which Fleur was discarding onto the floor.

'Very,' echoed the hairdresser in the corner. Surreptitiously he glanced at his watch. He was supposed to be back down in the salon in forty minutes. Trevor wouldn't be pleased. Perhaps he should phone down to explain the situation. Perhaps . . .

'All right!' said Fleur. 'I've decided.' She pushed up the veil and beamed around the room. 'I'm going to wear this one today.'

'A very wise choice, madam,' said the saleswoman in relieved tones. 'It's a lovely hat.'

'Lovely,' whispered the hairdresser.

'So if you could just pack the other five into boxes for me . . .' Fleur smiled mysteriously at her reflection and pulled the dark silk gauze down over her face again. The woman from Take Hat! gaped at her.

'You're going to buy them all?'

'Of course I am. I simply can't choose between them. They're all too perfect.' Fleur turned to the hairdresser. 'Now, my sweet. Can you come up with something special for my hair which will go under this hat?' The young man stared back at her and felt a dark pink colour begin to rise up his neck.

'Oh. Yes. I should think so. I mean . . .' But Fleur had already turned away.

'If you could just put it all onto my hotel bill,' she was saying to the saleswoman. 'That's all right, isn't it?'

'Perfectly all right, madam,' said the saleswoman eagerly. 'As a guest of the hotel, you're entitled to a fifteen per cent concession on all our prices.'

'Whatever,' said Fleur. She gave a little yawn. 'As long as it can all go on the bill.'

'I'll go and sort it out for you straight away.'

'Good,' said Fleur. As the saleswoman hurried out of the room, she turned and gave the young hairdresser a ravishing smile. 'I'm all yours.'

Her voice was low and melodious and curiously accentless. To the hairdresser's ears it was now also faintly mocking, and he flushed slightly as he came over to where Fleur was sitting. He stood behind her, gathered together the ends of her hair in one hand and let them fall down in a heavy, red-gold movement.

8

'Your hair's in very good condition,' he said awkwardly.

'Isn't it lovely?' said Fleur complacently. 'I've always had good hair. And good skin, of course.' She tilted her head, pushed her hotel robe aside slightly, and rubbed her cheek tenderly against the pale, creamy skin of her shoulder. 'How old would you say I was?' she added abruptly.

'I don't . . . I wouldn't . . .' the young man began to flounder.

'I'm forty,' she said lazily. She closed her eyes. 'Forty,' she repeated, as though meditating. 'It makes you think, doesn't it?'

'You don't look . . .' began the hairdresser in awkward politeness. Fleur opened one glinting, pussy-cat-green eye.

'I don't look forty? How old do I look, then?'

The hairdresser stared back at her uncomfortably. He opened his mouth to speak, then closed it again. The truth was, he thought suddenly, that this incredible woman didn't look any age. She seemed ageless, classless, indefinable. As he met her eyes he felt a thrill run through him; a dart-like conviction that this moment was somehow significant. His hands trembling slightly, he reached for her hair and let it run like slippery flames through his fingers.

'You look as old as you look,' he whispered huskily. 'Numbers don't come into it.'

'Sweet,' said Fleur dismissively. 'Now, my pet, before you start on my hair, how about ordering me a nice glass of champagne?'

The hairdresser's fingers drooped in slight disappointment, and he went obediently over to the telephone. As he dialled, the door opened and the woman from Take Hat! came back in, carrying a pile of hat boxes. 'Here we are,' she exclaimed breathlessly. 'If you could just sign here . . .'

'A glass of champagne, please,' the hairdresser was saying. 'Room 301.'

'I was wondering,' began the saleswoman cautiously to Fleur. 'You're quite sure that you want all six hats in black? We do have some other super colours this season.' She tapped her teeth thoughtfully. 'There's a lovely emerald green which would look stunning with your hair . . .'

'Black,' said Fleur decisively. 'I'm only interested in black.'

An hour later, Fleur looked at herself in the mirror, smiled and nodded. She was dressed in a simple black suit which had been cut to fit her figure precisely. Her legs shimmered in sheer black stockings; her feet were unobtrusive in discreet black shoes. Her hair had been smoothed into an exemplary chignon, on which the little black hat sat to perfection.

The only hint of brightness about her figure was a glimpse of salmon-pink silk underneath her jacket. It was Fleur's rule always to wear some colour no matter how sombre the outfit or the occasion. In a crowd of dispirited black suits, a tiny splash of salmon-pink would draw the eye unconsciously towards her. People would notice her but wouldn't be quite sure why. Which was just as she liked it.

Still watching her reflection, Fleur pulled the gauzy veil down over her face. The smug expression disappeared from her face, to be replaced by one of grave, inscrutable sadness. For a few moments she stared silently at herself. She picked up her black leather Osprey bag and held it soberly by her side. She nodded slowly a few times, noticing how the veil cast hazy, mysterious shadows over her pale face.

Then, suddenly, the telephone rang, and she sprang back into life.

'Hello?'

'Fleur, where have you been? I have tried to call you.' The heavy Greek voice was unmistakable. A frown of irritation creased Fleur's face.

'Sakis! Sweetheart, I'm in a bit of a hurry . . .'

'Where are you going?'

'Nowhere. Just shopping.'

'Why do you need to shop? I bought you clothes in Paris.'

'I know you did, darling. But I wanted to surprise you with something new for this evening.' Her voice rippled with convincing affection down the phone. 'Something elegant, sexy . . .' As she spoke, she had a sudden inspiration. 'And you know, Sakis,' she added carefully, 'I was wondering whether it wouldn't be a good idea to pay in cash, so that I get a good price. I can draw money out from the hotel, can't I? On your account?'

'A certain amount. Up to ten thousand pounds, I think.'

'I won't need *nearly* that much!' Her voice bubbled over with amusement. 'I only want one outfit! Five hundred maximum.'

'And when you have bought it you will return straight to the hotel.'

'Of course, sweetheart.'

'There is no of course. This time, Fleur, you must not be late. Do you understand? You-must-not-be-late.' The words were barked out like a military order and Fleur flinched silently in annoyance. 'It is quite clear. Leonidas will pick you up at three o'clock. The helicopter will leave at four o'clock. Our guests will arrive at seven o'clock. You must be ready to greet them. I do not want you to be late like last time. It was . . . it was unseemly. Are you listening? Fleur?'

'Of course I'm listening!' said Fleur. 'But there's someone knocking at the door. I'll just go and see who it is . . .' She waited a couple of seconds, then firmly replaced the receiver. A moment later, she picked it up again.

'Hello? Could you send someone up for my luggage, please?'

Downstairs, the hotel lobby was calm and tranquil. The woman from Take Hat! saw Fleur walking past the boutique, and gave a little wave, but Fleur ignored her.

'I'd like to check out,' she said, as soon as she got to the reception desk. 'And to make a withdrawal of money. The account is in the name of Sakis Papandreous.'

'Ah, yes.' The smooth, blond-haired receptionist tapped briefly at her computer, then looked up and smiled at her. 'How much money would you like?' Fleur beamed back at her.

'Ten thousand pounds. And could you order me two taxis?' The woman looked up in surprise.

'Two?'

'One for me, one for my luggage. My luggage is going to Chelsea.' Fleur lowered her eyes beneath her gauzy veil. 'I'm going to a memorial service.'

'Oh dear, I am sorry,' said the woman, handing Fleur several pages of hotel bill. 'Someone close to you?'

'Not yet,' said Fleur, signing the bill without bothering to check it. She watched as the cashier counted thick wads of money into two crested envelopes, then tenderly took them both, placed them in her Osprey bag and snapped it shut. 'But you never know.'

* * *

Richard Favour sat in the front pew of St Anselm's Church with his eyes closed, listening to the sounds of people filling the church – muted whisperings and shufflings, the tapping of heels on the tiled floor, and 'Jesu, Joy of Man's Desiring' being played softly on the organ.

He had always hated 'Jesu, Joy of Man's Desiring'; it had been the suggestion of the organist at their meeting three weeks previously, after it had become apparent that Richard could not name a single piece of organ music of which Emily had been particularly fond. There had been a slightly embarrassed silence as Richard vainly racked his brains, then the organist had tactfully murmured, '"Jesu, Joy of Man's Desiring" is always very popular . . .' and Richard had agreed in hasty relief.

Now he gave a dissatisfied frown. Surely he could have thought of something more personal than this turgid, over-popular tune? Emily had certainly been a music-lover, always going to concerts and recitals when her health allowed it. Had she never once turned to him, eyes alight, saying, 'I love this piece, don't you?' He screwed up his eyes and tried to remember. But the only vision that came to him was of Emily lying in bed, eyes dulled, wan and frail and uncomplaining. A spasm of guilty regret went through him. Why had he never asked his wife what her favourite piece of music was? In thirty-three years of marriage, he had never asked her. And now it was too late. Now he would never know.

He rubbed his forehead wearily, and looked down at the engraved order of service on his lap. The words stared back up at him. *Service of Memorial and Thanksgiving for the life of Emily Millicent Favour.* Simple black lettering, plain white card. He had

13

resisted all attempts by the printers to introduce such prized features as silver borders or embossed angels. Of that, he thought, Emily would have approved. At least . . . he hoped she would.

It had taken Richard several years of marriage to Emily to realize that he didn't know her very well, and several more for him to realize that he never would. At the beginning, her serene remoteness had been part of her appeal, along with her pale, pretty face and the neat, boyish figure which she kept as resolutely hidden as she did her innermost thoughts. The more she had kept herself hidden, the more tantalized Richard had become; he had approached their wedding day with a longing bordering on desperation. At last, he had thought, he and Emily would be able to reveal their secret selves to each other. He had yearned to explore not only her body but her mind, her person; to discover her most intimate fears and dreams; to become her lifelong soulmate.

They'd been married on a bright, blustery day, in a little village in Kent. Emily had looked composed and serene throughout; Richard had supposed she was simply better than him at concealing the nervous anticipation that surely burned as intensely within her as it did in him — an anticipation which had become stronger as the day was swallowed up and the beginning of their life together drew near.

Now he closed his eyes, and remembered those first, tingling seconds, as the door had shut behind the porter and he was alone with his wife for the first time in their Eastbourne hotel suite. He'd gazed at her as she took off her hat with the smooth, precise movements she always made, half-longing for her to throw the silly thing down and rush into his arms, and half-longing for this delicious, uncertain waiting to last for ever. It had seemed that Emily was deliberately delaying the moment of their coming together; teasing him with her cool, oblivious manner, as though she knew exactly what was going through his mind.

And then, finally, she'd turned, and met his eye. And he'd taken a breath, not knowing quite where to start; which of his pent-up thoughts to release first. And she'd looked straight at him with remote blue eyes and said, 'What time is dinner?'

Even then, he'd thought she was still teasing. He'd thought she was purposely prolonging the sense of anticipation, that she was deliberately stoppering up her emotions until they became too overwhelming to control, when they would flood out in a huge gush to meet and mix with his. And so, patiently, awed by her apparent self-control, he'd waited. Waited for the gush; the breaking of the waters; the tears and the surrender.

But it had never happened. Emily's love for him had never manifested itself in anything more than a slow drip-drip of fond affection; she'd responded to his every caress, his every confidence, with the same degree of lukewarm interest. When he tried to spark a more powerful reaction in her, he'd been met first by incomprehension, then, as he grew more strident, by an almost frightened resistance.

Eventually he'd given up trying. And gradually, almost without his realizing, his own love for her had begun to change in character. Over the years, his emotions had stopped pounding at the surface of his soul like a hot, wet tidal wave and had receded and solidified into something firm and dry and sensible. And Richard, too, had become firm and dry and sensible. He'd learned to keep his own counsel, to gather

15

his thoughts dispassionately and say only half of what he was really thinking. He'd learned to smile when he wanted to beam, to click his tongue when he wanted to scream in frustration; to restrain himself and his foolish thoughts as much as possible.

Now, waiting for her memorial service to begin, he blessed Emily for those lessons in self-restraint. Because if it hadn't been for his ability to keep himself in check, the hot, sentimental tears which bubbled at the back of his eyes would now have been coursing uncontrollably down his cheeks, and the hands which calmly held his order of service would have been clasped over his contorted face, and he would have been swept away by a desperate, immoderate grief.

The church was almost full when Fleur arrived. She stood at the back for a few moments, surveying the faces and clothes and voices in front of her; assessing the quality of the flower arrangements; checking the pews for anyone who might look up and recognize her.

But the people in front of her were an anonymous bunch. Men in dull suits; ladies in uninspired hats. A flicker of doubt crossed Fleur's mind. Could Johnny have got this one wrong? Was there really any money lurking in this colourless crowd?

'Would you like an order of service?' She looked up to see a long-legged man striding across the marble floor towards her. 'It's about to start,' he added with a frown.

'Of course,' murmured Fleur. She held out her pale, scented hand. 'Fleur Daxeny. I'm so glad to meet you . . . Sorry, I've forgotten your name . . .'

'Lambert.'

'Lambert. Of course. I remember now.' She paused,

16

and glanced up at his face, still wearing an arrogant frown. 'You're the clever one.'

'I suppose you could say that,' said Lambert, shrugging.

Clever or sexy, thought Fleur. All men want to be one or the other – or both. She looked at Lambert again. His features looked overblown and rubbery, so that even in repose he seemed to be pulling a face. Better just leave it at clever, she thought.

'Well, I'd better sit down,' she said. 'I expect I'll see you later.'

'There's plenty of room at the back,' Lambert called after her. But Fleur appeared not to hear him. Studying her order of service with an absorbed, solemn expression, she made her way quickly to the front of the church.

'I'm sorry,' she said, pausing by the third row from the front. 'Is there any room? It's a bit crowded at the back.'

She stood impassively while the ten people filling the row huffed and shuffled themselves along; then, with one elegant movement, took her place. She bowed her head for a moment, then looked up with a stern, brave expression.

'Poor Emily,' she said. 'Poor sweet Emily.'

'Who was that?' whispered Philippa Chester as her husband returned to his seat beside her.

'I don't know,' said Lambert. 'One of your mother's friends, I suppose. She seemed to know all about me.'

'I don't think I remember her,' said Philippa. 'What's her name?'

'Fleur. Fleur something.'

'Fleur. I've never heard of her.'

'Maybe they were at school together or something.'

'Oh yes,' said Philippa. 'That could be it. Like that other one. Joan. Do you remember? The one who came to visit out of the blue?'

'No,' said Lambert.

'Yes you do. *Joan.* She gave Mummy that hideous glass bowl.' Philippa squinted at Fleur again. 'Except this one looks too young. I like her hat. I wish I could wear little hats like that. But my head's too big. Or my hair isn't right. Or something.'

She tailed off. Lambert was staring down at a piece of paper and muttering. Philippa looked around the church again. So many people. All here for Mummy. It almost made her want to cry.

'Does my hat look all right?' she said suddenly.

'It looks great,' said Lambert without looking up.

'It cost a bomb. I couldn't believe how much it cost. But then, when I put it on this morning, I thought . . .'

'Philippa!' hissed Lambert. 'Can you shut up? I've got my reading to think about!'

'Oh yes. Yes, of course you have.'

Philippa looked down, chastened. And once again she felt a little pinprick of hurt. No-one had asked her to do a reading. Lambert was doing one, and so was her little brother Antony, but all she had to do was sit still in her hat. And she couldn't even do that very well.

'When I die,' she said suddenly, 'I want *everyone* to do a reading at my memorial service. You, and Antony, and Gillian, and all our children . . .'

'If we have any,' said Lambert, not looking up.

'If we have any,' echoed Philippa morosely. She looked around at the sea of black hats. 'I might die before we have any children, mightn't I? I mean, we don't know when we're going to die, do we? I could die

18

tomorrow.' She broke off, overcome by the thought of herself in a coffin, looking pale and waxy and romantic, surrounded by weeping mourners. Her eyes began to prickle. 'I could die tomorrow. And then it would be . . .'

'Shut up,' said Lambert, putting away his piece of paper. He stretched his hand down out of sight and casually pinched Philippa's fleshy calf. 'You're talking rubbish,' he murmured. 'What are you talking?'

Philippa was silent. Lambert's fingers gradually tightened on her skin, until suddenly they nipped so viciously that she gave a sharp intake of breath.

'I'm talking rubbish,' she said, in a quick, low voice.

'Good girl,' said Lambert. He released his fingers. 'Now, sit up straight and get a grip.'

'I'm sorry,' said Philippa breathlessly. 'It's just a bit . . . overwhelming. There are so many people here. I didn't know Mummy had all these friends.'

'Your mother was a very popular lady,' said Lambert. 'Everyone loved her.'

And no-one loves me, Philippa felt like saying. But instead, she prodded helplessly at her hat and tugged a few locks of wispy hair out from under the severe black brim, so that by the time she stood up for the first hymn, she looked even worse than before.

Chapter Two

'The day thou gavest, Lord, is ended,' sang Fleur. She
forced herself to look down at the hymn-book and pretend that she was reading the words. As though she
didn't know them off by heart; as though she hadn't
sung them at too many funerals and memorial services
to count. Why did people always choose the same
dreary hymns for funerals? she thought. Didn't they
appreciate how boring it made things for the regular
funeral gatecrasher?

The first funeral that Fleur had gatecrashed had been
by accident. Wandering down a little Kensington back
street one dull morning, wondering if she might be
able to get herself a job in an expensive art gallery, she
had seen an assembly of smart people milling on the
pavement outside a small but distinguished Catholic
church. With an aimless curiosity, she had slowed
down as she reached them; slowed down, and then
stopped. She had stood, not quite in the group but not
quite out of it, and listened as hard as she could to as
many conversations as possible. And gradually she'd
realized, as she heard talk of trusts, of family dia-
monds, of Scottish islands, that these people had
money. Serious money.

Then, suddenly, the spattering rain had turned into
a drenching pour, and the people on the pavement
had unfurled twenty-five umbrellas in unison, like a
flock of blackbirds taking off. And it had seemed

entirely natural for Fleur to choose a benevolent looking elderly man, and to meet his eye tentatively, and to
creep, with a grateful smile, under the shelter of his
Swaine Adeney Brigg dome of black silk. It hadn't been
easy to talk, above the rain and the chatter, and the cars
swooshing by, so they'd simply smiled at each other,
and nodded. And by the time the choir had stopped
rehearsing, and the church doors had opened, they'd
assumed the companionship of old friends. He'd
ushered her into the church, and handed her an order
of service, and they'd taken seats together near the
back.

'I didn't know Benjy awfully well,' the elderly man
had confided as they sat down. 'But he was a dear
friend of my late wife's.'

'He was a friend of my father's,' Fleur had replied,
glancing down at the order of service, and quickly
committing the name 'Benjamin St John Gregory' to
memory. 'I didn't know him at all. But it's nice to show
respect.'

'I agree,' the elderly man had said, beaming at her
and extending his hand. 'Now let me introduce myself.
My name's Maurice Snowfield.'

Maurice Snowfield had lasted for three months. He
hadn't been quite as rich as Fleur had hoped, and his
gentle, absent-minded manner had nearly driven her
crazy. But by the time she left his Wiltshire house, she
had enough of his money to pay two terms of her
daughter Zara's school fees in advance, and a brand
new wardrobe of black suits.

'. . . till all thy creatures own thy sway.' There was a
rustling sound around the church, as everyone closed
their hymn-book, sat down, and consulted the order of
service. Fleur took the opportunity to open her bag and
look again at the little note which Johnny had sent her,

clipped to a cutting from a newspaper announcements column. The announcement was of the memorial service of Emily Favour, at St Anselm's Church on 20 April. 'A good bet,' Johnny had scribbled. 'Richard Favour very rich, very quiet.'

Fleur peered at the front pew. She could see the man with the rubbery face, who had given the first reading, and, next to him, a mousy blonde woman in a terrible hat. Then there was a teenaged boy, and an older woman in an even more terrible hat . . . Fleur's eyes passed quickly along and then stopped. Sitting at the other end of the pew was an unobtrusive, greying man. He was leaning forward, with his shoulders hunched, his head resting on the wooden panel in front of him.

She stared critically at him for a few seconds. No, he wasn't pretending – he had loved his wife. He missed her. And, judging by his body language, he didn't talk to his family about it.

Which made things so much easier. The truly grief-stricken were the easiest targets – the men who couldn't imagine ever falling in love again; who vowed to remain faithful to their dead wives. In Fleur's experience, all that meant was that when they did fall for her they were convinced that it must be real love.

They'd asked Richard if he wanted to give the eulogy.

'You must be used to giving speeches,' the vicar had said, 'business speeches. This would be much the same – just a description of your wife's character, maybe an anecdote or two, some mention of the charities she was involved with, anything that reminds the congregation of the real Emily . . .' And then he'd tailed away at Richard's sudden bleak expression, and added gently, 'You don't have to – perhaps you'd find it too upsetting?'

And Richard had nodded.

'I think I would,' he'd muttered.

'Quite understandable,' the vicar had said briskly. 'You're not alone.'

But he *was* alone, Richard had thought. He was alone in his misery; isolated in the knowledge that his wife had died and no-one but him would ever realize just how little he'd known her. The loneliness which he'd felt throughout his marriage now seemed unbearably intensified; distilled into a bitterness not unlike anger. The real Emily! he felt like shouting. What did I ever know of the real Emily?

And so the job of giving the eulogy had fallen to their old friend, Alec Kershaw. Richard sat up straight as Alec approached the lectern, patted together the little white cards in front of him, and looked up over his rimless half-moon spectacles at the congregation.

'Emily Favour was a brave, charming and generous woman,' he began, in raised, formal tones. 'Her sense of duty was matched only by her sense of compassion and her devotion to helping others.'

Alec paused, and glanced at Richard. And as he saw Alec's expression, Richard felt a jolt of understanding pass through him. Alec hadn't really known Emily, either. These words were hollow; conventional – designed to do the job rather than speak the truth.

Richard began to feel a ridiculous sensation of alarm – panic, almost. Once this eulogy had been heard, once the service was over and the congregation had left the church, then that would be it. That would be the official version of Emily Favour's character. Story finished; file closed; nothing more to learn. Could he bear it? Could he bear to live with the final assessment of his wife as nothing more than a collection of well-meaning clichés?

23

'Her charity work was unparalleled – in particular her work for the Rainbow Fund and St Bride's Hospice. I think many of us will remember the first Greyworth Golf Club Christmas auction, an event which has become a regular fixture in all our diaries.'

Fleur felt a yawn creeping through her body. Was this man never going to stop?

'And, of course, mention of Greyworth Golf Club brings us to another most important aspect of Emily Favour's life. What some might describe as a hobby . . . a game. Of course, the rest of us know that it's a *far* more serious matter than that.'

Several members of the congregation tittered obligingly, and Fleur looked up. What was he talking about?

'When she married Richard, Emily had the choice of becoming golf widow or golf partner. Golf partner she became. And despite the ill health which dogged her, she developed an enviably steady game, as all of us who witnessed her fine winning performance in the Ladies' Foursome can verify.'

Golf widow or golf partner, thought Fleur idly. Widow or partner. Well, that's easy – widow wins, every time.

After the service, Richard made his way to the west door, as the vicar had suggested, in order to greet friends and family. 'People appreciate an opportunity to show their condolences personally,' the vicar had said. Now Richard wondered whether this was really true. Most of the congregation scuttled past him, throwing hurried, indistinct phrases of sympathy at him like superstitious charms. A few stopped, met his gaze directly, shook his hand; even embraced him. But these were, surprisingly often, the people he barely knew: the representatives from law firms and private banks; the wives of business acquaintances.

'On to the Lanesborough,' Lambert was saying self-importantly on the other side of the door. 'Drinks at the Lanesborough.'

An elegant woman with red hair stopped in front of Richard and held out a pale hand. Weary of shaking hands, Richard took it.

'The thing is,' the woman said, as though carrying on a conversation they'd already begun, 'the loneliness won't last for ever.' Richard gave a little start, and felt the drooping eyelids of his mind jerk open.

'What did you say?' he began. But the woman was gone. Richard turned to his fifteen-year-old son, Antony, who was standing beside him.

'Who was that?' he said. Antony shrugged.

'Dunno. Lambert and Philippa were talking about her. I think she might have known Mum at school.'

'How did she know . . .' began Richard, and stopped. He had been going to say, How did she know I was lonely? But instead, he turned and smiled at Antony, and said, 'You read very well.' Antony shrugged.

'I s'pose.' In the unconscious movement which he repeated every three minutes or so, Antony put a hand up to his face and rubbed his brow – and for a few moments the dark red birthmark which leapt across his eye like a small lizard was masked. Every three minutes of his waking life, without even knowing that he did it, Antony hid his birthmark from view. As far as Richard knew he'd never been teased because of the birthmark; certainly at home, everybody had always behaved as though it wasn't there. Nevertheless, Antony's hand shot up to his face with almost desperate regularity, and occasionally hovered there for longer, for hours at a time, protecting the little red lizard from scrutiny like a watchful guardian angel.

'Well,' said Richard.

'Yeah,' said Antony.

'Perhaps we should be going.'

'Yeah.'

And that was it. Conversation over. When had he stopped talking to Antony? Richard wondered. How had those adoring, unembarrassed soliloquies addressed to his infant son managed to turn, over the years, into such empty, public exchanges?

'Right,' he said. 'Well. Let's go, then.'

The Belgravia Room at the Lanesborough was nicely full when Fleur arrived. She accepted a glass of buck's fizz from a tanned Australian waiter and made her way directly towards Richard Favour. When she got near, she changed path very slightly, as though to walk straight past him.

'Excuse me.' His voice hit the back of her head, and Fleur felt a small dart of triumph. Sometimes she could spend half an hour walking back and forth before the object of her attention spoke to her.

She turned, as quickly as possible without looking rushed, and gave Richard Favour the warmest, widest smile she could muster. Playing hard to get with widowers was, she had come to realize, a complete waste of time. Some lacked the energy for pursuit; some lacked confidence; some began to grow suspicious during the very process of winning her. Better to leap straight into their lives; to become part of the status quo as quickly as possible.

'Hello again,' said Fleur. She took a sip of buck's fizz and waited for him to speak. If any beady-eyed family members were watching, they would see him chatting her up – not the other way round.

'I wanted to say thank you,' said Richard, 'for your kind words. I thought you spoke – as though you knew what this process is like.'

Fleur looked tenderly down at her drink for a few moments, deciding which story to choose. Eventually she looked up, and gave him a brave smile.

'I'm afraid I do. I've been through it myself. A while ago now.'

'And you survived it.'

'I survived it,' echoed Fleur. 'But it wasn't easy. It can be hard just knowing who to talk to. Often one's family is simply too close.'

'Or not close enough,' said Richard, thinking, bleakly, of Antony.

'Exactly,' said Fleur. 'Not close enough to know what you're really going through; not close enough to . . . to share the grief.' She took another sip of buck's fizz, and looked at Richard. He suddenly looked desolate. Drat, she thought. Have I gone too far?

'Richard?' Fleur looked up. The rubbery man was bearing down on them. 'Derek Cowley's just arrived. You remember – software director of Graylows.'

'I saw him in the church,' said Richard. 'Who on earth invited him?'

'I did,' said Lambert. 'He's a useful contact.'

'I see.' Richard's face tightened.

'I've had a chat with him,' Lambert continued obliviously, 'but he wants to talk to you, too. Could you have a word? I haven't mentioned the contract yet . . .' He broke off, as though noticing Fleur for the first time. I get it, thought Fleur, narrowing her eyes. Women don't count.

'Hello there,' he said. 'Sorry, what was your name?'

'Fleur,' said Fleur. 'Fleur Daxeny.'

'That's right. And you're – what? An old school friend of Emily's?'

'Oh no.' Fleur smiled prettily at him.

'I thought you were a bit young for that,' said Lambert. 'So how did you know Emily?'

'Well, it's interesting,' said Fleur, and took another thoughtful sip. It was surprising just how often a tricky question could be stalled by pausing to sip at a drink or eat a cocktail snack. More often than not, during the silence, someone passing by would see that conversation had temporarily come to a standstill and take the opportunity to join the group – and her answer would be conveniently forgotten.

But today no-one interrupted them, and Lambert was still looking at her with blunt curiosity.

'It's interesting,' said Fleur again, directing her gaze at Richard. 'I only met your wife twice. But each time, she had a great effect on me.'

'Where did you meet?' said Lambert.

'At a lunch,' said Fleur. 'A big charity lunch. We were at the same table. I complained about the food, and Emily said she quite agreed but she wasn't the sort to complain. And then we just started talking.'

'What did you talk about?' Richard peered at Fleur.

'Everything,' said Fleur. She looked back at Richard; noticed his yearning eyes. 'I confided in her about all sorts of things,' she said slowly, lowering her voice so that Richard unconsciously leaned forward, 'and she confided in me. We talked about our lives . . . and our families . . . and the choices we'd made . . .'

'What did she say?' Richard's question burst forth from him before he could stop it. Fleur shrugged.

'It was a long time ago now. I'm not sure if I even remember exactly.' She smiled. 'It was nothing, really.

28

I expect Emily forgot all about me long ago. But I . . . I always remembered her. And when I saw the memorial announcement, I couldn't resist coming along.' Fleur lowered her eyes. 'It was rather presumptuous. I hope you don't mind.'

'Of course I don't mind,' said Richard. 'Any friend of Emily's is absolutely welcome.'

'Funny she never mentioned you,' said Lambert, looking at her critically.

'I would have been surprised if she had,' replied Fleur, smiling at him. 'It was really nothing. A couple of long conversations, many years ago.'

'I wish . . . I wish I knew what she'd told you.' Richard gave an embarrassed little laugh. 'But if you don't remember . . .'

'I remember bits.' Fleur smiled tantalizingly at him. 'Little snippets. Some of it was quite surprising. And some was quite . . . personal.' She paused, and glanced sidelong at Lambert.

'Lambert, you go and talk to Derek Cowley,' said Richard at once. 'I might have a word with him later on. But now I'd like . . . I'd like to talk a little further with Mrs Daxeny.'

Fifteen minutes later, Fleur emerged from the Lanesborough and got into a taxi. In her pocket was Richard Favour's telephone number and in her diary was an appointment for lunch with him the next day.

It had been so easy. The poor man was quite obviously desperate to hear what she had to say about his wife – but too well-mannered to interrupt her as she digressed, apparently unwittingly, on to other subjects. She'd fed him a few innocuous lines, then suddenly glanced at her watch and exclaimed that she must be shooting off. His face had fallen and for a few seconds he'd seemed resigned to the disappointment of ending the conversation there. But then, almost as Fleur was giving up on him, he'd pulled out his diary and, in a slightly shaking voice, asked Fleur if she might like to have lunch with him. Fleur suspected that making lunch appointments with strange women was not something Richard Favour had done very often. Which was fine by her.

By the time the taxi pulled up in front of the Chelsea mansion block where Johnny and Felix lived, she had scribbled down on a piece of paper all the facts she could remember about Emily Favour. 'Ill-health', she underlined. 'Golf', she underlined twice. It was a pity she didn't know what the woman looked like. A photograph would have been useful. But then, she didn't intend to talk about Emily Favour for very long. Dead wives were, in her experience, best avoided.

As she hopped out of her taxi, she saw Johnny on the pavement outside the front door of the mansion block, watching carefully as something was unloaded from a delivery van. He was a dapper man in his late fifties, with nut-brown hair and a permanent suntan. Fleur had known him for twenty years; he was the only person she had never lied to.

'Darling!' she called. 'Johnn-ee! Did you get my luggage all right?' He turned at the sound of his name, frowning petulantly at the interruption. But when he saw it was Fleur, the frown disappeared.

'Sweetheart!' he cried. 'Come and see this.'

'What is it?'

'It's our new epergne. Felix bid for it yesterday. Quite a snip, we thought. Careful!' he suddenly snapped. 'Don't knock it!'

'Is Felix in?'

'Yes he is. Go on up. I said careful, you moron!'

As she mounted the stairs to the first floor, she could hear Wagner coming, loud and insistent, from Johnny's flat; as she stepped inside, the volume seemed to double.

'Felix!' she called. But he couldn't hear her. She went into the drawing room to see him standing in front of the mirror, a portly middle-aged man, singing along with Brünnhilde in a shrieking falsetto.

When Fleur had first heard Felix's high, fluting voice, she had thought there must be something horrendously wrong with him. But she'd soon learned that he made his living from this strange sound, singing services in churches and cathedrals. Sometimes she and Johnny would go to hear Felix singing Evensong at St Paul's Cathedral or Westminster Abbey, and would see him solemnly processing and bowing in his white frills. More rarely, they would see him attired in tails, singing in a performance of Handel's *Messiah* or Bach's *St Matthew Passion*.

Fleur didn't enjoy the sound of Felix's voice, and found the *St Matthew Passion* very boring indeed. But she always sat in the front row and applauded vigorously and joined Johnny in his cries of 'Bravo!' Because Fleur owed Felix a great deal. Memorial services, she could find out about from the papers – but it was Felix who always knew about the funerals. If he wasn't singing at them himself, he knew someone who was. And it was at the smaller, more intimate funerals that Fleur had always done best.

When Felix saw her reflection he gave a little jump, and stopped singing.

'Not really my range,' he shouted over the music. 'A bit low for me. How was the memorial service?'

'Fine!' shouted Fleur. She went over to the CD player

31

and turned the volume down. 'Fine,' she repeated. 'Quite promising. I'm having lunch with Mr Favour tomorrow.'

'Oh well done!' said Felix. 'I was going to tell you about a funeral we're doing tomorrow. Rather nice; they've asked for "Hear My Prayer". But if you're fixed up . . .'

'You'd better tell me anyway,' said Fleur. 'I'm not entirely convinced about this Favour family. I'm not sure there's any money.'

'Oh really?'

'Terrible hats.'

'Hmm. Hats aren't everything.'

'No.'

'What did Johnny say about them?'

'What did Johnny say about what?' Johnny's high voice came through the doorway. 'Careful, you oaf! In there. Yes. On the table.'

A man in overalls entered the room and placed on the table a large object, shrouded in brown paper.

'Let me see!' exclaimed Johnny. He began to tear the paper off in strips.

'A candelabra,' said Fleur. 'How nice.'

'It's an epergne,' corrected Johnny. 'Isn't it beautiful?'

'Clever little me,' said Felix. 'To find such a gorgeous thing.'

'I bet it cost a fortune,' said Fleur sulkily. 'You could have given that money to a good cause, you know.'

'Like you? I don't think so.' Johnny took out a handkerchief and began to polish the epergne. 'If you want money so badly, why did you leave the lovely Sakis?'

'He wasn't lovely. He was an overbearing bully. He used to order me about, and shout at me . . .'

'. . . and buy you suits from Givenchy.'

'I know,' said Fleur regretfully. 'But I couldn't stand him for one more moment. And besides, he wouldn't give me a Gold Card.' She shrugged. 'So there was no point.'

'Why any of these men ever gives you a credit card is quite beyond me,' said Felix.

'Yes,' said Fleur. 'Well, it would be, wouldn't it?'

'*Touché*,' said Felix cheerfully.

'But you did pretty well out of him, didn't you?' said Johnny.

'Little bits, here and there. Some cash. But not enough.' Fleur sighed, and lit a cigarette. 'What a bloody waste of time.'

'That'll be a pound in the swear box, thank you,' said Felix at once. Fleur rolled her eyes and felt in her bag for her purse. She looked up.

'Can you change a fifty-pound note?'

'Probably,' said Felix. 'Let me look in the box.'

'You know, Fleur,' said Johnny, still polishing, 'your little bits and pieces probably add up to what most people call a fortune.'

'No they don't,' said Fleur.

'How much have you got stashed away now?'

'Not enough.'

'And how much is enough?'

'Oh Johnny, stop quizzing me!' said Fleur irritably. 'It's all your fault. You told me Sakis would be a pushover.'

'I told you nothing of the sort. I merely told you that according to my sources he was a multimillionaire and emotionally vulnerable. Which turned out to be absolutely true.'

'He'll be even more vulnerable tonight when he re-alizes you've scooted,' said Felix, depositing Fleur's fifty-pound note in a large tin decorated with pink cherubs.

'Don't start feeling sorry for him,' exclaimed Fleur.

'Oh I don't! Any man who allows himself to be duped by you deserves everything he gets.' Fleur sighed.

'I had a good time on his yacht, at any rate.' She blew out a plume of smoke. 'It's a pity, really.'

'A great pity,' said Johnny, standing back to admire the epergne. 'Now I suppose we've got to find you someone else.'

'And you needn't expect another rich Greek,' put in Felix. 'I don't often get asked to sing at Orthodox bashes.'

'Did you go to the Emily Favour memorial service?'

'Yes I did,' said Fleur, stubbing out her cigarette. 'But I wasn't impressed. Is there really any money there?'

'Oh *yes*,' said Johnny, looking up. 'At least, there should be. My chum at de Rouchets told me that Richard Favour has a personal fortune of millions. And then there's the family company. There should be plenty of money.'

'Oh well, I'm having lunch with him tomorrow. I'll try and find out.' Fleur wandered over to the mantelpiece and began to leaf through the stiff, engraved invitations addressed to Johnny and Felix.

'You know, perhaps you should lower your sights a little,' suggested Felix. 'Settle for a plain old millionaire once in a while.'

'Come on. A million goes nowhere these days,' said Fleur. 'Nowhere! You know that as well as I do. And I need security.' Her eye fell on a silver-framed photograph of a little girl with fair, fluffy hair haloed in the sunlight. '*Zara* needs security,' she added.

'Dear Zara,' said Johnny. 'We haven't heard from her

for a while. How is she?'

'Fine,' said Fleur vaguely. 'At school.'

'Which reminds me,' said Johnny. He glanced at Felix. 'Have you told her?'

'What? Oh that. No.'

'What is it?' said Fleur suspiciously.

'Someone telephoned us last week.'

'Who?'

'Hal Winters.' There was a short silence.

'What did he want?' said Fleur eventually.

'You. He wanted to get in touch with you.'

'And you told him . . .'

'Nothing. We said we didn't know where you were.'

'Good.' Fleur exhaled slowly. She met Johnny's eye, and quickly looked away.

'Fleur,' said Johnny seriously, 'don't you think you should call him?'

'No,' said Fleur.

'Well I do.'

'Well I don't! Johnny, I've told you before. I don't talk about him.'

'But . . .'

'Do you understand?' exclaimed Fleur angrily. 'I don't talk about him!'

And before he could say anything else, she picked up her bag, tossed back her hair and walked quickly out of the room.

Chapter Three

Lambert put the phone down and stared at it for a few seconds. Then he turned to Philippa.

'Your father's a fool,' he exclaimed. 'A bloody fool!'

'What's he done?' asked Philippa nervously.

'He's got involved with some bloody woman, that's all. I mean, at his age!'

'And so soon after Mummy's death,' put in Philippa.

'Exactly,' said Lambert. 'Exactly.' He looked at Philippa approvingly, and she felt a glow of pleasure spread over her neck. Lambert didn't often look approvingly at her.

'That was him phoning, to say he's bringing this woman along to lunch today. He sounded . . .' Lambert contorted his face reflectively, and Philippa looked away quickly, before she could find herself articulating the thought that she was married to an extremely ugly man. 'He sounded drunk,' Lambert concluded.

'At this time in the morning?'

'Not *alcohol* drunk,' said Lambert impatiently. 'Drunk with . . .' He broke off, and for a few moments, he and Philippa looked at each other.

'With happiness,' said Philippa eventually.

'Well, yes,' said Lambert grudgingly. 'I suppose that must be it.'

Philippa leaned forward towards the mirror and began to apply liquid eyeliner shakily to her eyelid.

'Who is she?' she asked. 'What's her name?'

'Fleur.'

'Fleur? The one from the memorial service? The one with the lovely hat?'

'For God's sake, Philippa! Do you think I asked him about her hat? Now, hurry up.' And without waiting for an answer, he left the room.

Philippa gazed silently at her reflection; at her watery blue eyes and pale, mousy hair and slightly flushed cheeks. Through her mind rushed a torrent of imaginary words; words Lambert might have said if he had been a different person. He might have said, 'Yes darling, I expect that's the one' . . . or he might have said, 'Philippa, my love, I only had eyes for you at the memorial service' . . . or he might have said, 'The one with the lovely hat? You had the loveliest hat of all.' And then she would have said, in the confident, teasing tones she could never recreate in real life, 'Come on, sweetheart. Even you must have noticed that hat!' And then he would have said, 'Oh *that* hat!' And then they both would have laughed. And then . . . and then he would have kissed her on the forehead, and then . . .

'Philippa!' Lambert's voice came ringing sharply through the flat. 'Philippa, are you ready?' Philippa jumped.

'I'll be five minutes!' she called back, hearing the wobble in her voice and despising it.

'Well, get on with it!'

Philippa began to search confusedly through her make-up bag for the right shade of lipstick. If Lambert had been a different person, perhaps he would have called back, 'Take your time', or 'No hurry, dearest', or maybe he would have come back into the room, and smiled at her, and fiddled with her hair, and she would have laughed, and said, 'You're holding me up!' and he would have said, 'I can't help it when you're so gorgeous!' And then he would have kissed her finger-tips . . . and then . . .

In the corner of the room, the phone began to ring in a muted electronic burble. Lost in her own private dream-world, Philippa didn't even hear it.

In the study, Lambert picked up the phone.

'Lambert Chester here.'

'Good morning, Mr Chester. It's Erica Fortescue from First Bank here. I wonder if I might have a quick word?'

'I'm about to go out. Is it important?'

'It's about your overdraft, Mr Chester.'

'Oh.' Lambert looked cautiously towards the door of the study – then, to make sure, kicked it shut. 'What's the problem?'

'You seem to have exceeded your limit. Quite sub-stantially.'

'Rubbish.' Lambert leaned back, reached inside his mouth and began to pick his teeth.

'The balance on that account is currently a debit of over three hundred thousand pounds. Whereas the agreed limit was two hundred and fifty.'

'I think you'll find,' said Lambert, 'it was raised again last month. To three hundred and fifty thousand.'

'Was that confirmed in writing?'

'Larry Collins fixed it up for me.'

'Larry Collins has left the bank.' Erica Fortescue's voice came smoothly down the line.

Fuck, thought Lambert. Larry's been sacked. Stupid bugger.

'Well, he confirmed it in writing before he left,' he said quickly. He could easily knock up some letter.

'There's nothing in our files.'

'Well I expect he forgot.' Lambert paused, and his face twisted into a complacent sneer. 'Maybe he also forgot to tell you that in two years' time I'll be coming into more money than either of you has ever seen.' That'll sort you, he thought, you stupid officious bitch.

'Your wife's trust fund? Yes, he did tell me about it. Has that been confirmed?'

'Of course it has. It's all set up.'

'I see.'

'And you're still worried about my pathetic little overdraft?'

'Yes, Mr Chester, I am. We don't generally accept spouses' assets as collateral on sole accounts.' Lambert stared at the phone in anger. Who did this tart think she was? 'Another thing . . .'

'What?' He was beginning to feel rattled.

'I was interested to see that there's no mention of the trust fund in your wife's file here. Only in your own file. Is there a reason for that?'

'Yes there is,' snapped Lambert, his guard down. 'It's not mentioned in my wife's file because she doesn't know about it.'

The files were empty. All empty. Fleur stared at them in disbelief, flicking a few of them open, checking for stray documents, bank statements, anything. Then, hearing a noise, she quickly pushed the drawers of the metal cabinet shut and hurried over to the window. When Richard came into the room, she was leaning out, breathing in the London fumes rapturously.

'Such a wonderful view,' she exclaimed. 'I adore Regent's Park. Do you often visit the Zoo?'

'Never,' said Richard, laughing. 'Not since Antony was little.'

'We must go,' said Fleur. 'While you're still in London.'

'This afternoon, perhaps?'

'This afternoon we're going to Hyde Park,' said Fleur firmly. 'It's all arranged.'

'If you say so.' Richard grinned. 'But now we'd better get going if we're not going to be late for Philippa and Lambert.'

'OK.' Fleur smiled charmingly at Richard and allowed herself to be led from the room. At the door she glanced fleetingly around, wondering if she'd missed something. But the only businesslike piece of furniture she could see was the filing cabinet. No desk; no bureau. His paperwork must all be somewhere else. At the office. Or at the house in Surrey.

On the way to the restaurant, she allowed her hand to fall easily into Richard's, and as their fingers linked she saw a tiny flush spread across his neck. He was such a buttoned-up English gentleman, she thought, trying not to laugh. After four weeks, he had progressed no further than kissing her, with dry, diffident, out-of-practice lips. Not like brutish Sakis, who had dragged her off to a hotel room after their very first lunch date. Fleur winced at the memory of Sakis's thick, hairy thighs; his barked commands. Much better this way. And to her surprise, she rather liked being treated like a high-school virgin. She walked along beside Richard with a smile on her face, feeling wrapped up and protected and smug, as though she really did have a virtue to protect; as though she were saving herself for that special moment.

Whether she could wait that long was another matter. Four weeks of lunches, dinners, films and art galleries — and she still had no hard evidence that Richard Favour had serious money. So he had a few nice suits; a London flat; a Surrey mansion; a reputation of wealth. That didn't mean anything. The houses might be mortgaged up to the hilt. He might be about to go bust. He might be about to ask *her* for money. It had happened to her once before – and ever since, Fleur had been wary. If she couldn't find hard proof of money she was wasting her time. Really, she should have been off by now. On to the next funeral; the next sucker. But . . .

Fleur paused in her thoughts, and tucked Richard's arm more firmly under her own. If she was honest with herself, she had to admit that her self-confidence had slightly fallen since she'd left Sakis. In the last few weeks she had attended three funerals and five memorial services – but so far Richard Favour was her only promising catch. Meanwhile Johnny and Felix, sweet as they were, had begun to get fidgety at the sight of her luggage littering their spare room. She didn't usually spend so long between men ('resting', as Felix put it); usually it was straight out of one bed and into another.

If only, thought Fleur, she could speed Richard up a bit: secure a place in his bed; work her way into his household. Then she'd be able to assess his finances properly and at the same time solve the problem of a place to stay. Otherwise – if things didn't work out soon – she would be forced to take the sort of steps she'd vowed she'd never stoop to. She would have to find a flat of her own. Maybe even look for a job. Fleur shuddered, and her jaw tightened in determination. She would just have to get Richard into bed. Once that had happened, everything would become easy.

As they turned into Great Portland Street, Richard felt Fleur nudge him.

'Look!' she said in a low voice. 'Look at that!'

Richard turned his head. On the other side of the road were two nuns standing on the pavement, apparently engaged in a bitter dispute.

'I've never seen nuns arguing before,' said Fleur, giggling.

'I don't think I have either.'

'I'm going to talk to them,' said Fleur suddenly. 'Wait here.'

Richard watched in astonishment as Fleur strode across the road. For a few moments she stood on the pavement opposite, a vibrant figure in her scarlet coat, talking to the black-habited nuns. They seemed to be nodding and smiling. Then all of a sudden she was coming back across the road towards him, and the nuns were walking away in apparent harmony.

'What happened?' exclaimed Richard. 'What on earth did you say?'

'I told them the Blessed Virgin Mary was grieved by discord.' Fleur grinned at Richard's incredulous expression. 'Actually, I told them how to get to the tube station.'

Richard gave a sudden laugh.

'You're a remarkable woman!' he said.

'I know,' said Fleur complacently. She tucked her hand under his arm again, and they began to walk.

Richard stared at the pale spring sunlight dappling the pavement, and felt a bubbling exhilaration rise through his body. He had known this woman for a mere four weeks, and already he couldn't imagine life without her. When he was with her, drab everyday events seemed transformed into a series of shiny moments to relish; when he wasn't with her, he was wishing that he was. Fleur seemed to turn life into a game – not the rigid maze of rules and conventions to which Emily had so tirelessly adhered, but a game of chance; of who dares wins. He found himself waiting with a childish excitement to hear what she would say next; what plan she would surprise him with. He had seen more of London over the last four weeks than ever before; laughed more than ever before; spent more money than he had for a long time.

Often his mind would return to Emily, and he would feel a pang of guilt – guilt that he was spending such a lot of time with Fleur, that he was enjoying himself so much, that he had kissed her. And guilt that his original motivation for pursuing Fleur – to discover as much about Emily's hidden character as he could – seemed to have taken second place to that of simply being with her. Sometimes in his dreams he would see Emily's face, pale and reproachful; he would wake in the night, curled up in grief and sweating with shame. But by morning Emily's image had always faded, and all he could think about was Fleur.

'She's stunning!' said Lambert in outraged tones.

'I *told* you,' said Philippa. 'Didn't you notice her at the memorial service?'

Lambert shrugged.

'I suppose I thought she was quite attractive. But . . . just look at her!' Just look at her next to your father! he wanted to say.

They watched in silence as Fleur took off her scarlet coat. Underneath she was wearing a clinging black dress; she gave a little wriggle and smoothed it down over her hips. Lambert felt a sudden stab of angry desire. What the hell was a woman like that doing with Richard, when he was stuck with Philippa?

'They're coming,' said Philippa. 'Hello, Daddy!'

'Hello darling,' said Richard, kissing her. 'Lambert.'

'Richard.'

'And this is Fleur.' Richard couldn't stop the smirk of pride spreading across his face.

'I'm so glad to meet you,' said Fleur, smiling warmly at Philippa and holding out her hand. After a moment's hesitation, Philippa took it. 'And Lambert, of course, I've already met.'

'Very briefly,' said Lambert, in discouraging tones. Fleur gave him a curious look, then smiled again at Philippa. Slightly unnerved, Philippa smiled back.

'I'm sorry we're a little late,' said Richard, shaking out his napkin. 'We ahm . . . we got into a contretemps with a pair of nuns. Nuns on the run.' He glanced at Fleur and with no warning they both began to laugh.

Philippa looked uneasily at Lambert, who raised his eyebrows.

'I'm sorry,' said Richard, still chuckling. 'It's too long to explain. But it was terribly funny.'

'I expect it was,' said Lambert. 'Have you ordered drinks?'

'I'll have a Manhattan,' said Richard.

'A what?' Philippa stared at him.

'A Manhattan,' repeated Richard. 'Surely you've heard of a Manhattan?'

'Richard was a Manhattan virgin until last week,' said Fleur. 'I just adore cocktails. Don't you?'

'I don't know,' said Philippa. 'I suppose so.' She took a sip of her fizzy water and tried to remember the last time she'd had a cocktail. Then, to her disbelief, she noticed her father's hand creeping under the table to meet Fleur's. She glanced at Lambert; he was gazing, transfixed, at the same thing.

'And I'll have one too,' said Fleur cheerfully.

'I think I'd better have a gin,' said Philippa. She felt slightly faint. Was this really her father? Holding hands with another woman? She couldn't believe it. She'd never even seen him holding hands with her mother. And here he was, grinning away as though Mummy had never existed. He wasn't behaving like her father, she thought. He was behaving as though . . . as though he were a normal man.

Lambert was the tricky one, thought Fleur. It was he who kept giving her suspicious looks; who kept quizzing her on her background and probing her on exactly how well she'd known Emily. She could almost see the phrase 'gold-digger' forming itself in his mind. Which was good if it meant there was some money to be had – but not if it meant he was going to rumble her. She would have to butter him up.

So, as the puddings arrived, she turned to him and adopted a deferential, almost awed expression.

'Richard's told me that you're his company's computer expert.'

'That's right,' said Lambert, sounding bored.

'How marvellous. I know nothing about computers.'

'Most people don't.'

'Lambert designs computer programs for the company,' said Richard, 'and sells them to other firms. It's quite a profitable sideline.'

'So are you going to be another Bill Gates?'

'Actually, my approach is completely different from Gates's,' said Lambert coldly. Fleur looked at him to see if he was joking but his eyes were hard and humourless. Goodness, she thought, trying not to laugh. Never underestimate a man's vanity.

'But you still might make billions?' Lambert shrugged.

'Money doesn't interest me.'

'Lambert doesn't bother about money,' put in Philippa, giving an uncertain little laugh. 'I do all our book-keeping.'

'A task eminently suited to the female mind,' said Lambert.

'Hang on a minute, Lambert,' protested Richard. 'I don't think that's quite fair.'

'It may not be fair,' said Lambert, digging a spoon into his chocolate mousse, 'but it's true. Men create, women administrate.'

'Women create babies,' said Fleur.

'Women *produce* babies,' said Lambert. 'Men create them. The woman is the passive partner. And who determines the sex of a baby? The man or the woman?'

'The clinic,' said Fleur. Lambert looked displeased.

'You don't seem to appreciate the point of what I'm saying,' he began. 'Quite simply . . .' But before he could continue, he was interrupted by a ringing, female voice.

'Well, what a surprise! The Favour family *en masse*!' Fleur looked up. A blonde woman in an emerald green jacket was bearing down on them. Her eyes swivelled from Richard to Fleur, to Lambert, to Philippa, and back to Fleur. Fleur returned her gaze equably. Why did these women have to wear so much make-up? she wondered. The woman's eyelids were smothered in bright blue frosting; her eyelashes stuck straight out from her eyes in black spikes; on one of her teeth there was a tiny smear of lipstick.

'Eleanor!' said Richard. 'How nice to see you. Are you up with Geoffrey?'

'No,' said Eleanor. 'I'm having lunch with a girl-friend; then we're off to the Scotch House.' She shifted the gilt chain strap of her bag from one shoulder to the other. 'Actually, Geoffrey was saying only the other day that he hadn't seen you at the club recently.' Her voice held a note of enquiry; again her eyes slid towards Fleur.

'Let me introduce you,' said Richard. 'This is a friend of mine, Fleur Daxeny. Fleur, this is Eleanor Forrester. Her husband is captain of the golf club down at Greyworth.'

'How nice to meet you,' murmured Fleur, rising from her seat slightly to shake hands. Eleanor Forrester's hand was firm and rough; almost masculine except for the red-painted nails. Another golfer.

'Are you an old friend of Richard's?' asked Eleanor.

'Not really,' said Fleur. 'I met Richard for the first time four weeks ago.'

'I see,' said Eleanor. Her spiky eyelashes batted up and down a few times. 'I see,' she said again. 'Well, I suppose I'd better be off. Will you be playing in the Spring Meeting, any of you?'

'I certainly will,' said Lambert.

'Oh, I expect I will too,' said Richard. 'But who knows?'

'Who knows,' echoed Eleanor. She looked again at Fleur, and her mouth tightened. 'Very nice to meet you, Fleur. Very interesting indeed.'

They watched in silence as she walked briskly away, her blond hair bouncing stiffly on the collar of her jacket.

'Well,' exclaimed Lambert when she was out of earshot. 'That'll be all over the club tomorrow.'

'Eleanor was a really good friend of Mummy's,' said Philippa apologetically to Fleur. 'She probably thought . . .' She broke off awkwardly.

'You know, you'll have to watch it,' said Lambert to Richard. 'You'll get back to Greyworth and find everyone's been talking about you.'

'How nice,' said Richard, smiling at Fleur, 'to be the centre of attention.'

'It may seem funny now,' said Lambert. 'But if I were you . . .'

'Yes, Lambert? What would you do?'

A note of steel had crept into Richard's voice, and Philippa shot Lambert a warning look. But Lambert ploughed on.

'I'd be a bit careful, Richard. Frankly, you don't want people getting the wrong idea. You don't want people gossiping behind your back.'

'And why should they gossip behind my back?'

'Well I mean, it's obvious, isn't it? Look, Fleur, I don't want to offend you, but you understand, don't you? A lot of people were very fond of Emily. And when they hear about you . . .'

'Not only will they hear about Fleur,' said Richard loudly, 'but they will meet her, since she will be coming down to stay at Greyworth as soon as possible. And if you have a problem with that, Lambert, then I suggest you keep well away.'

'I only meant . . .' began Lambert.

'I know what you meant,' said Richard. 'I know only too well what you meant. And I'm afraid I think a lot less of you for it. Come on Fleur, let's leave.'

Out on the pavement, Richard took Fleur's arm.

'I'm so sorry about that,' he said. 'Lambert can be most objectionable.'

'It's quite all right,' said Fleur quietly. My God, she thought, I've had it a lot more objectionable than that. There was the daughter who tried to pull my hair out, the neighbour who called me a slut . . .

'And you will come down to Greyworth? I'm sorry, I should have asked first.' Richard looked at her anxiously. 'But I promise you'll enjoy it down there. We can go for long walks, and you can meet the rest of the family . . .'

'And learn to play golf?'

'If you'd like to.' He smiled. 'It's not compulsory.' He paused awkwardly. 'And of course, you'd . . . you'd have your own room. I wouldn't want you to . . . to . . .'

'Wouldn't you?' said Fleur softly. 'I would.' She raised herself on tiptoe and gently kissed Richard on the lips. After a moment, she softly pushed her tongue inside his mouth. Immediately, his body stiffened. With shock? With desire? She casually ran a hand down the back of his neck and waited to find out.

Richard stood completely still, with Fleur's mouth open against his, her words echoing in his mind, trying to marshal his thoughts and yet completely unable to. He felt suddenly rigid, almost paralysed with excitement. After a few moments Fleur moved her lips softly to the corner of his mouth, and he felt his skin explode with delicious sensation. This was how it should have been with Emily, he thought dizzily, trying not to keel over with headiness. This was how it should have felt with his beloved wife. But Emily had never aroused him like this woman – this bewitching woman whom he'd only known for four weeks. He had never felt anticipation like this before. He'd never felt like . . . like *fucking* a woman before.

'Let's get a cab,' he said, in a blurred voice, pulling himself away from Fleur. 'Let's go back to the flat.' He could hardly bear to speak. Each word seemed to sully the moment; to spoil the conviction inside him that he was on the brink of a perfect experience. But one had to break the silence. One had somehow to get off the street.

'What about Hyde Park?'

Richard felt as though Fleur were torturing him.

'Another day,' he managed. 'Come on. Come on!'

He hailed a taxi, bundled her inside, mumbled an address to the taxi driver and turned back to Fleur. And at the sight of her, his heart nearly stopped. As Fleur had leaned back on the black leather taxi seat, her dress had mysteriously hitched itself up until the top of one of her black stockings was just visible.

'Oh God,' he said, indistinctly, staring at the sheer black lace. Emily had never worn black lace stockings.

And suddenly a cold flash of fear went through him. What was he about to do? What had happened to him? Images of Emily came flashing through his mind. Her sweet smile; the feeling of her hair between his fingers. Her slim legs; her neat little buttocks. Cosy, un-demanding times; nights of fondness.

'Richard,' said Fleur huskily, running a finger gently along his thigh. Richard flinched in panic. He felt ter-rified. What had seemed so clear on the pavement now seemed muddied by memories that would not leave his mind alone; by a guilt that rose up, choking his throat till he could hardly breathe. Suddenly he felt close to tears. He could not do this. He would not do it. And yet desire for Fleur still whirled tormentingly about his body.

'Richard?' said Fleur again.

'I'm still married,' he found himself saying. 'I can't do this. I'm still married to Emily.' He stared at her, waiting for some relief to his agony; some internal acknowledgement that he was doing the right thing. But there was none. He felt awash with conflicting emotions, with physical needs, with mental anguish. No direction seemed the right one.

'You're not really married to Emily any more,' said

Fleur, in slow soft tones. 'Are you?' She put up a hand and began to caress his cheek, but he jerked away.

'I can't!' Richard's face was white with despair. He sat forward with taut cheeks and glittering eyes. 'You don't understand. Emily was my wife. Emily's the only one . . .' His voice cracked and he looked away.

Fleur thought for a moment, then quickly adjusted her dress. By the time Richard had gained control of himself and looked back towards her the lacy stockings had disappeared under a sea of decorous black wool. He looked silently at her.

'I must be a great disappointment to you,' he said eventually. 'I'd quite understand if you decided . . .' he shrugged.

'Decided what?'

'That you didn't want to see me any more.'

'Richard, don't be so silly!' Fleur's voice was soft, compassionate, and just a little playful. 'You don't imagine that I'm only after you for one thing?' She gave him a tiny smile, and after a few seconds Richard grinned back. 'We've been having such wonderful times together,' continued Fleur. 'I'd hate either of us to feel pressured . . .'

As she was speaking, she caught a glimpse of the taxi driver's face in the rear-view mirror. He was staring at them both in transparent astonishment, and Fleur suddenly wanted to giggle. But instead she turned to Richard and in a quieter voice, said,

'I'd love to come down and stay at Greyworth and I'd be very happy to have my own bedroom. And if things move on . . . they move on.'

Richard looked at her for a few seconds, then suddenly grasped her hand.

'You're a wonderful woman,' he said huskily. 'I feel . . .' He clasped her hand tighter. 'I feel suddenly very close to you.' Fleur stared back at him silently for a moment, then modestly lowered her eyes.

Bloody Emily, she thought. Always getting in the way. But she said nothing, and allowed Richard's hand to remain clutching hers, all the way back to Regent's Park.

Chapter Four

Two weeks later, Antony Favour stood in the kitchen of The Maples, watching as his Aunt Gillian whipped cream. She was whipping it by hand, with a grim expression and a mouth which seemed to grow tighter at each stroke of the whisk. Antony knew for a fact that inside one of the kitchen cupboards lived an electric whisk; he'd used it himself to make pancakes. But Gillian always whipped cream by hand. She did most things by hand. Gillian had been living in the house since before Antony was born, and for as long as he could remember she'd been the one who did all the cooking, and told the cleaner what to do, and walked around after the cleaner had left, frowning, and polishing again over surfaces which looked perfectly clean. His mother had never really done any of that stuff. Some of the time she'd been too ill to cook, and the rest of the time she'd been too busy playing golf.

A vision of his mother came into Antony's mind. Small, and thin, with silvery blond hair and neat tartan trousers. He remembered her blue-grey eyes; her expensive rimless spectacles; her faint flowery scent. His mother had always looked neat and tidy; silver and blue. Antony looked surreptitiously at Gillian. Her dull grey hair had separated into two heavy clumps; her cheeks were bright red; her shoulders were hunched up in their mauve cardigan. Gillian had the same blue-grey eyes as his mother, but apart from that,

Antony thought, it was difficult to believe that they'd been sisters.

He looked again at Gillian's tense expression. Ever since Dad had called to tell them he'd be bringing this woman to stay, Gillian had been walking around looking even more grim than usual. She hadn't said anything – but then, Gillian didn't often say very much. She never had an opinion; she never said when she was pissed off. It was up to you to guess. And now, Antony guessed, she was seriously pissed off.

Antony himself wasn't quite sure how he felt about this woman. He'd lain in bed the night before, thinking about his mother and his father and this new woman, waiting for a sudden gut reaction; a stab of emotion to point him in the right direction. But nothing. He'd had no particularly negative emotions, nor any positive ones, just a kind of astonished acknowledgement that this thing was happening; that his father was seeing another woman. Occasionally the thought would hit him as he was in the middle of something else, and he'd feel so shocked that he would have to stare ahead and breathe deeply and blink several times, to stop his eyes filling with tears, for Christ's sake. But other times it seemed completely natural; almost something he'd been expecting.

He'd got used to telling people that his mother was dead; perhaps telling them that his father had a girlfriend was just the next step along. Sometimes it even made him want to laugh.

Gillian had finished whipping the cream. She shook the whisk and dumped it in the sink without even licking it. Then she sighed heavily and rubbed her forehead with her hand.

'Are we having pavlova?' said Antony.

'Yes,' said Gillian. 'With kiwi fruit.' She shrugged. 'I don't know if it's what your father wants. But it'll just have to do.'

'I'm sure it'll be great,' said Antony. 'Everyone loves pavlova.'

'Well, it'll just have to do,' repeated Gillian. She looked wearily about the kitchen and Antony followed her gaze. He loved the kitchen; it was his favourite room. About five years ago his parents had had it done up like a huge farmhouse kitchen, with terracotta tiles everywhere, and an open fire, and a huge wooden table with really comfortable chairs. They'd bought five million pots and pans and stuff, all out of expensive catalogues, and hung garlic on the walls and got a woman to come in and arrange dried flowers all over the place.

Antony could have spent all day in the kitchen – in fact, now they'd installed a telly on the wall, he often did. But Gillian seemed to hate it. She'd hated it as it was before – 'all white and clinical', she'd called it – and she still hated it, even though she'd been the one to choose the tiles and tell the designer where everything should go. Antony didn't understand it.

'Can I help?' he said. 'Can I peel the potatoes or something?'

'We're not having potatoes,' said Gillian irritably, as if he should have known. 'We're having wild rice.' She frowned. 'I hope it's not too difficult to cook.'

'I'm sure it'll be delicious,' said Antony. 'Why don't you use the rice cooker?'

His parents had given Gillian a rice cooker three Christmases ago. The year before that they'd given her an electrical juicer; since then there had been an automatic herb shredder, a bread slicer and an ice-cream maker. As far as Antony knew, she'd never used any of them.

'I'll manage,' said Gillian. 'Why don't you go out-side? Or do some revision?'

'Honestly, I don't mind helping,' said Antony.

'It's quicker if I do it myself.' Gillian gave another heavy sigh and reached for a cookery book. Antony looked at her silently for a few moments, then shrugged and walked out.

It was a nice day, and he was, he thought, quite glad to get out into the sunshine. He wandered out of the drive of The Maples and along the road towards the clubhouse. All the roads on the Greyworth estate were private and you had to have a security pass to get in, so most of the time there were hardly any cars; just people who had houses on the estate or who were members of the golf club.

Maybe, Antony thought as he walked, there was time for a quick nine holes before Dad arrived. He was supposed to be revising for his exams this week; that was the reason he was at home. Ahead of him stretched a week-long home study period. But Antony didn't need to study – he knew all the stuff they were going to ask. Instead he was planning to spend his days lazing around, playing golf, a bit of tennis maybe. It depended on who was around. His best friend, Will, was away at school like him, and Will's school didn't have home study periods. 'You jammy bastard,' Will had written. 'Just don't blame me if you fail every-thing.' Antony had to agree. It was bloody jammy. His dad hadn't been at all impressed. 'What are we paying your fees for,' he'd exclaimed, 'if all they do is send you back home?' Antony didn't know. He didn't care. It wasn't his problem.

The road to the clubhouse was downhill, lined with grass and trees and the gates to other people's houses. Antony glanced at each driveway as he passed, assessing from the presence of cars who was at home and who wasn't. The Forresters had a new white Jeep, he noticed, pausing by their gate. Very nice.

'Hey Antony! Like my Jeep?' Antony started, and looked up. Sitting on the grass about fifty yards down the road were Xanthe Forrester and Mex Taylor. Their legs were entwined in a tangle of 501s and they were both smoking. Antony fought with a desire to turn round and pretend he hadn't heard. Xanthe was about his own age; he'd known her for ever. She'd always been a bitchy little girl; now she was just a bitch. She always managed to make him feel stupid and awkward and ugly. Mex Taylor was new to Greyworth. All Antony knew was that he was in the upper sixth at Eton and played off seven and all the girls thought he was great. Which was enough.

He walked slowly down the hill towards them, trying not to rush, trying to keep his breath steady, trying to think of something clever to say. Then, as he neared them, Xanthe suddenly put out her cigarette and began kissing Mex, clutching his head and writhing about as though she were in some stupid movie. Antony told himself furiously that she was just showing off. She probably thought he was jealous. She probably thought he'd never snogged anyone in his life before. If only she knew. At school, they were bussed off to dances nearly every weekend, and Antony always came away with a couple of love bites and a phone number, no problem. But that was at school, where there was no childhood history; where people took him for what he was. Whereas Xanthe Forrester, Fifi Tilling – all that little clique – still thought of him as square old

Antony Favour, good for a round of golf but not much else.

Suddenly Xanthe pulled herself away from Mex.

'My phone! It's vibrating!' She darted a wicked look at Mex, glanced at Antony, then pulled her mobile phone from the bright red leather holster on her hip. Antony looked awkwardly at Mex and, in spite of himself, felt his hand shoot up protectively to his eye, covering his birthmark.

'Hi? Fifi! Yeah, I'm with Mex!' Xanthe's voice was triumphant.

'Want a smoke?' said Mex casually to Antony. Antony considered. If he said yes, he would have to stay and talk to them. And someone might see him and tell his dad, which would be a real hassle. But if he said no, they'd think he was square.

'OK.'

Xanthe was still babbling away into her phone, but as Antony lit up, she paused and said with a giggle, 'Antony! Smoking! That's a bit daring for you, isn't it?' Mex gave Antony an amused look and Antony felt himself flushing.

'It's so cool!' said Xanthe, putting her phone away. 'Fifi's parents are away until Friday. We're all meeting at hers tonight,' she added to Mex. 'You, me, Fifi and Tania. Tania's got some stuff.'

'Sounds good,' said Mex. 'What about . . .' He jerked his head towards Antony. Xanthe pulled the briefest of faces at Mex, then turned to Antony.

'D'you want to meet up, Antony? We're watching *Betty Blue* on Fifi's laser disc.'

'I can't, I'm afraid,' said Antony. 'My dad's . . .' He paused. He wasn't about to tell Xanthe that his dad had a girlfriend. 'My dad's coming home,' he said weakly.

'Your dad's coming home?' said Xanthe incredulously. 'You can't come out because your dad's coming home?'

'I think that's really nice,' said Mex kindly. 'I wish I was that close to my dad.' He smirked at Xanthe. 'It would help if I didn't hate his guts.'

Xanthe burst into peals of laughter.

'I wish I was closer to my dad,' she said. 'Maybe then he would have given me a Jag instead of a Jeep.' She lit up another cigarette.

'How come you've got a Jeep? said Antony. 'You can't drive yet. You're only fifteen.'

'I can drive on private roads,' retorted Xanthe. 'Mex is teaching me. Aren't you, Mex?' She lay back on the grass and ran her fingers through her blond curls. 'And that's not all he's teaching me. Know what I mean?' She blew a circle of smoke into the air. 'Actually, you probably don't.' She winked at Mex. 'I don't want to shock Antony. He still kisses with his mouth closed.'

Antony stared at Xanthe in furious embarrassment, searching in his mind for some witty put-down. But the co-ordination between his brain and his mouth seemed to have disappeared.

'Your dad,' said Xanthe musingly. 'Your dad. What did I hear about him the other day?' Suddenly she sat up. 'Oh yes! He's got a floosie, hasn't he?'

'No he hasn't!'

'Yes he has! Mum and Dad were talking about it. Some woman in London. Really pretty, apparently. Mum caught them having lunch.'

'She's just a friend,' said Antony desperately. All his nonchalance had disappeared. Suddenly he hated his father; even hated his mother for dying. Why couldn't everything have stayed as it was?

'I heard about your mum,' said Mex. 'Rough.'

You don't know anything about it! Antony wanted to shout. But instead he stubbed out his cigarette awkwardly with his foot, and said,

'I've got to go.'

'Too bad,' said Xanthe. 'You were really turning me on, standing there in those sexy trousers. Where'd you get them? A jumble sale?'

'Catch you later,' said Mex. 'Have a nice time with your dad.'

As Antony began to walk off, he heard a suppressed snigger, but he didn't look back until he reached the corner. Then he allowed himself a quick glance behind him. Xanthe and Mex were kissing again.

Quickly he rounded the corner and sat down on a low stone wall. Through his mind ran all the phrases he'd heard from grown-ups over the years. *People who tease you are just immature . . . Don't take any notice – then they'll get bored . . . If they attach more importance to your looks than your personality, then they're not worth having as friends.*

So what was he supposed to do? Ignore everyone except Will? End up with no friends at all? The way he saw it, he had two choices. Either he could be lonely, or he could get on with the crowd. Antony sighed. It was all very well for grown-ups. They didn't know what it was like. When was the last time someone had been bitchy to his dad? Probably never. Grown-ups weren't bitchy to each other. They just weren't. In fact, grown-ups, thought Antony morosely, should stop complaining. They had it bloody easy.

Gillian sat at the huge wooden table in her dead sister's kitchen, looking blankly at a heap of French beans. She felt weary, almost too weary to raise the knife. Since Emily's death an apathy had been creeping up on her which alarmed and confused her. She knew no other way of dealing with it than by throwing herself whole-heartedly into the household tasks which filled her day. But the harder she worked, the less energy she seemed to have. When she sat down for a break she felt like stopping for ever.

She leaned forward on her elbows, feeling lethargic and heavy. She could feel her own weight sinking into the farmhouse chair, the mass of her solid, unbeautiful body. Ample breasts encased in a sensible bra, bulky legs hidden under a skirt. Her cardigan was thick and weighty; even her hair felt heavy today.

For a few minutes, she stared down at the table, tracing the grain of the wood with her finger, trying to lose herself in the whorls and loops, trying to pretend she felt normal. But as her finger reached a dark woody knot, she stopped. There was no point pretending to herself. She didn't just feel heavy. She didn't just feel apathetic. She felt scared.

The phone call from Richard had been brief. No explanation beyond the fact that he was bringing a woman down to stay and she was called Fleur. Gillian stared at her stubby, roughened fingertip and bit her lip. She should have realized that this would happen; that sooner or later Richard would find a . . . a female companion. But somehow she had imagined every-thing carrying on as normal: Richard, Antony and herself. Not so very different from when Emily had been alive – from all the times that the three of them had sat eating supper together, with Emily upstairs in bed.

She was a fool. Of course everything couldn't have continued like that for ever. For one thing, Antony was nearly grown up. Before long he'd be leaving school and going off to university. And did she expect to carry on living at The Maples then? Just her and Richard? She had no idea what Richard thought of her. Did he see her as any more than Emily's sister? Did he consider her a friend? Part of the family? Or did he expect her to leave, now that Emily was dead? She had no idea. In all the years she'd lived in his house, she'd rarely spoken to Richard directly. Their communications, such as they were, had always been through Emily. And now that Emily had gone, they didn't communicate at all. In the months since her death they had discussed nothing more significant than arrangements for meals. Gillian had not questioned her position; neither had Richard.

But now everything was different. Now there was a woman called Fleur. A woman she knew nothing about.

'You'll *love* her,' Richard had added just before putting the phone down. This Gillian doubted. Of course, he'd meant 'love' in the casual, modern use of the word. She'd heard it bandied about by the women in the clubhouse bar – I *love* your dress . . . Don't you just *love* this scent. Love, love love. As though it meant nothing; as though it weren't a sacrosanct word, a precious syllable, to be used sparingly. Gillian loved human beings, not handbags. She knew with a fierce certainty whom she loved, whom she had loved, whom she would always love. But in her adult life she had never uttered the word aloud.

Outside, a cloud moved, and a shaft of sunlight landed on the table.

'It's a nice day,' said Gillian, listening to her voice fall into the dead silence of the kitchen. She'd been talking to herself more and more, recently. Sometimes, with Richard up in London and Antony away at school, she was alone in the house for days at a time.

Empty, lonely days. She didn't have any friends at Greyworth; when the rest of the family were away, the phone soon stopped trilling. Many of Emily's friends had gained the impression over the years that Gillian was more a paid housekeeper than a member of the family – an impression which Emily had never bothered to correct.

Emily. Gillian's thoughts paused. Her little sister Emily, dead. She closed her eyes and rested her head in her hands. What kind of world was it where a younger sibling died before the elder? Where a married sister's frail body might be almost destroyed by repeated miscarriages, while her spinster sister's sturdy frame was never put to the test? Gillian had nursed Emily through each miscarriage, nursed her through the birth of Philippa and – much later – Antony. She'd watched as Emily's body gradually gave up; watched as everything faded away. And now she was left alone, living in a family that wasn't really hers, waiting for the arrival of her sister's replacement.

Maybe it was time to leave and start on a new life. After Emily's generous bequest she was now financially independent. She could go anywhere, do anything. A series of visions flipped through her mind like the pictures in a retirement plan brochure. She could buy a cottage by the sea. She could take up gardening. She could travel.

Into Gillian's thoughts crept the memory of an offer made many years ago, an offer which had thrilled her so much that she'd run and told Emily straight away. A trip round the world, with Verity Standish.

'You remember Verity,' she'd said excitedly to Emily, who stood by the fireplace, fiddling with a piece of porcelain. 'She's just taking off! Flying to Cairo in

October and going on from there. She wants me to come too! Isn't it exciting?'

And she'd waited for Emily to smile, to ask questions, to welcome Gillian's delight as wholeheartedly as Gillian had welcomed Emily's own many happinesses over the years. But Emily had turned, and without waiting for Gillian's breath to subside, had said, 'I'm pregnant. Four months.'

Gillian had caught her breath and stared at Emily, startled tears of delight springing into her eyes. She had thought – everyone had thought – that Emily would never have another child. Every one of her pregnancies since Philippa had ended in miscarriage before twelve weeks; it had seemed unlikely that she would ever carry another baby to term.

She'd hurried over and clasped Emily's hands in joy. 'Four months! Oh, Emily!' But Emily's blue eyes had bored into Gillian's reproachfully.

'Which means the baby's due in December.'

Suddenly Gillian had realized what she meant. And for once in her life she'd tried to resist Emily's dominance.

'You won't mind if I still go on the trip?' She'd adopted a cheery, matter-of-fact voice. 'Richard will be very supportive, I'm sure. And I'll be back in January, I can take over then.' She had begun to falter. 'It's just that this is such a wonderful . . .'

'Oh you go!' Emily had exclaimed in a brittle voice. 'I can easily hire a maternity nurse. And a nanny for Philippa. It'll be fine.' She'd flashed Gillian a little smile, and Gillian had stared back at her with a miserable wariness. She knew this game of Emily's; knew that she was always too slow to anticipate the next move.

'And I'll probably keep the nanny on after you come

back.' Emily's silvery voice had travelled across the room and lodged itself like a painful splinter in Gillian's chest. 'She can have your room. You won't mind, will you? You'll probably be living elsewhere by then.'

She should have gone anyway. She should have called Emily's bluff and gone with Verity. She could have travelled for a few months, come back and joined the family again. Emily wouldn't have rejected her help. She felt sure of that now. *She should have gone.* The words echoed bitterly in her mind and she felt her entire body tense up as the regrets of fifteen years circled around her like poisoned blood.

But she had not gone. She had caved in, as she'd always caved in to Emily, and she had stayed for the birth of Antony. And it was after his birth that she'd realized that she could never go; that she could never leave the house by her own choice. Because Emily didn't love little Antony. But Gillian loved him more than anything else in the world.

'So, tell me about Gillian,' said Fleur, leaning comfortably back in her seat.

'Gillian?' said Richard absently. He put on his indicator. 'Go on, let me in, you idiot.'

'Yes, Gillian,' said Fleur, as the car changed lanes. 'How long has she been living with you?'

'Oh, years. Since . . . I don't know, since Philippa was born, maybe.'

'And do you get on well with her?'

'Oh yes.'

Fleur glanced at Richard. His face was blank and uninterested. So much for Gillian.

'And Antony,' she said. 'I haven't met him yet either.'

'Oh, you'll like Antony,' said Richard. A sudden enthusiasm came into his face. 'He's a good lad. Plays off twelve, which is pretty good for his age.'

'Marvellous,' said Fleur politely. The more time she spent with Richard, the more clear it was becoming that she was going to have to take up this appalling game. She tried to imagine herself in a pair of golfing shoes, with tassles and spikes, and gave a little shudder.

'It's lovely country round here,' she said, looking out of the window. 'I didn't realize Surrey had sheep.'

'The odd sheep,' said Richard. 'The odd cow, too.' He paused, and his mouth began to twitch humorously. Fleur waited. The twitching mouth meant he was going to make a joke. 'You'll meet some of Surrey's finest cows down at the golf club,' said Richard eventually, and gave a snort of laughter. Fleur giggled along, amused at him rather than the joke. Was this really the same stiff, dull man she'd met six weeks ago? She could hardly believe it. Richard seemed to have plunged into a life of merriment with an almost zealous determination. Now it was he who phoned her up with outlandish suggestions, who cracked jokes, who planned outings and amusements.

In part he was trying to compensate, she guessed, for the lack of physical intimacy in their relationship; a lack which he clearly believed troubled her as much as it troubled him. She had told him once or twice that it didn't matter – but not too convincingly; not too unflatteringly. And so, to allay both their frustrations, he'd begun to fill their nights with substitutes. If he could not entertain her in bed, he could entertain her in theatres and cocktail bars and night clubs. Every morning he called her at ten o'clock with a plan for the evening. To her surprise, Fleur had started to look forward to his calls.

'Sheringham St Martin!' she suddenly exclaimed, noticing a sign out of the window.

'Yes, it's a pretty village,' said Richard.

'That's where Xavier Formby's opened his new restaurant. I was reading about it. The Pumpkin House. Apparently it's wonderful. We must go some time.'

'Let's go right now,' said Richard at once. 'Have supper there. Perfect! I'll give them a call, see if there's a table.'

Without pausing, he reached down to his phone and punched in the number for Directory Enquiries. Fleur looked at him carefully. Was there any reason for her to point out that this Gillian character had probably organized dinner for them already? Richard didn't seem to care – in fact he seemed almost oblivious of Gillian. In some families it was well worth winning round the womenfolk – but what was the point here? She might as well play along with Richard. After all, he was the one with the money. And if he wanted to go out to dinner, who was she to persuade him otherwise?

'You have?' Richard was saying. 'Well, we'll be right along.' Fleur beamed at him.

'You're so clever.'

'*Carpe diem*,' said Richard. 'Seize the day.' He smiled at her. 'You know, when I was a boy I never understood that saying. I thought it was "sees" as in "to see". Sees the day. It never seemed to make sense.'

'But it makes sense now?' said Fleur.

'Oh yes,' said Richard. 'It makes more and more sense.'

The phone rang at seven o'clock, just as Antony had finished laying the table. As Gillian answered, he stood back to admire it. There were lilies in vases, and lacy white napkins and candles waiting to be lit, and from the kitchen was coming a wonderful smell of roast lamb. Time for a gin, thought Antony. He looked at his watch. Surely his father would be here soon?

Suddenly Gillian appeared at the door of the dining room, wearing the blue dress she always put on for special occasions. Her face was grim, but that didn't necessarily mean anything.

'That was your father,' she said. 'He won't be here till later.'

'Oh. How much later?' Antony straightened a knife.

'About ten, he said. He and this woman are eating out.' Antony's head shot up.

'Eating out? But they can't!'

'They're at the restaurant now.'

'But you've made supper! Did you tell him? Did you say there was roast lamb waiting in the oven?' Gillian shrugged. She had the resigned, weary expression on her face that Antony hated.

'Your father can eat out if he likes,' she said.

'You should have said something!' cried Antony.

'It's not for me to tell your father what to do.'

'But if he'd realized, I'm sure . . .' Antony broke off and looked at Gillian in frustration. Why the hell hadn't she said something to Dad? When he got back and saw what he'd done, he'd feel terrible.

'Well, it's too late now. He didn't say which restaurant he was at.'

She looked almost pleased, thought Antony, as though she got some satisfaction from having all her efforts wasted.

'So we'll just eat it all ourselves?' He sounded aggressive, he knew, but he didn't care.

'I suppose so.' Gillian looked down at herself. 'I'll go and get out of this dress,' she said.

'Why don't you keep it on?' said Antony, desperate

somehow to salvage the occasion. 'You look nice.'

'It'll get all creased. There's no point messing it up.' She turned, and made her way towards the stairs.

Well fuck it, thought Antony. If you don't want to make an effort, then neither do I. He remembered Xanthe Forrester and Mex Taylor that morning. They had actually invited him out, hadn't they? Maybe they weren't so bad, after all.

'I might go out then,' he said. 'If we're not having a big dinner or anything.'

'All right,' said Gillian, without looking back.

Antony went over to the phone and dialled Fifi Tilling's number.

'Hello?' Fifi's voice was bubbling over with fun; there was music in the background.

'Hi, it's Antony. Antony Favour.'

'Oh right. Hi, Antony. Hey, everyone,' she called, 'Antony's on the phone.' In the background, he thought he could hear sniggers.

'I wasn't going to be free this evening,' he said awkwardly, 'but now I am. So I could come round or something. Xanthe said everyone was getting together.'

'Oh. Yeah.' There was a pause. 'Actually we're all about to go out to a club.'

'Great. Well, I'm on for that.' Did he sound friendly and laid-back, or anxious and desperate? He couldn't tell.

'The thing is, actually, the car's full.'

'Oh, right.' Antony looked at the receiver; not sure. Was she trying to say . . .

'Sorry about that.' Yes, she was.

'No problem.' He tried to sound casual. Amused, even. 'Maybe another time.'

'Oh. Yeah. Sure.' Fifi sounded vague. She wasn't even listening to him.

'Well, bye then,' said Antony.

'Bye Antony. See you around.'

Antony put the phone down and felt a wave of humiliation rise through him. They would have found room for him if they'd wanted to. He looked down at his hands and saw that they were shaking. He felt hot with embarrassment, even though he was alone in the room.

It was all his bloody dad's fault – if he'd arrived on time, that phone call wouldn't have happened. Antony leaned back in his chair. He found that thought gratifying. Yeah, it was his dad's fault. An invigorating resentment began to wash through him. And it was Gillian's fault too. What was her bloody problem? Why hadn't she just given his dad some grief and told him to come right home?

For a few minutes he sat, fiddling with a napkin, thinking how pissed off he was with them both, and looking at the table which he'd laid. What an effort for nothing. Well, it could all just stay there. He wasn't about to put everything away again.

Then it occurred to him that Gillian might call down and suggest that he did exactly that, so before she could he got up and wandered into the kitchen. The lamb was still roasting away in the oven, and sitting majestically on the table was the pavlova, smothered in whipped cream and decorated with kiwi fruit. Antony looked at it. If they weren't going to do supper properly, then there was no harm in him having a bit, was there? He pulled out a chair, picked up the remote control and zapped it several times at the screen of the television. Then, as the kitchen filled with the glitzy sound of a game show, he picked up a spoon, dug it into the shiny meringue, and began to munch.

Chapter Five

Breakfast had been laid in the conservatory.

'What a lovely room,' said Fleur politely, looking at Gillian's face, searching for eye contact. But Gillian was looking down at her plate. She had not once met Fleur's eye since she and Richard had arrived the night before.

'We like it,' said Richard cheerfully. 'Especially in the spring. In the summer, it sometimes gets too hot.'

There was another silence. Antony put down his teacup and everyone seemed to listen intently to the little tinkle.

'We built the conservatory about . . . ten years ago,' continued Richard. 'Is that right, Gillian?'

'I expect so,' said Gillian. 'More tea, anyone?'

'Yes please,' said Fleur.

'Right. Well I'll make another pot, then,' said Gillian, and she disappeared into the kitchen.

Fleur took a bite of toast. Things were going rather well, she thought, despite the uneaten roast lamb and pavlova. It had been the boy, Antony, who had confronted them the night before, almost as soon as they had got inside the door, and informed them that Gillian had spent all day cooking. Richard had looked horror-struck, and Fleur had put on a most convincing show of dismay. Fortunately, no-one seemed to blame her. Equally fortunately, it was obvious this morning that no-one was going to mention the matter again.

'Here you are.' Gillian had returned with the teapot.

'Wonderful,' said Fleur, smiling into Gillian's unreceptive face. It was going to be easy, she thought, if all she would have to deal with were awkward silences and a few resentful glares. Glares didn't bother her at all; neither did raised eyebrows; neither did sidelong comments. That was the blessedness of preying on the reserved British middle classes, she thought, sipping at her tea. They never seemed to talk to each other; they never wanted to rock the boat; they seemed almost more willing to lose all their money than to undergo the embarrassment of a direct confrontation. Which meant that for someone like her, the way was clear.

She looked curiously at Gillian. For someone who presumably had access to funds, Gillian was wearing particularly hideous clothes. Dark green trousers – slacks, Fleur supposed they would be called – and a blue embroidered cotton shirt with short, workmanlike sleeves. As she leaned over with the teapot, Fleur glimpsed Gillian's upper arms – solid slabs of white, opaque, almost dead-looking skin.

Antony's clothes were a bit better. Fairly standard jeans and a rather nice red shirt. It was a shame about his birthmark. Had they not been able to treat it? Possibly not, because it stretched right across his eye. If he'd been a girl, of course, he'd have been able to wear make-up . . . Other than that, thought Fleur, he was a handsome boy. He took after his father.

Fleur's gaze flitted idly over to Richard. He was leaning back in his chair, looking out of the conservatory into the garden, with an apparent look of contentment on his face, as though he were beginning a holiday. As he felt her eyes on him, he glanced up and smiled. Fleur smiled back. It was easy to smile at Richard, she thought. He was a good man, kind and considerate, and not nearly as dull as she had first feared. These last few weeks had been fun.

But it was money she needed, not fun. She hadn't persevered so hard in order to end up with a limited income and holidays in Majorca. Fleur gave an inward sigh, and took another sip of tea. Sometimes the effort of pursuing money quite exhausted her; sometimes she began to think that Majorca would not be so bad after all. But that was weakness. She hadn't come so far simply to give up. She would achieve her goal. She *had* to achieve it. Apart from anything else, it was the only goal she had.

She looked up at Richard and smiled.

'Is this the largest house on the Greyworth estate?'

'I don't think so,' said Richard. 'One of the largest, I suppose.'

'The Tillings have got eight bedrooms,' volunteered Antony. 'And a snooker room.'

'There you are.' Richard grinned. 'Trust Antony to be on the ball.'

Antony said nothing. He found the sight of Fleur across the table from him unsettling. Was this woman really going out with his dad? She was gorgeous. Gorgeous! And she made his dad look different. When the two of them had arrived the night before, all smart and glamorous looking, they'd looked as if they came from someone else's family. His dad didn't look like his dad. And Fleur certainly didn't look like anyone's mum. But she wasn't a floosie, either, thought Antony. She wasn't a dolly-bird. She was just . . . beautiful.

Reaching for his cup, Richard saw Antony staring at Fleur with undisguised admiration. And in spite of himself, he felt a little dart of pride. That's right, my boy, he felt like saying. Life's not over for me yet. At

73

the back of his mind ran guilty thoughts like a train: remembered images of Emily sitting just where Fleur now sat; memories of family breakfasts with Emily's tinkling laugh rising above the conversation. But he stamped on them every time they surfaced; refused to allow his sentimentality to get the better of him. Life was for living; happiness was for taking; Fleur was a wonderful woman. Sitting in the bright sunshine, there seemed nothing more to it than that.

After breakfast, Richard disappeared to get ready for golf. As he had explained to Fleur, today was the Banting Cup. Any other Saturday, he would have forgone golf to show her around the place. But the Banting Cup . . .

'Don't worry,' Fleur had said at once. 'I'll be fine.'

'We can meet up for a drink afterwards,' Richard had added. 'Gillian will bring you down to the clubhouse.' He'd paused, and his brow had wrinkled. 'Do you mind?'

'Of course not,' Fleur had said, laughing. 'I'll have a lovely morning on my own.'

'You won't be on your own!' Richard had said. 'Gillian will look after you.'

Now Fleur eyed Gillian thoughtfully. She was taking clean plates from the dishwasher and stacking them in a pile. Every time she bent down she gave a little sigh; every time she stood up she looked as though the effort might kill her.

'Lovely plates,' said Fleur, getting up. 'Simply beautiful. Did you choose them?'

'What, these?' said Gillian. She looked at the plate in her hand as though she hated it. 'Oh no. Emily chose them. Richard's wife.' She paused, and her voice became harsher. 'She was my sister.'

'I see,' said Fleur.

Well, it hadn't taken long to get on to that subject, she thought. The dead, blameless wife. Perhaps she had underestimated this Gillian. Perhaps the attack would begin now. The pursed lips, the hissed threats. *You're not welcome in my kitchen.* She stood, watching Gillian and waiting. But Gillian's face remained impassive; pale and pouchy like an undercooked scone.

'Do you play golf?' said Fleur eventually.

'A little.'

'I don't play at all, I'm afraid. I must try to learn.'

Gillian didn't reply. She had begun to put the plates back on the dresser. They were hand-painted pottery plates, each decorated with a different farm-yard animal. If they were going to be displayed, thought Fleur, they should at least go the right way up. But Gillian didn't seem to notice. Each plate went back on the dresser with a crash, until the top shelf and half the second shelf were filled with animals at assorted angles. Then all of a sudden the animals came to an end and she began to fill the rest of the shelves with blue and white patterned china. No! Fleur wanted to exclaim. Can't you see how ugly that looks? It would take two minutes to make it look nice.

'Lovely,' she said, as Gillian finished. 'I adore farm-house kitchens.'

'It's difficult to keep clean,' said Gillian glumly. 'All these tiles. You chop vegetables and all the bits go in between.'

Fleur looked around vaguely, wondering what she could find to say on the subject of chopped vegetables. The room reminded her uncomfortably of a kitchen in Scotland in which she'd shivered for an entire shooting season, only to discover at the end that her titled host was not only heavily in debt, but had been two-timing her all along. Bloody upper classes, she thought savagely. Waste-of-time losers.

'Excuse me,' said Gillian. 'I've got to get to that cupboard.' She reached down, past Fleur, and emerged with a grater.

'Let me help,' said Fleur. 'I'm sure there's something I can do.'

'It's easier if I do it myself.' Gillian's shoulders were hunched and her eyes refused to meet Fleur's. Fleur gave an inward shrug.

'OK,' she said. 'Well, I might pop upstairs and do some bits and pieces. What time are we going to the clubhouse?'

'Twelve,' said Gillian, without looking up.

Plenty of time, thought Fleur, as she made her way up the stairs. With Richard and Antony both out and Gillian grating away in the kitchen, now was the perfect opportunity to find out what she needed. She walked slowly down the corridor, mentally valuing as she went. The wallpaper was dull but expensive; the pictures were dull and cheap. All the good paintings had obviously been crammed into the drawing room downstairs, where visitors could see them. Emily Favour, she thought, had probably been the sort of woman to wear expensive dresses and cheap underclothes.

She walked straight past the door to her bedroom and turned down a tiny flight of stairs. The beauty of being new to a house was that one could always claim to be lost. Especially since the guided tour the night before had been so vague. 'Down there's my office,' Richard had said, gesturing towards the stairs. And Fleur had not so much as flickered, but had given a tiny yawn and said, 'All that wine's making me feel snoozy!'

Now she descended the flight of stairs with determination. At last she was starting on the real business in hand. Behind that door she would discover the true extent of Richard's potential – whether he was worth bothering with, and how much she could take him for. She would quickly work out whether it was worth waiting for a particular time in the year; if there were any unusual factors she should take into account. She suspected not. Most men's financial affairs were remarkably similar. It was the men themselves who differed.

The thought of a new project filled her with a slight exhilaration, and she felt her heart beat more quickly as she reached for the door handle and pushed. But the door didn't budge. She tried again – but it was no good. The door to the office was locked.

For a few seconds she stared at the glossy white panels in outrage. What kind of man locked the door to the office in his own house? She tried the handle one more time. Definitely locked. She felt like giving it a little kick. Then self-discipline took over. There was no point lingering there and risking being seen. Quickly she turned and retreated up the steps, down the corridor and into her room. She sat down on her bed and gazed crossly at her reflection in the mirror. What was she going to do now? That door stood between her and all the details she needed. How could she proceed without the right information?

'Damn and blast,' she said aloud. 'Blast and damn. Damn and blast.' Eventually the sound of her own voice cheered her. It wasn't so bad. She would work something out. Richard couldn't keep the office locked all the time – and if he did, she would just have to find the key. Meanwhile . . . Fleur ran an idle hand through her hair. Meanwhile, she could always have a nice long bath and wash her hair.

At half-past eleven Gillian came trudging up the stairs. Fleur thought for a moment then, still wearing her dressing gown, she came out onto the landing. Gillian would prove a distraction, if nothing else.

'Gillian, what shall I wear to the clubhouse?' she asked. She tried to meet Gillian's eye. 'Tell me what to wear.' Gillian gave a little shrug.

'There aren't really any rules. Fairly smart, I suppose.'

'Too vague! You'll have to come and help me decide. Come on!' Fleur went back into her room and after a moment's hesitation, Gillian followed.

'My smartest clothes are all black,' said Fleur. 'Does anyone at the golf club wear black?'

'Not really,' said Gillian.

'I didn't think so.' Fleur gave a dramatic little sigh. 'And I so wanted to blend in. Can I see what you're wearing?'

'I'm not wearing anything special,' said Gillian in a rough, almost angry voice. 'Just a blue dress.'

'Blue! I tell you what . . .' Fleur rummaged around in one of her bags. 'Do you want to borrow this?' She produced a long blue silk scarf and draped it over Gillian's shoulder. 'Some fool gave it to me. Do I look the sort of woman who can wear blue?' She rolled her eyes at Gillian and lowered her voice. 'He also seemed to think I was size eight and liked wearing red underwear.' She shrugged. 'What can you do?'

Gillian stared back at Fleur, feeling her colour rise. Something unfamiliar was happening at the back of her throat. It felt a bit like laughter.

'But it should suit you perfectly,' said Fleur. 'It's exactly the same colour as your eyes. I wish I had blue eyes!' She scrutinized Gillian's eyes and Gillian began to feel hot.

'Thank you,' she said abruptly. She looked down at the blue silk. 'I'll try it. But I'm not sure it'll suit the dress.'

'Shall I come and help you? I know how to tie these things.'

'No!' Gillian almost shouted. Fleur was overwhelming her. She had to get away. 'I'll just go now and change. And I'll see.' She hurried out of the room.

In the safety of her own bedroom Gillian stopped. She picked up the end of the scarf and rubbed the smooth fabric across her face. It smelt sweet. Like Fleur. Sweet and soft and bright.

Gillian sat down at her dressing table. Fleur's voice rang in her ears. A bubble of laughter was still at the back of her throat. She felt enlivened; out of breath; almost overcome. That's charm, she suddenly thought. Real charm wasn't the gushing and kisses of the frosted women at the golf club. Emily had been called a charming woman, but her eyes had held splinters of ice and her tinkling laugh had been saccharine and humourless. Fleur's eyes were warm and all-inclusive and when she laughed she made everyone else want to laugh too. That was real charm. Of course Fleur didn't really mean any of it. She didn't really want blue eyes; she didn't really need Gillian's advice. Nor – Gillian was sure – did she want to blend in with the others at the golf club. But, just for a few seconds, she'd made Gillian feel warm and wanted and in on the joke. Never before had Gillian been in on the joke.

* * *

The clubhouse at Greyworth had been built in an American colonial style, with a large wooden veranda overlooking the eighteenth green.

'Is this the bar?' asked Fleur as they arrived. She looked around at the tables and chairs; the gins; the flushed, jolly faces.

'The bar's in there. But in the summer everyone sits outside. It's terribly hard to get a table.' Gillian looked around, eyes screwed up. 'I think they're all taken.' She sighed. 'What would you like to drink?'

'A Manhattan,' said Fleur. Gillian looked at her dubiously.

'What's that?'

'They'll know.'

'Well . . . all right then.'

'Wait a moment,' said Fleur. She reached towards Gillian and tugged at the ends of the blue scarf. 'You need to drape it more. Like this. Don't let it get wrinkled up. OK?' Gillian gave a tiny shrug.

'It's all such a fuss.'

'The fuss is what makes it fun,' said Fleur. 'Like having seams on your stockings. You have to check them every five minutes.'

Gillian's expression became gloomier still.

'Well, I'll get the drinks,' she said. 'I expect there'll be an awful queue.'

'Do you want some help?' Fleur asked.

'No, you'd better stay out here and wait for a table.'

She began to walk towards the glass doors leading to the bar. As she reached them she slowed very slightly, almost imperceptibly reached for the ends of the scarf, and pulled them into place. Fleur gave a tiny smile. Then, moving unhurriedly, she turned and looked around the veranda. She was aware that she had begun to attract a few interested glances. Red-faced golfing men were leaning across to their chums; sharp-eyed golfing women were nudging each other.

Quickly Fleur assessed the tables on the veranda. Some overlooked the golf course, some didn't. Some had parasols, others didn't. The best one was in the corner, she decided. It was large and round, and there were only two men sitting at it. Without hesitating, Fleur walked over and smiled at the plumper of the two men. He was dressed in a bright yellow jersey and halfway down a silver tankard of beer.

'Hello,' she said. 'Are you two alone?' The plump man became a degree pinker and cleared his throat.

'Our wives will be joining us.'

'Oh dear.' Fleur began to count the chairs. 'Might there still be room for my friend and me? She's just getting our drinks.'

The men glanced at each other.

'The thing is,' continued Fleur, 'I'd so like to look at the golf course.' She began to edge towards the table. 'It's very beautiful, isn't it?'

'One of the best in Surrey,' said the thinner man gruffly.

'Just look at those trees!' said Fleur, gesturing. Both men followed her gaze. By the time they turned back, she was sitting down on one of the spare chairs. 'Have you been playing today?' she said.

'Now look here,' said one of the men awkwardly. 'I don't mean to . . .'

'Did you play in the Banting Cup? What exactly *is* the Banting Cup?'

'Are you a new member? Because if you are . . .'

'I'm not a member at all,' said Fleur.

'You're not a member? Do you have a guest pass?'

'I'm not sure,' said Fleur vaguely.

'This is bloody typical,' said the thinner man to the

yellow-jerseyed man. 'Absolutely no bloody security.' He turned to Fleur. 'Now look, young woman, I'm afraid I'm going to have to ask you . . .'

'Young woman?' said Fleur, sparkling at him. 'You are kind.'

He stood up angrily.

'Are you aware that this is a private club and that trespassers will be prosecuted? Now I think the best thing is for you and your friend . . .'

'Oh, here comes Gillian,' interrupted Fleur. 'Hello, Gillian. These nice men are letting us sit at their table.'

'Hello, George,' said Gillian. 'Is anything wrong?'

There was a tiny silence, during which Fleur turned unconcernedly away. A confused, embarrassed conversation broke out behind her. The men hadn't realized that Fleur's friend was Gillian! They'd had no idea. They'd thought . . . No, of course they hadn't thought. Well, anyway . . . a small world, wasn't it? What a small world. And there were the drinks.

'Mine's the Manhattan,' said Fleur, turning round. 'How do you do? My name is Fleur Daxeny.'

'Alistair Lennox.'

'George Tilling.'

'I've found my guest pass,' said Fleur. 'Do you want to see it?' Both the men began to harrumph awkwardly.

'Any friend of Gillian's . . .' began one.

'Actually, I'm more a friend of Richard's,' said Fleur.

'An old friend?'

'No, a new friend.'

There was a pause, during which a flash of comprehension passed through George Tilling's eyes. Now you remember, thought Fleur. I'm that piece of gossip your wife was trying to tell you while you were reading the newspaper. Now you wish you'd listened a bit harder, don't you? And she gave him a tiny smile.

'You realize you're the subject of a lot of gossip?' said Alec, as they reached the seventeenth green. Richard gave a little smile, and took out his putter.

'So I gather.' He looked up at his old friend; kindly and concerned. 'What you don't realize is that being the subject of gossip is actually quite fun.'

'It's no joke,' said Alec. His Scottish accent was becoming more pronounced, as it always did when he was anxious. 'They're saying . . .' He broke off.

'What are they saying?' Richard held up a hand. 'Let me putt first.'

With no hesitation he sank the ball from ten feet.

'Good shot,' said Alec automatically. 'You're playing well today.'

'What are they saying? Come on, Alec. You might as well get it off your chest.' Alec paused. A look of pain passed across his face.

'They're saying that if you persist with this woman, you might not be nominated for captain after all.' Richard's mouth tightened.

'I see,' he said. 'And have any of them actually met "this woman", as you so charmingly put it?'

'I think Eleanor's been saying . . .'

'Eleanor met Fleur once, briefly, in a London restaurant. She has absolutely no right . . .'

'Rights and wrongs don't come into it. You know that. If the club takes against Fleur . . .'

'Why should they?'

'Well . . . She's quite different from Emily, isn't she?'

Richard had known Alec since the age of seven and had never before in his life felt like hitting him. But now he felt a surge of violent anger against Alec; against them all. He watched in silence as Alec muffed his putt, feeling his fists clench and his jaw tighten. As the ball eventually plopped into the hole, Alec looked up and met his tense stare.

'Look,' he said apologetically. 'You may not care what the club thinks. But . . . well, it's not just the club. I'm worried for you. You have to admit that Fleur seems to have taken over your entire life.' He replaced the flag and they began to walk slowly towards the eighteenth tee.

'You're worried for me,' repeated Richard. 'And what exactly are you worried about? That I might be enjoying myself too much? That I might be happier now than I've ever been in my life before?'

'Richard . . .'

'Well what, then?'

'I'm just worried you'll be hurt, I suppose.' Alec looked away awkwardly.

'My word,' said Richard. 'We are becoming frank with one another.'

'You know what I mean.'

'All I know is that I'm happy, Fleur's happy, and the rest of you should mind your own business.'

'But you've just plunged in . . .'

'Yes, I've plunged in. And do you know what? I've discovered that plunging in is the best way to live.'

They had reached the tee. Richard took out his ball and looked straight at Alec.

'Have you ever plunged into anything in your life?' Alec was silent. 'I didn't think so. Well, you know, maybe you should try it.'

Richard placed his ball on the tee and, with a set jaw, took a few practice swings. The eighteenth was long and tricky, looping round a little lake to the right. Richard and Alec had always agreed that it was safer to play round the lake than to risk losing a ball in the water. But today, without looking at Alec, Richard hit the ball boldly to the right, directly towards the lake. They both watched in silence as the little ball soared over the surface of the water and landed safely on the fairway.

'I think . . . you made it,' said Alec faintly.

'Yes,' said Richard. He didn't sound surprised. 'I made it. You probably would too.'

'I don't think I'd try.'

'Yes well,' said Richard. 'Maybe that's the difference between us.'

Chapter Six

To Fleur's astonishment, it was four weeks later. The July sun streamed into the conservatory every morning, Antony was home from school for the holidays, Richard's lower arms were turning brown. Talk at the clubhouse was of nothing but flights, villas and house-sitters.

Fleur was now a familiar figure at the clubhouse. Most mornings, when Richard had gone off to the office, she and Gillian had taken to strolling down to the Greyworth health club – for which Richard had bought Fleur a season's membership. They would swim a little, sit in the Jacuzzi a little, drink a glass of fresh passion fruit juice and stroll back again. It was a pleasant, gentle routine, which even Gillian now appeared to enjoy – despite her initial resistance. Persuading her to come along the first time had been almost impossible and Fleur had only succeeded by appealing to Gillian's sense of duty as a hostess. Most of Gillian's life, it seemed, was governed by a sense of duty – a concept completely alien to Fleur.

She took a sip of coffee and shut her eyes, feeling the sun on her face. Breakfast was over; the conservatory was now empty apart from her. Richard had gone off for a meeting with his lawyer; he'd be coming back later for a round of golf with Lambert and some business contact or other. Antony was off somewhere doing, she supposed, teenage things. Gillian was upstairs, supervising the cleaner. Supervision – another concept completely alien to Fleur. One either did a task oneself, she thought, or one left it to other people and didn't bother about it. But then, she'd always been lazy. And she was becoming lazier. Too lazy.

A pang of self-reproach darted through her. She'd been living in Richard Favour's house for four weeks. Four weeks! And what had she accomplished in that time? Nothing. After the initial attempt on his office she'd let the subject of money slip comfortably from her mind; let herself slide into an easy sunlit existence in which one day melted into another and suddenly she was four weeks older. Four weeks older and not a penny richer. She hadn't even gone near his office again. For all she knew, it was unlocked and stashed full of gold bullion.

'A penny for your thoughts,' said Gillian, appearing at the door of the conservatory.

'They're worth more than a penny,' retorted Fleur cheerfully. 'A lot more.'

She looked quizzically at Gillian's attire. She was wearing a tangerine-coloured dress with a nasty, fussy neckline and, draped straight across it, Fleur's blue scarf. Not a day went by now without Gillian wearing that scarf, always in exactly the way Fleur had shown her – no matter what the outfit. Fleur supposed she should be flattered, but instead she was beginning to feel irritated. Was the only answer to supply the woman with a scarf in every colour?

'We'd better be off in a moment,' said Gillian. 'I don't know what the form is. Maybe everybody arrives late. Fashionably late.' She attempted a little laugh.

'Fashionably late is out,' said Fleur idly. 'Although I

suppose it might still be fashionable in Surrey.'

This afternoon, she thought to herself. This afternoon she'd have another shot. Perhaps while Richard was out on the golf course. She could keep Gillian in the kitchen by suggesting that she make a cake. And maybe she could find some reason to borrow Richard's keys. She would be in and out before anyone even wondered where she was.

'I don't know who'll be there,' Gillian was saying. 'I've never been to this kind of thing before.'

Gillian seemed unusually loquacious, thought Fleur. She raised her eyes and Gillian met them imploringly. My God, she's nervous, thought Fleur. I'm the impostor and she's the one who's nervous.

They were about to walk down to Eleanor Forrester's house, to have brunch and look at the range of jewellery which Eleanor energetically sold whenever she had the chance. Gillian had apparently never been to one of Eleanor's brunch mornings before. Reading between the lines, thought Fleur, Gillian had never been asked before.

Fleur's own instinct, when Eleanor had asked her, had been to turn the invitation down. But then she'd seen Richard's delighted smile, and she'd remembered her own guiding principle. If a man smiles, do it again; if he smiles again, don't stop.

'Of course,' she'd said, darting a glance at Gillian's stiff, averted cheek. 'We'd love to come, wouldn't we Gillian?' After that, she hadn't known which to enjoy most, the embarrassed expression on Gillian's face or the discomfited one on Eleanor Forrester's.

Gillian was shifting from one foot to another and mangling the end of the scarf in her anxious fingers. For the sake of the scarf if nothing else, Fleur got to her feet.

'OK,' she said. 'Let's go and look at this woman's baubles.'

Eleanor's garden was large and sloping with many arbours and wrought-iron benches. Two trestle tables had been erected on the lawn; one covered with food, the other with jewellery.

'Have some buck's fizz!' exclaimed Eleanor as they arrived. 'I don't have to ask if you're driving, do I? Did you hear about poor James Morrell?' she added in an undertone. 'Banned for a year. His wife's *furious*. Now, go and sit down. A lot of the girls are here already.'

The 'girls' were aged between thirty-five and sixty-five. They were all tanned, fit and vivacious. Many wore brightly coloured clothes with what looked like expensive appliqué work. Little tennis players careered across bosoms; little golfers danced up and down arms, endlessly striking tiny beaded golf balls.

'Aren't these fun?' said one woman, noticing Fleur's gaze. 'Foxy sells them! Polo shirts, trousers, everything, really. Foxy Harris. I'm sure she'll tell you about them when she arrives.'

'I'm sure she will,' murmured Fleur.

'Emily had quite a collection of Foxy's clothes,' chimed in another woman, dressed entirely in pink. 'She always looked absolutely lovely in them.'

Fleur said nothing.

'Were you a close friend of Emily's, Fleur?' asked the pink woman.

'Not really,' said Fleur.

'No, I thought you couldn't have been,' said the woman. 'I suppose I knew her the best out of all of us. I expect she mentioned me. Tricia Tilling.'

Fleur gestured vaguely with her hand.

'We all miss her,' said Tricia. She paused as though

lost in memories. 'And of course, Richard was devoted to her. I used to think, I'll never see a couple as much in love as Richard and Emily Favour.' Fleur was aware of Gillian shifting awkwardly beside her. 'They were *made* for each other,' continued Tricia. 'Like . . . gin and tonic.'

'What a beautiful thought,' said Fleur.

Tricia's eyes met hers appraisingly.

'That's a lovely watch, Fleur,' she said. 'Did Richard buy that for you?' She gave a little laugh. 'George is always buying me little things here and there.'

'Is he?' said Fleur. She idly fingered the watch and said nothing more. From the corner of her eye she was aware of Tricia's satisfied face.

'You know,' said Tricia, as though beginning on a new subject, 'poor Graham Loosemore has got into an awful pickle. You remember Graham?' There was a murmur of assent.

'Well, he went to the Philippines on holiday – and married a local girl! All of eighteen. They're living together in Dorking!' There was a general gasp. 'She's after his money, of course.' Tricia drew up her face as though gathering the neck of a shoe-bag. 'She'll have a baby so she can claim support, and then she'll be off. She'll probably get . . . half the house? That's two hundred thousand pounds! And all for a silly mistake. The fool!'

'Maybe he's not a fool,' said Fleur idly, and winked at Gillian.

'What?' snapped Tricia.

'How much would you pay a strapping young Filipino to make love to you every night?' Fleur grinned at Tricia. 'I'd pay quite a lot.' Tricia goggled at Fleur.

'Just exactly what are you saying?' she whispered, in

tones prepared to be astounded.

'I'm saying . . . maybe this girl is worth it.'

'Worth it?'

'Maybe she's worth two hundred thousand pounds. To him, at any rate.'

Tricia stared at Fleur as though suspecting trickery.

'These wealthy widowers have to be very careful,' she said eventually. 'They're terribly vulnerable.'

'So are wealthy widows,' said Fleur casually. 'I find I have to be on my guard constantly.' Tricia stiffened. But before she could speak, Eleanor Forrester's voice interrupted the group.

'More buck's fizz? And then I'll start the presentation. Did I tell you all about poor James Morrell?' she added, handing round glasses. 'Banned for a year! And he was only a tiny bit over the limit! I mean, which of us hasn't been a tiny bit over?'

'Me,' said Fleur, putting her glass down on the grass without drinking from it. 'I don't drive.'

A babble broke out around her. How could Fleur not drive? How did she manage? What about the school run? The shopping?

Tricia Tilling's voice rose truculently above the rest.

'I suppose you have a chauffeur, do you, Fleur?'

'Sometimes,' said Fleur.

Suddenly, without meaning to, she remembered sitting behind her father's driver in Dubai, leaning out of the window into the hot dusty street and being told in Arabic to sit still. They'd been driving past the gold souk. Where had they been going? Fleur couldn't remember.

'Now, are we ready?' Eleanor's voice pierced Fleur's consciousness. 'I'll start with brooches. Aren't these fun?'

She held up a gold tortoise and a diamanté spider

and began to talk. Fleur stared ahead politely. But the words washed over her. Memories, unbidden, were flooding into her mind. She was sitting with Nura el Hassan and they were giggling. Nura was dressed in pale silk; her small brown hands were holding a string of beads. They were a present; a ninth birthday present. She'd put them round Fleur's neck and they'd both giggled. Fleur hadn't admired the beads aloud. If she had done so, Nura would have been obliged, under custom, to give the beads to Fleur. So Fleur had simply smiled at Nura, and smiled at the beads, to let Nura know that she thought they were very pretty. Fleur knew Nura's customs better than her own. She had never known anything else.

Fleur had been born in Dubai, to a mother who ran off to South Africa with her lover six months later and a rather older father who equated bringing up a child with throwing money at it. In the shifting, rootless world of Dubai expatriates, Fleur learned to lose friends as easily as she made them, to greet a new intake at the British School at the beginning of every year and say goodbye to them at the end; to use people for the brief period that she had them – and then discard them before she herself was discarded. Throughout, only Nura had remained constant. Many Islamic families would not allow the Christian – in truth, heathen – Fleur to play with their children. But Nura's mother admired the pretty, insolent little red-head; pitied the businessman who was having to raise a daughter as well as hold down a demanding job.

And then, when Fleur was only sixteen, her father had suddenly suffered massive liver failure. He had died leaving Fleur a surprisingly small amount of money: not enough for her to continue living in the luxury apartment; not enough for her to stay on at the British School. The el Hassan family had kindly taken Fleur in to live with them while her future was decided. For a few months, she and Nura had slept in next-door bedrooms. They had become closer than ever; had discussed and compared themselves endlessly. At the age of sixteen, Nura was considered ready to marry; her parents were in the process of arranging a match. Fleur was alternately aghast and fascinated at the thought.

'How can you stand it?' she would exclaim. 'Marrying some man who'll just boss you about?' Nura always simply shrugged and smiled. She was a remarkably pretty girl, with smooth skin, dancing eyes and rounded features verging already on plumpness.

'If he is too bossy, I will not marry him,' she said once.

'Won't your parents make you?'

'Of course not. They will let me meet him and then we will talk about it.'

Fleur stared at her. Suddenly she felt jealous. Nura's life was being comfortably mapped out for her, while her own wavered uncertainly in front of her like a broken spider's web.

'Perhaps I could marry, like Nura,' she said the next day to Nura's mother, Fatima. She gave a little laugh, as though she were joking, but her eyes scanned Fatima's face sharply.

'I'm sure you will marry,' said Fatima. 'You will find a handsome Englishman.'

'Maybe I could marry an Arab,' said Fleur. Fatima laughed.

'Would you convert to Islam?'

'I might,' said Fleur desperately, 'if I had to.'

Fatima looked up. 'Are you serious?'

Fleur gave a tiny shrug. 'You could . . . find me some-one.'

'Fleur.' Fatima rose and took Fleur's hands. 'You know you would not make a suitable bride for an Arab. It is not just that you are not Islamic. You would find the life too difficult. Your husband would not allow you to answer back in the way that we do. You would not be allowed to go out without his permission. My husband is very liberal. Most are not.'

'Are you going to find a liberal man for Nura?'

'We hope so, yes. And you will find a man too, Fleur. But not here.'

Two days later the betrothal was announced. Nura was to marry Mohammed Abduraman, a young man from one of the wealthiest families in the Emirates. It was generally acknowledged that she had done very well indeed.

'But do you love him?' asked Fleur that night.

'Of course I love him,' said Nura. But her eyes were distant, and she wouldn't discuss it further.

Immediately the family was plunged into prep-aration. Fleur wandered about, unnoticed, watching with disbelief the amount of money being spent on the wedding. The bolts of silk, the food, the gifts for all the guests. Nura was whisked away into a whirl of veils and scented oils. Soon she would be whisked away for ever. Fleur would be on her own. What was she to do? The el Hassan family didn't want her any more. Nobody wanted her any more.

At nights she lay quite still, smelling the sweet musky scent of the house, allowing the tears to trickle down the sides of her face, trying to plot her future. Nura's parents thought she should go back to England, to the aunt in Maidenhead whom she'd never met.

'Your family is the most important,' Fatima had said, with the confidence of one surrounded by an extended web of loyal family members. 'Your own family will care for you.'

Fleur knew she was wrong. It was different in England. Her father's sister had never shown any interest in her. She was going to have to rely on herself.

And then Nura's betrothal party had been held. It was an all-female affair, with sweetmeats and games and much giggling. Halfway through, Nura took out a little box.

'Look,' she said. 'My betrothal ring.'

On her hand it looked almost incongruous, a huge diamond set in an intricate web of gold. The room was filled with satisfactory gasps; even by Arabic standards it was enormous.

That's got to be worth a hundred thousand dollars, thought Fleur. At least. A hundred thousand dollars, sitting on Nura's finger. It's not even as though she's ever going to be able to show it off properly. She'll probably hardly ever wear it. A hundred thousand dollars. What could you do with a hundred thousand dollars?

And then, before she could stop herself, it happened. Fleur put her cup down, stared straight at Nura and said,

'I do so admire your diamond ring, Nura. I admire it greatly. I wish I had one like it.'

The room fell silent. Nura turned pale; her lips began to quiver. Her eyes met Fleur's, shocked and hurt. There was an infinitesimal pause, during which no-one seemed to breathe. Everyone in the room leaned forward. Then, slowly and carefully, Nura loosened the diamond ring from her finger, reached out and dropped it into Fleur's lap. She looked at it for a moment, then rose and left the room. Fleur's last image of Nura was two dark, betrayed eyes.

That night, Fleur had sold the diamond for a hundred and twenty thousand dollars. She'd caught a flight to New York the next morning and she'd never seen Nura again.

Now, nearly twenty-five years later, sitting in Eleanor Forrester's garden, Fleur felt a wrenching in her chest, a hotness in her eyes. If I end up mediocre, she thought furiously – if I end up the English housewife I could have been all along – then the diamond was for nothing. I lost Nura for nothing. And I can't stand that. I can't *stand* it.

She blinked hard, and looked up, and focused anew on the gilt chain which Eleanor Forrester was holding aloft. I'll buy a necklace, she thought, and I'll have brunch, and then I'll take Richard Favour for everything I can.

Oliver Sterndale leaned back in his chair and looked at Richard with mild exasperation.

'You do realize,' he said for the third time, 'that once this money goes into trust, it's not your money anymore?'

'I know,' said Richard. 'That's the whole point. It'll be the children's.'

'It's a lot of money.'

'I know it's a lot of money.'

They both looked down at the numbers in front of them. The figure in question was underlined at the bottom of the page – a single one followed by a trail of noughts like a little caterpillar.

'It's not that much,' said Richard. 'Not really. And I do want the children to have it. Emily and I agreed.'

Oliver sighed, and began to tap his pen against his hand.

'Death duties . . .' he began.

'This isn't about death duties. This is about . . . security.'

'You can give your children security without signing over vast amounts of money to them. Why not buy Philippa a house?'

'Why not give her a vast amount of money?' There was the glimmer of a smile on Richard's face. 'In the end it doesn't make much difference.'

'It makes a huge difference! All sorts of things could happen to make you regret handing over your entire fortune prematurely.'

'Hardly my entire fortune!'

'A substantial part of it.'

'Emily and I discussed it. We agreed that it would be perfectly possible to live comfortably on the remainder. And there's always the company.'

The lawyer leaned back in his chair, thoughts battling against each other in his face.

'When did you decide all this?' he asked at last. 'Remind me.'

'Around two years ago.'

'And did Emily know then that . . .'

'That she was going to die? Yes, she did. But I don't see what relevance that has.' Oliver stared at Richard. For a moment he seemed about to say something, then he sighed and looked away.

'Oh, I don't know,' he muttered. 'What I *do* know,' he stated more firmly, 'is that by giving away such a large quantity of money you may be hampering your own future.'

'Oliver, don't be melodramatic!'

'What you and Emily may not have considered is the

possibility that your life might change to some degree after she died. I understand you have a . . . friend staying at the moment.'

'A woman, yes.' Richard smiled. 'Her name's Fleur.'

'Well then.' Oliver paused. 'It may seem a ridiculous idea now. But what would happen if you were, say, to remarry?'

'It doesn't seem a ridiculous idea,' said Richard slowly. 'But I can't see what it has to do with giving this money to Philippa and Antony. What does money have to do with marriage?' The lawyer looked aghast.

'You're not serious?'

'Half-serious.' Richard relented. 'Look, Oliver, I'll think about it. I won't rush into anything. But you know, I'm going to have to do something with the money sooner or later. I've been gradually liquidizing it over the last few months.'

'It won't do any harm in a deposit account for a while. Better to lose a bit of income than rush into the wrong decision.' Oliver suddenly looked up. 'You haven't told either of the children about this plan? They aren't expecting it?'

'Oh no. Emily and I agreed it would be better for them not to know. And also that they should wait till the age of thirty before coming into control of the money. We didn't want them thinking they didn't have to make an effort in life.'

'Very wise. And no-one else knows?'

'No. No-one else.'

Oliver sighed and pressed the buzzer on his desk for more coffee.

'Well, I suppose that's something.'

The money was his. Practically his. As soon as Philippa turned thirty . . . Lambert's grip tightened irritably on the steering wheel. What was so magic about the age of thirty? What would she have at the age of thirty that she didn't have at the age of twenty-eight?

When Emily had first told him about Philippa's money, he'd thought she meant straight away. Next week. He'd felt an exploding exhilaration rush through his body, which must have shown in his face, because she'd smiled – a satisfied smile – and said, 'She won't come into it till she's thirty, of course.' And he'd smiled back knowingly, and said 'Of course,' when really he'd been thinking, Why not? Why the fuck not!

Bloody Emily. Of course she'd done it deliberately. Told him early so she could watch him waiting. It was just another of her power games. Lambert smiled unwillingly to himself. He missed Emily. She'd been the only one in this whole blasted family that he'd really clicked with, from the moment they'd first met. It had been at a company reception, soon after he'd been taken on as technical director. She'd been standing quietly next to Richard, listening to the jovial anecdotes of the marketing director – a man whom, it later transpired, she despised. Lambert's eyes had caught hers off-guard – and in an instant he'd seen through that gentle, docile manner to the steely contempt behind. He'd seen the real Emily. As she'd met his gaze she'd clearly realized how much she'd given away. 'Introduce me to this nice young man,' she'd immediately said to Richard. And as Lambert's hand had met hers, her mouth had twisted up in a faint acknowledgement.

Two weeks later he'd been invited to The Maples for the weekend. He'd bought a new blazer, played golf with Richard and taken walks round the garden with Emily. She had done most of the talking. She'd spoken on a series of vague, apparently unconnected topics.

Her dislike of the marketing director; her admiration for those who understood computers; her desire for Lambert to become acquainted with the rest of her family. Some weeks after that, the marketing director had been fired for sending out a computer mailshot full of embarrassing mistakes. It was about the same time, remembered Lambert, that Richard had upgraded Lambert's company car. 'Emily's been chiding me,' he'd said with a smile. 'She thinks we'll lose you if we don't treat you properly!'

And then he'd been invited down to The Maples again, and introduced to Philippa. Philippa's boyfriend Jim had been there too, a long-limbed lad of twenty-two who had just left university and wasn't quite sure what he wanted to do next. But as Emily had later explained to everyone in the clubhouse bar, Lambert had quite literally swept Philippa off her feet. 'On the sixteenth hole!' she'd added, with a little laugh. 'Philippa lost her ball in that boggy patch. She got stuck, and Lambert just lifted her up and carried her back to the fairway!' Now Lambert frowned at the memory. Philippa had been heavier than he expected; he'd nearly pulled a muscle heaving her up out of that mud. On the other hand, she'd also been richer than he'd expected. He'd married Philippa thinking he was buying himself financial security. The news that he was in fact going to be extremely rich had come as an unexpected prize.

He glanced out of the car window. The dreary suburbs of outer London were beginning to turn into Surrey; they'd be at Greyworth in half an hour. Philippa was silent in the seat next to him, engrossed in one of her romantic novels. His wife, the millionairess. The multimillionairess, if Emily had been speaking the truth. Except she wasn't a millionairess, not yet. A familiar resentment ran through Lambert and he felt his teeth begin to grind together. It was unreasonable, treating Philippa like a child who couldn't be trusted. If she was to have the money anyway, then why not give it to her straight away? And why keep it a secret from her? Neither she nor Antony seemed to have any inkling that they were potentially very rich people: that they would never have to work if they didn't want to; that life was going to be easy for them. When Philippa sighed and fretted over the price of a new pair of shoes, Lambert felt like shouting, For God's sake, you could afford twenty pairs if you wanted them! But he never did. He didn't want his wife planning how to spend her money. He had plans enough of his own.

He glanced in his rear-view mirror at a Lagonda roaring up the fast lane and his grip tightened covetously on the wheel. Two years, he thought. Only two years to go. His only problem at the moment was the bank. Lambert frowned. He had to think of a solution to the bank problem. Fucking morons. Did they want the business of a potentially very rich person, or what? In the last few weeks, one idiot after another had been calling him, asking to arrange a meeting, querying his overdraft again and again. He was going to have to do something, before they got it into their little heads to call Philippa. She didn't know anything about it. She didn't even know he had that third account.

Again, Lambert went over the possibilities in his mind. The first was to ignore the bank completely. The second was to go along and see them, admit he didn't have the funds to pay off the overdraft and get an extension on it until Philippa came into her money. A two-year extension? It wasn't inconceivable. But neither was it very likely. They might decide they needed more assurance than that. They might decide to call his employer for a guarantee. Lambert scowled. They'd call Richard. He could just imagine Richard's sanctimonious attitude. Perfect, organized Richard, who never even had a gas bill outstanding. He would call Lambert into his office. He would talk about living within one's means. He'd quote fucking Dickens at him.

No. That wouldn't do. Lambert paused, and took a deep breath. The third option was somehow to keep the piranhas at the bank happy. Lob a healthy chunk of money at them. Fifty thousand pounds or so. At the same time, he could imply that he considered their lack of trust in him most surprising, bearing in mind his future prospects. He could talk about taking his money elsewhere. Put the wind up them properly. Lambert smiled grimly to himself. That was the best option of the three. By far the best. It had almost no disadvantages — just one. Which was that he didn't have fifty thousand pounds. Not yet.

Chapter Seven

As they pulled into the drive of The Maples, Philippa looked up from her romantic novel with bleary eyes.

'Are we here already?'

'No, we're on fucking Mars.'

'I haven't finished! Give me two minutes. I must just see what happens. I mean, I know what's going to happen, but I must just see . . .' She tailed off. Already her eyes were back down on the page, greedily devouring the text like a box of Milk Tray.

'For God's sake,' said Lambert. 'Well, I'm not sitting around here.' He got out of the car and banged the door shut. Philippa didn't flicker.

The front door was open but the house felt empty. Lambert stood in the hall and cautiously looked around. No sign of Gillian. Richard's car wasn't there; maybe he and his redhead had gone out together. Maybe no-one was about. Maybe he had the house to himself.

Lambert felt a thrill of satisfaction. He hadn't expected this. He'd thought he would have to creep about at night, or maybe even wait until another time. But this was perfect. He could put his plan into action at once.

Swiftly he mounted the broad staircase. The corridor upstairs was quiet and motionless. He stopped at the top of the stairs, listening for sounds of life. But there were none. Looking behind him to check once more that he wasn't being observed, Lambert moved cautiously towards Richard's office. It was a tucked-away room, completely separate from the bedrooms and usually kept locked. If anyone saw him there it would be impossible to pretend that he'd strayed there on the way somewhere else.

Not that it should matter, thought Lambert, fingering the key in his pocket. Richard trusted him. After all, he'd given him a key to the office – just in case of emergency, he'd said. If questioned, Lambert could always say that he'd been after some piece of information to do with the company. In fact Richard kept very little company information at home. But he would give Lambert the benefit of the doubt. People generally did.

The office door was closed. But as he tried to turn the key he realized that it was unlocked. Quickly he put the key away in his pocket. This way, if anyone saw him, he would be on safe ground. ('I saw the door was open, Richard, so I thought I'd better just check . . .') He went inside, and quickly headed for the filing cabinet. Bank statements, he muttered under his breath. Bank statements. He opened a drawer and began to flip through the files.

Fifty thousand pounds wasn't a lot of money. Not for someone like Richard, it wasn't. Richard had so much money, he could easily spare that much. He would never even notice it was missing. Lambert would borrow fifty grand, use it to solve his problems with the bank and then put it back. Five thousand pounds here, ten thousand pounds there – he'd take it out in bits and pieces, then put it back again when he had the chance. As long as the bottom lines added up at the end of the year, no-one would be the wiser.

Forging Richard's signature wasn't a problem.

Setting up the transfers wasn't a problem. Deciding which accounts to go into was more tricky. He didn't want to find he'd wiped out the housekeeping account, or this year's holiday fund. Knowing Richard, every bit of money, large or small, was probably allocated to something or other. He would have to be careful.

Lambert closed the top drawer and opened the second one down. He began to flip through the files. Suddenly a sound made him stop, fingers still poised. Something was behind him. Something – or someone . . .

He spun round, and felt his face freeze in disbelief. Sitting at Richard's desk, legs calmly crossed, was Fleur. His mind began to race. Had she been there all the time? Had she seen him . . .

'Hello Lambert,' said Fleur pleasantly. 'What are you doing in here?'

Philippa finished the last page of her book and leaned back, feeling both satisfied and slightly sick. Words and images jangled in her mind; in her nostrils the aroma of car upholstery mingled uneasily with the lingering smell of Lambert's driving peppermints. She opened the door and breathed in dazedly, trying to wrench herself away from fiction, into reality. But in her mind she was still on the Swiss Alps with Pierre, the dashing ski instructor. Pierre's manly mouth was on hers; his hands were in her hair; music was playing in the background . . . When Gillian suddenly banged on the car she gave a little shriek and jumped, bashing her head against the window frame.

'I've been picking strawberries,' said Gillian. 'Do you want a drink?'

'Oh,' said Philippa. 'Yes. I could do with a cup of coffee.'

She got out of the car with stiff, stumbling legs, shook herself down and followed Gillian into the house. Pierre and the Alps began to recede from her mind like an ill-remembered dream.

'Is Daddy out?' she said, sitting feebly down on a kitchen chair.

'He's at a meeting with Oliver Sterndale,' said Gillian. 'Antony's out, too.' She began to run water into the kettle.

'I suppose we are a bit early. What about . . .' Philippa pulled a tiny face.

'What about what?'

'You know. Fleur!'

'What about her?' said Gillian shortly.

'Well . . . where is she?'

'I don't know,' said Gillian. She paused. 'We only got back from Eleanor's brunch a short while ago.'

'Eleanor's brunch?'

'Yes.'

'You went to Eleanor Forrester's brunch?'

'Yes.' Gillian's face seemed to close up under Philippa's astonished gaze. 'A lot of nonsense, really,' she added roughly.

'Did you buy anything?'

'I did in the end. This.' Gillian pulled aside her blue scarf to reveal a little gold tortoise sitting on her lapel. She frowned. 'I don't know if I'm wearing it right. It'll probably pull at the fabric and spoil the dress.'

Philippa stared at the little tortoise. Gillian never bought brooches. Neither did she usually go to Eleanor's brunches. It had always been Philippa and her mother who went, while Gillian stayed behind. Gillian had always stayed behind. And now, thought Philippa with a sudden jealousy, it was Gillian and

Fleur who had gone, and she who had been left behind.

Fleur did so enjoy shocking men. It was almost worth the inconvenience of being interrupted to see Lambert's face staring speechlessly at her. Almost, but not quite. For things had been going so well until he'd arrived. She'd found the office door unlocked, had quickly slipped in and begun to look for what she wanted. And she would have found it, too, if she hadn't been interrupted. Richard was obviously a highly organized person. Everything in his office was filed and listed and paperclipped. She'd headed first of all to his desk, in search of recent correspondence – and had been rootling through his desk drawer when the door opened and Lambert came in.

Immediately, she had sunk underneath the desk, with an ease borne of practice. For a few minutes she'd wondered whether or not to get up. Should she keep still and wait until he'd gone? Or might Lambert glance over and spot her? Certainly it would be better to surprise him than to be discovered cowering under the furniture.

Then she'd noticed that Lambert didn't look quite at ease himself. His demeanour was almost . . . shifty. What was he doing, leafing through the filing cabinet? Did Richard know? Was something going on that she should know about? If so, it might be in her interests to let him know that she'd seen him. She'd thought for a moment, then before Lambert could slip away, she'd stood up, sat down casually on Richard's chair, and waited for him to turn round. Now she looked with relish at his bulging eyes; his rising colour. Something was going on. But what?

'Is this your office, too?' she asked, in tones almost innocent enough to fool. 'I didn't realize.'

'Not exactly,' said Lambert, regaining his composure slightly. 'I was just checking something for the company. For the company,' he repeated, more belligerently. 'There's a lot of highly confidential stuff in here. In fact, I'm wondering what you're doing in here at all.'

'Oh, me!' said Fleur. 'Well, I was just looking for something that I left here last night.'

'Something you left here?' He sounded disbelieving. 'What was it? Shall I help you look?'

'Don't worry,' said Fleur, getting up and coming towards him. 'I found it.'

'You found it,' said Lambert, folding his arms. 'Might I ask what it was?'

Fleur paused, then opened her hand. Inside was a pair of black silky knickers.

'They were underneath the desk,' she said confidentially. 'So easy to mislay. But I didn't want the cleaner to be shocked.' She glanced at his scarlet face. 'You're not shocked, are you, Lambert? You did ask.'

Lambert didn't reply. He seemed to be having trouble breathing.

'It might be better not to mention this to Richard,' said Fleur, moving close to Lambert and looking him straight in the eye. 'He might be a little . . . coy.' She paused for a moment, breathing a little more quickly than usual and leaning very slightly towards Lambert's face. He looked transfixed.

And suddenly she was gone. Lambert remained exactly where he was; still feeling her breath on his skin, still hearing her voice in his ear, replaying the scene in his mind. Fleur's underwear – her black silky underwear – had been under the desk. Which must mean that she and Richard . . . Lambert swallowed. She and Richard . . .

With a bang, he closed the filing cabinet drawer and turned away He couldn't concentrate any more; he couldn't focus. He couldn't think about statements and balances. All he could think about was . . .

'Philippa!' he barked down the stairs. 'Come up here!' There was silence. 'Come up here!' he repeated. Eventually Philippa appeared.

'I was talking to Fleur,' she complained, hurrying up the stairs.

'I don't care. Come in here.' He took Philippa's hand and led her quickly to the end bedroom in which they always stayed. It had been Philippa's as a child, a fantasy land of roses and rabbits, but as soon as she left home, Emily had torn down the wallpaper and replaced it with dark green tartan.

'What do you want?' Philippa wrenched her arm out of Lambert's grasp.

'You. Now.'

'Lambert!' She looked uneasily at him. He was staring at her with a glassy, unfocused gaze. 'Get that dress off.'

'But Fleur . . .'

'Fuck Fleur.' He watched as Philippa hurriedly pulled her dress over her head, then closed his eyes and pulled her close, squeezing her flesh painfully between his fingers. 'Fuck Fleur,' he repeated in a blurry voice. 'Fuck Fleur.'

Richard arrived back from his meeting to find Fleur reclining in her usual spot in the conservatory.

'Where are Philippa and Lambert?' he asked. 'Their car's in the drive.' He looked at his watch. 'We tee off in half an hour.'

'Oh, I expect they're around somewhere,' murmured Fleur. 'I did catch a glimpse of Lambert earlier.' She stood up. 'Let's have a quick walk around the garden.'

As they walked, she took Richard's arm and said casually,

'I suppose you and Lambert know each other pretty well. Now that you're family.' She looked carefully at his face as she spoke, and saw a fleeting expression of distaste appear on it, which was quickly supplanted by one of reasonable, civilized tolerance.

'I've certainly got to know him better as a person,' said Richard. 'But I wouldn't say—'

'You wouldn't call yourself his friend? I gathered that. So you don't have long talks with him? Confide in him?'

'There's a generation gap,' said Richard defensively. 'It's understandable.'

'Completely understandable,' said Fleur, and rewarded herself with a little smile. What she had suspected was indeed the case. The two never spoke. Which meant Lambert was not going to accost Richard with tales of sex on the floor of his office. He wasn't going to check out her story; she was safe.

What Lambert's own story was, she had no idea. Once upon a time she might have felt compelled to find out. But experience had taught her that in every family there was someone with a secret. There was always one family member with a hidden agenda; sometimes there were several. Trying to use internal arguments for her own gain never worked. Family disputes were always irrational, always long-standing and the warriors always flipped over to the other side as soon as anyone else touched them. The best thing was to ignore everyone else and pursue her own goal as quickly as she could.

They walked on for a few minutes silently, then Fleur said,

'Did you have a good meeting?' Richard shrugged, and gave her a tense little smile.

'It made me think. You know, I still feel that there were parts of Emily which I knew nothing about.'

'Was the meeting about Emily?'

'No . . . but it concerned some affairs we discussed before she died.' Richard frowned. 'I was trying to remember her reasoning; her motivation for doing things,' he said slowly. 'And I realized that I don't *know* why she wanted certain things done. I suppose she didn't tell me – or I've forgotten what she said. And I never knew her character well enough to work it out now.'

'Perhaps I could help,' said Fleur. 'If you told me what it was all about.' Richard looked at her.

'Maybe you could. But I feel . . . this is something I've got to puzzle out for myself. Can you understand that?'

'Of course,' said Fleur lightly and squeezed his arm affectionately. Richard gave a little laugh.

'It's not really important. It won't affect anything I do. But–' he broke off and met Fleur's eyes. 'Well, you know how I feel about Emily.'

'She was full of secrets,' said Fleur, trying not to yawn. Hadn't they talked enough about this blessed woman already?

'Not secrets,' said Richard. 'I hope not secrets. Simply . . . hidden qualities.'

As soon as he had come, Lambert's proxy affection for Philippa vanished. He unfastened his lips from her neck and sat up.

'I've got to get going,' he said.

'Couldn't we just lie here for a bit?' said Philippa wistfully.

'No we couldn't. Everyone'll be wondering where we are.' He tucked his shirt in and smoothed his hair down and suddenly he was gone.

Philippa heaved herself onto her elbows and looked around the silent room. In her mind, she had begun to organize Lambert's quick fuck into an example of his passion for her; an anecdote to be confided to the bubbly friends that she would one day have. 'Honestly, he was *so* desperate for me . . . We just disappeared off together . . .' Giggles. 'It was so romantic . . . Lambert's always like that, a real man of the moment . . .' More giggles. Admiring looks. 'Oh Phil, you're so lucky! . . . I can't *remember* the last time we had sex . . .'

But now, slicing through the laughing voices, there was another voice in her head. Her mother's voice. 'You disgusting girl.' An icy blue stare. Philippa's diary being waved incriminatingly in the air. Her secret adolescent fantasies, opened up and exposed.

As though the last fifteen years had never happened, Philippa began to feel a teenager's panic and humiliation begin to rise through her. Her mother's voice, cutting through her thoughts again. 'Your father would be shocked if he saw this. A girl of your age, thinking about sex!'

Sex! The word had rung shockingly through the air, edged with sordid, unspeakable images. Philippa's embarrassment had suffused her face; her lungs. She had wanted to scream; she'd been unable to look her mother in the eye. The next term she'd allowed several of the sixth-formers from the neighbouring boys' boarding school to screw her behind the hedges on the hockey pitches. Each time the experience had been painful and embarrassing and she'd silently wept as it

112

was happening. But then, she'd thought miserably, as one sixteen-year-old after another panted beer-breath into her face, that was all she deserved.

Lambert came downstairs to find Fleur and Richard arm in arm in the hall.

'Fleur's decided to come with us round the golf course,' said Richard. 'Isn't that a splendid idea?' Lambert looked at him, aghast.

'What do you mean?' he exclaimed. 'She can't come with us! This is a business game.'

'I won't get in your way,' said Fleur.

'We'll be having confidential business discussions.'

'On a golf course?' said Fleur. 'They can't be that confidential. Anyway, I won't be listening.'

'Fleur very much wants to see the course,' said Richard. 'I don't think there's any harm.'

'You don't mind, do you Lambert?' said Fleur. 'I've been here four weeks, and all I've seen is the eighteenth green.' She smiled at him from under her lashes. 'I'll be as quiet as a little mouse.'

'Perhaps Philippa could come along too,' suggested Richard.

'She's already fixed up to have tea with Tricia Tilling,' said Lambert at once. God help us, he thought, they didn't want a gaggle of women trailing around after them.

'Dear Tricia Tilling,' said Fleur. 'We had a lovely chat this morning.'

'Fleur's becoming quite a regular fixture at the club!' said Richard, beaming fondly at her.

'I bet she is,' said Lambert.

There was a sound on the stairs and they all looked up. Philippa was descending, looking rather flushed.

'Hello Fleur,' she said breathlessly. 'I was going to

say, how about coming with me to Tricia's this afternoon? I'm sure she wouldn't mind.'

'I'm otherwise engaged,' said Fleur. 'Unfortunately.'

'Fleur's accompanying us around the golf course,'
said Richard with a smile. 'A most unexpected treat.'

Philippa looked at Lambert. Why didn't he ask her to
come round the golf course, too? If he'd asked her, she
would have cancelled tea with Tricia Tilling. She
began to imagine the phone call she'd make. 'Sorry,
Tricia, Lambert says I've simply got to go along . . .
something about bringing him good luck!' An easy
laugh. 'I know . . . these men of ours – aren't they something else?'

'Philippa!' She jumped, and the relaxed, laughing
voices in her head vanished. Lambert was looking
impatiently at her. 'I said would you look in at the pro
shop and ask if they've mended that club yet.'

'Oh, all right,' said Philippa. She watched as the
three of them left – Richard laughing at something
Fleur had said; Lambert swinging his cashmere
sweater over his shoulders. They were off to have a
good time, and she was consigned to an afternoon with
Tricia Tilling. She gave a gusty sigh of resentment.
Even Gillian had more fun than her.

Gillian sat in the conservatory shelling peas and
watching as Antony mended a cricket bat. He'd always
been good with his hands, she thought. Careful,
methodical, reliable. At the age of three, his nursery
school teachers had been bemused at his paintings –
always a single colour, completely covering the sheet
of paper. Never more than one colour; never a single
missed spot. Bordering on the obsessive. Perhaps these
days, she thought, they would worry that he was too
tidy for a three-year-old; take him off for counselling or

114

workshops. Even back then, she'd sometimes detected a note of concern in the teachers' eyes. But no-one had said anything. For it had been obvious that Antony was a well-loved, well-cared-for child.

Well loved. Gillian stared fiercely out of the window. Well loved by everyone except his own mother. His own shallow selfish mother. A woman who'd recoiled with dismay at the sight of her own baby. Who had peered at the tiny disfigurement as though she could see nothing else, as though she weren't holding a perfect, healthy baby for whom she and everyone else ought to have been eternally grateful.

Of course, Emily had never said anything to the outside world. But Gillian had known. She'd watched as Antony had grown into a chuckling, beaming toddler, running around the house, arms outstretched, ready to embrace the world – confident that it must love him as much as he loved all of it. And then she'd watched as the little boy had gradually become aware that his mother's face perpetually held an expression of slight disapproval towards him; that she occasionally shrank from him when no-one else was watching; that she only fully relaxed when his face was averted and she couldn't see the tiny lizard leaping across his eye. The first day Antony had raised his little hand to his eye, concealing his birthmark from the world, Gillian had waited until the evening and confronted Emily. All her frustrations and anger had erupted in a tearful tirade, while Emily sat at her dressing table, brushing her hair; waiting. Then, when Gillian had finished, she'd looked round with a cold, contemptuous stare. 'You're just jealous,' she'd said. 'It's unhealthy! You wish Antony were your baby. Well, he's not yours, he's mine.'

Gillian had stared at Emily in shock, suddenly less

sure of herself. Did she really wish Antony were hers? Was she unhealthy?

'You know I love Antony,' Emily had continued. 'Everyone knows I love him.' She'd paused. 'Richard's always saying how wonderful I am with him. And who cares about a birthmark? We never even notice it.' Her eyes had narrowed. 'In fact I'm surprised at you, Gillian, mentioning it all the time. We think the best thing is to ignore it.'

Somehow she'd twisted and reversed Gillian's words until Gillian had felt confused and unsure of her own motives. Was she becoming a frustrated, jealous spinster? Did her love for Antony border on possessiveness? It was Emily, after all, who was his natural mother. And so she'd backed down and said nothing more. And, after all, Antony had grown up a pleasant, problem-free child.

'There!' Antony held out the cricket bat.

'Well done,' said Gillian. She watched as he stood up and tried the bat out. He was tall now; an adult, practically. But sometimes as she caught a glimpse of his sturdy arms or smooth neck, she saw again in him that happy, chunky baby who had laughed up at her from his cot; whose hands she'd held as he took his first few steps; whom she'd loved from the moment he was born.

'Careful,' she said gruffly, as he swung the bat towards a large, painted plant pot.

'I *am* being careful,' he said irritably. 'You always fuss.'

He took a few imaginary swings. Gillian silently shelled a few more peas.

'What are you going to do this afternoon?' she asked at last.

'Dunno,' said Antony. 'I might get a video out. Or even a couple. It's so *boring*, with Will away.'

'What about the others? Xanthe. And that new boy, Mex. You could organize something with them.'

'Yeah, maybe.' His face closed up and he turned away, swinging the bat viciously through the air.

'Careful!' exclaimed Gillian. But it was too late. As he swung back, there was a crack and then a crash as he hit a terracotta pot off its stand and onto the tiled floor.

'Look what you've done!' Her voice snapped roughly through the air. 'I told you to be careful!'

'I'm sorry, OK?'

'It's all over the floor!' Gillian stood up and gazed despairingly at the pieces of terracotta, the clumps of earth, the fleshy leaves.

'Honestly. It's not such a disaster.' He bent down and picked up a piece of terracotta. A clod of earth fell onto his shoe.

'I'd better get a brush.' Gillian sighed heavily and put down the peas.

'I'll do it,' said Antony. 'It's no big deal.'

'You won't do it properly.'

'I will! Isn't there a broom around here somewhere?' Antony's eyes swept the conservatory and suddenly stopped as his gaze reached the door. 'Jesus Christ!' he exclaimed. The piece of terracotta fell out of his hand, smashing on the floor.

'Antony! I've told you before—'

'Look!' he interrupted. 'Who's that?'

Gillian turned and followed his gaze. Standing on the other side of the door was a girl with long, white-blond hair, dark eyebrows and a suspicious expression.

'Hi,' she said through the glass. Her voice was high-pitched and had an American accent. 'I guess you weren't expecting me. I've come to stay. I'm Zara. I'm Fleur's daughter.'

117

Chapter Eight

By the time they came off the eighteenth green, Lambert was bright red, sweating and grimacing with frustration. Fleur had dominated the attention all the way round the course, sashaying along beside Richard as though she were at a tea party, interrupting the discussion to ask endless questions, behaving as though she had as much right to be there as Lambert did himself. Bloody impertinent bitch.

A remark made by his old housemaster suddenly came into Lambert's mind. *I'm all for equality in women . . . they're all equally inferior to men!* A little chuckle had gone around the select group of sixth-formers whom Old Smithers had been entertaining with sherry. Lambert had chortled particularly loudly, acknowledging the fact that he and Old Smithers had always shared the same sense of humour. Now his frown softened slightly; a reminiscent look passed over his features. For a few moments he found himself wishing he was a sixth-former once again.

It was a fact which Lambert rarely admitted to himself that the happiest and most successful years of his life had, so far, been those spent at school. He had attended Creighton – a minor public school in the Midlands – and had soon found himself one of the brightest, strongest and most powerful boys in the school. A natural bully, he had soon established around himself a sycophantic entourage, mildly terrorizing younger boys and sneering in packs at the local lads in the town. The boys at Creighton were for the most part third-rate plodders who would never again in their lives achieve the superior status which was accorded to them in this little town; therefore they made the most of it, striding around the streets in their distinctive greatcoats and flamboyant ties, braying loudly and picking fights with what were known as the townies. Lambert had rarely actually fought himself but had become known as the author of a great number of disparaging remarks about the 'plebs' which had eventually given him the reputation of a wit. The masters – themselves insular, bored and discouraged with life – had not reprimanded him but tacitly encouraged him in this role; had fed his pompous, superior manner with winks and chortles and snobbish asides. Lambert's timid mother had delighted in her tall, confident son with his loud voice and forthright views, which by the time he reached the sixth form, were dismissive of almost everyone at Creighton and almost everyone outside of Creighton, too.

The exception was his father. Lambert had always idolized his father – a tall, swaggering man with an overbearing manner which Lambert still unconsciously emulated. His father's moods had been violent and unpredictable, and Lambert had grown up desperate for his approval. When his father made fun of the young Lambert's rubbery-looking face or clipped him too vigorously round the head, Lambert would force himself to grin back and laugh; when he spent whole evenings bellowing at Lambert's mother, Lambert would creep upstairs to his bedroom, telling himself furiously that his father was right; his father was always right.

It had been Lambert's father who insisted he attend

Creighton School, as he had done. Who taught him to mock the other boys in the village; who took him to Cambridge for the day and proudly pointed out his old college. It was his father, Lambert believed, who knew about the world; who cared about his future; who would guide him in life.

And then, when Lambert was fifteen, his father announced that he had a mistress, that he loved her and that he was leaving. He said he'd come back and visit Lambert; he never did. Later they heard that he'd only lasted six months with the mistress; that he'd gone abroad; that no-one knew where he was.

Filled with a desperate, adolescent grief, Lambert had taken his anger out on his mother. It was her fault his father had left. It was her fault that there was now no money for holidays; that letters had to be written to the headmaster of Creighton, pleading for a reduction in the fees. As their situation grew more and more wretched, Lambert's swagger grew more pronounced; his contempt for the town plebs grew fiercer – and his idolatry for his absent father grew even stronger.

Against the advice of his masters, he tried for Cambridge – for his father's old college. He was granted an interview but on the strength of his interview he was turned down. The sense of failure was almost more than he could bear. Abruptly he announced that he was not going to waste his time with university. The masters remonstrated with him, but only mildly; he was on the way out of their lives and therefore of waning interest. Their attention was now focusing on the boys lower down the school; the boys Lambert had used to beat for burning his toast. What Lambert did with his life, they didn't really care. His mother, who did care, was roundly ignored.

And so Lambert had gone straight to London,

straight into a job in computing. The pompous manner which might have been rubbed off by Cambridge remained, as did his feeling of innate superiority. When others of inferior schooling were promoted above him, he retaliated by wearing his OC tie to work. When his flat mates organized weekend gatherings without him, he retaliated by driving back up to Creighton and displaying his latest car to anyone who would look. It was unthinkable to Lambert that those around him should not admire him and defer to him. Those who didn't, he dismissed as being too ignorant to bother with. Those who did, he secretly despised. He was unable to make friends; unable even to understand any relationship based on equality. Those who would tolerate his company for even a couple of hours had been few and were becoming fewer when he moved to Richard's company. And at that point his life had been transformed. He had married the boss's daughter and moved on to a new level and his status had become, in his own mind, assured for good.

Richard, he was certain, appreciated his superior attributes – his intellect, his breeding, his ability to make decisions – although not as fully as Emily had appreciated them. Philippa was a little fool who thought flowers looked nicer on a tie than Old Creightonian stripes. But Fleur . . . Lambert scowled, and wiped a drip of sweat from his brow. Fleur didn't obey the rules. She seemed heedless of his rank as Richard's son-in-law and almost oblivious of social convention. She was too slippery; he couldn't place her. What was her age exactly? What was her accent exactly? Where did she fit into his scheme of things?

'Lambert!' Philippa's voice interrupted his thoughts. She was coming towards the eighteenth green, merrily waving her bag at him.

'Philippa!' His head jerked up; in his state of frustration he felt almost glad to see his wife's familiar face, slightly flushed. Tea with Tricia had clearly metamorphosed into G and T with Tricia.

'I thought I'd catch you playing the eighteenth! But you've finished already! That was pretty quick!'

Lambert said nothing. When Philippa was in full voluble flight she would scoop everything up from a subject that could possibly be mentioned, leaving no crumbs for an answer.

'Good game?' Lambert shot a glance behind him. Richard and the two men from Briggs & Co. were some way behind, walking slowly, all listening to something Fleur was saying.

'Bloody awful game.' He stepped off the course and without waiting for the others began to stride towards the trolley shed, his spikes clattering noisily on the path.

'What happened?'

'That bloody woman. All she did was ask questions. Every fucking five minutes. "Richard, could you explain that again to a very stupid lay-woman?" "Richard, when you say cashflow, what exactly do you mean?" And I'm trying to impress these guys. Christ, what an afternoon.'

'Maybe she's just interested,' said Philippa.

'Of course she isn't interested. Why would she be interested? She's just a stupid tart who likes having all the attention.'

'Well, she certainly looks very good,' said Philippa wistfully, turning to survey Fleur.

'She looks terrible,' said Lambert. 'Far too sexy for a golf course.' Philippa giggled.

'Lambert! You're awful!' She paused, then added in needlessly hushed tones, 'We were talking about her

122

this afternoon, actually. Tricia and I.' She lowered her voice further. 'Apparently she's really rich! Tricia told me. She's got a chauffeur and everything! Tricia said she thought Fleur was super.' Philippa darted a bright-eyed glance at Lambert. 'Tricia thinks . . .'

'Tricia is a moron.' Lambert wiped the sweat off his brow again and wondered why the hell he was talking about Fleur to his wife. He turned and looked at Fleur sauntering along in her white dress, looking at him with her mocking green eyes. The arousal which he had fought all afternoon began to stir in him again.

'Christ what a fiasco,' he said coarsely, turning back, running a frustrated hand over Philippa's inferior buttocks. 'I need a bloody drink.'

Unfortunately the chaps from Briggs and Co. didn't have time for a drink. Regretfully they shook hands and, with one last admiring glance at Fleur, got back into their Saab and drove off. The others stood politely in the car park, watching them manoeuvre the car past rows of glossy BMWs, the occasional Rolls-Royce, a sprinkling of pristine Range Rovers.

Philippa felt a twinge of disappointment as their car disappeared through the gates. She had looked forward to meeting them, chatting to them, perhaps flirting a little, perhaps even organizing a dinner party for them and their wives. Since marrying Lambert two years before, she had only given one dinner party, for her parents and Antony. And yet at home she had an elegant dining room with a table big enough for ten, and a kitchen full of expensive saucepans, and a 'Dinner Party' book full of recipes and time-saving tips, laboriously copied out of magazines.

She had always thought that being married to

Lambert would mean she spent the evenings entertaining Lambert's friends: cooking elaborate dishes for them, perhaps striking up jolly acquaintanceships with their wives. But now it appeared that Lambert didn't have any friends. And neither, if she was honest, did she – only people at Greyworth who had been her mother's friends, and people from work, who were always leaving to go to other jobs and never seemed to be free in the evenings anyway. Her contemporaries from university had long since dispersed about the country; none of them lived in London.

Suddenly Fleur laughed at something Richard had said, and Philippa's head jerked up. If only Fleur could be her friend, she thought wistfully. Her best friend. They could go out to lunch, and have little private jokes which only they understood, and Fleur would introduce her to all *her* friends, and then Philippa would offer to host a dinner party for her in London . . . In her mind, Philippa's dining room became filled with amusing, delightful people. Candles burning, flowers everywhere, all her wedding china out of its wrappers. She would pop into the kitchen to check on the seafood brochettes with civilized laughter in her ears. Lambert would come in after her ostensibly to replenish glasses, but really to tell her how proud he was of her. He would put the glasses down, then draw her towards him in a slow embrace . . .

'Is that Gillian?' Fleur's voice, raised in astonishment, woke Philippa from her reverie. 'What's she doing here?'

Everyone looked up, and Philippa tried to catch Fleur's eye; to start the seeds of friendship between them. But Fleur didn't see her. Fleur was looking up at Richard as though no one else in the world existed.

* * *

Watching Gillian approach across the car park, Richard gradually pulled Fleur closer and closer to him until they were practically hip to hip.

'I'm so glad you came along,' he murmured in her ear. 'I'd forgotten how interminable these games can be. Especially when Lambert's involved.'

'I enjoyed it,' said Fleur, smiling demurely at him. 'And I certainly learned a lot.'

'Would you like some golf lessons?' said Richard immediately. 'I should have suggested it before. We can easily fix some up for you.'

'Maybe,' said Fleur. 'Or maybe you could teach me yourself.' She glanced up at Richard's face, still flushed from the sun, still exhilarated from his victory. He looked as relaxed and happy as she'd ever seen him.

'Hello Gillian,' said Richard, as she came within earshot. 'What good timing. We're just about to have a drink.'

'I see,' said Gillian distractedly. 'Are the people from Briggs and Co. still around?'

'No, they had to shoot off,' said Richard. 'But we're going to have a celebratory drink on our own.'

'Celebrate?' said Lambert. 'What's there to celebrate?'

'The preferential rate which Briggs and Co. have offered us,' said Richard, his mouth twisting into a smile. 'Which Fleur charmed them into offering us.'

'A preferential rate?' said Philippa, ignoring Lambert's disbelieving scowl. 'That's marvellous!' She smiled warmly at Fleur.

'It would be marvellous,' said Fleur, 'if they weren't a pair of utter crooks.'

'What?' They all stared at her.

'Didn't you think so?' she said.

'Well . . .' said Richard doubtfully.

'Of course I didn't think so!' said Lambert. 'These chaps are chums of mine.'

'Oh,' said Fleur. She shrugged. 'Well I don't want to offend anyone. But I thought they were crooks, and if I were you I wouldn't do business with them.'

Philippa glanced at Lambert. He was breathing heavily and his face was an even brighter scarlet than before.

'They cheat a little on the golf course, maybe,' said Richard uncomfortably. 'But . . .'

'Not just on the golf course,' said Fleur. 'Trust me.'

'Trust you?' exclaimed Lambert, as though unable to keep quiet any more. 'What the hell do you know about anything?'

'Lambert!' said Richard sharply. He looked fondly down at Fleur. 'Tell you what, darling, I'll think about it. Nothing's signed yet.'

'Good,' said Fleur.

'Fleur,' said Gillian quietly. 'You've got—'

'What do you mean, you'll think about it?' Lambert's scandalized voice exploded across hers. 'Richard, you're not taking this rubbish of Fleur's seriously?'

'All I've said, Lambert,' said Richard tightly, 'is that I'll think about it.'

'For Christ's sake, Richard! The deal's all set up!'

'It can be un-set up.'

'I don't believe I'm hearing this!'

'Fleur,' said Gillian more urgently. 'You've got a visitor back at the house.'

'Since when was Fleur consulted on company decisions?' Lambert's face was almost purple. 'Whose advice are you going to ask next? The milkman's?'

'I'm just giving an opinion,' said Fleur, shrugging. 'You can ignore it if you like.'

'Fleur!' Gillian's voice rose harshly into the air. Everyone turned to look at her. 'Your daughter's here.'

There was silence.

'Oh, is she?' said Fleur casually. 'Yes, I suppose it must be the end of term. How did she get here?'

'Your daughter?' said Richard, giving a little, uncertain laugh.

'I told you about my daughter,' said Fleur. 'Didn't I?'

'Did you?'

'Perhaps I didn't.' Fleur sounded unconcerned.

'The woman is a nutter!' muttered Lambert to Philippa.

'She just arrived out of the blue,' said Gillian, in tones of stupefaction. 'Is her name Sarah? I couldn't quite make it out.'

'Zara,' said Fleur. 'Zara Rose. Where is she now?' she added, almost as an afterthought.

'She's gone out for a walk,' said Gillian, as though this surprised her the most of all, 'with Antony.'

Antony looked again at Zara and tried to think of something to say. They'd been walking for ten minutes now in complete silence. Zara's hands were in her pockets and her shoulders were hunched up, and she was staring straight ahead as though she didn't want to catch anyone's eye. They were very thin shoulders, thought Antony, glancing at her again. In fact Zara was one of the thinnest people he'd ever seen. Her arms were long and bony; her ribs were practically visible through her T-shirt. No tits to speak of, even though she was . . . how old was she?

'How old are you?' he asked.

'Thirteen.' Her voice was American and raspy and not very friendly. She shook back her long white-blond hair and hunched her shoulders again. Her hair was bleached, thought Antony knowledgeably, pleased with himself for having noticed.

'And . . . where do you go to school?' This was more like it. Small talk.

'Heathland School for Girls.'

'Is it nice?'

'It's a boarding school.' She spoke as though that were answer enough.

'Did you . . . When did you move here from the States?'

'I didn't.' Oh ha-ha, thought Antony.

'Canada, then,' he said.

'I've lived in Britain all my life,' she said. She sounded bored. Antony stared at her, perplexed.

'But your accent . . .'

'I have an American accent. So what? It's my choice.' For the first time she turned towards him. Her eyes were extraordinary, he thought – green like Fleur's but deep-set and fierce-looking.

'You just decided to speak with an American accent?'

'Yup.'

'Why?'

'Just did.'

'How old were you?'

'Seven.'

They walked for a while in silence. Antony tried to remember himself at seven. Could he have made a decision like that? And stuck with it? He thought not.

'I guess your dad's rich, right?' Her voice rasped through the air and Antony felt himself blushing.

'Quite rich, I suppose,' he said. 'I mean, not that rich. But you know. Well off. Relatively speaking.' He knew he was sounding awkward and pompous, but there was nothing he could do about it. 'Why do you want to know?' he said, retaliating.

'No reason.' She took her hands out of her pockets and began to examine them. Antony followed her gaze. They were thin hands, tanned pale brown, with a single, huge silver ring on each. Why? thought Antony in sudden fascination. Why are you staring at your hands? Why are you frowning? What are you looking for?

Abruptly she seemed to get bored with her hands and thrust them back into her pockets. She turned to Antony.

'You mind if I smoke a joint?'

Antony's heart missed a beat. This girl was only thirteen. How could she be smoking joints?

'No . . . I don't mind.' He could hear his voice slipping higher and higher, into a register of slight panic.

'Where do you go to smoke? Or don't you?'

'Yes,' said Antony, too quickly. 'But mostly at school.'

'OK.' She shrugged. 'Well, there must be somewhere, in all this forest.'

'There's a place down here.' He led the way off the road and into the wood. 'People come here to—' How could this girl be only thirteen? She was two years younger than him. It was incredible. 'You know,' he finished feebly.

'Have sex.'

'Well.' His face felt hot; his birthmark seemed to throb with embarrassment. 'Yeah.' They had arrived at a little clearing. 'Here we are.'

'OK.' She crouched down on her haunches, took a little box from her pocket and efficiently began to roll a joint.

As she lit it and inhaled, Antony waited for her to look up and say Wow this is great stuff, like Fifi Tilling always did. But Zara said nothing. She had none of the excited self-consciousness that surrounded the drug-takers of his experience, in fact she seemed barely aware that he was there. She inhaled silently again, then passed the joint to him.

This afternoon, thought Antony, I was going to sit at home and watch a couple of crummy videos. And instead, here I am smoking dope with the most extra-ordinary thirteen-year-old girl I've ever met.

'Is your family friendly?' she asked suddenly.

'Well,' said Antony, feeling thrown again. Into his mind came the parties his parents had always held at Christmas. Decorations and mulled wine; everyone dressed up and having a jolly time. 'Well, yes,' he said, 'I think we're pretty friendly. You know. We've got loads of friends and stuff.'

His words rose into the silent forest air; Zara gave no indication that she'd heard him. Her face was covered in dappled shadows from the trees and it was difficult to make out an expression. After another pause she spoke again.

'What do you all think of Fleur?'

'She's great!' said Antony with genuine enthusiasm. 'She's such a laugh. I never thought—'

'Don't tell me. You never thought your dad would date again,' said Zara, and inhaled again on the joint. Antony looked curiously at her.

'No,' he said, 'I didn't. Well, you don't, do you? Think of your parents dating.' Zara was silent.

Suddenly there was a sound. Footsteps were coming towards them; indistinct voices were rising above the trees. In one swift movement Zara put out the joint and buried it in the earth. Antony leaned casually back on one elbow. A moment later, Xanthe Forrester and Mex Taylor arrived in the clearing. Xanthe was holding a bottle of vodka, her cheeks were flushed and her shirt was unbuttoned, revealing a pink gingham bra. When she saw Antony and Zara she stopped short.

'Antony!' she said in nonplussed tones. 'I didn't know you—'

'Hi Xanthe. This is Zara,' said Antony. He looked at Zara. 'This is Xanthe and Mex.'

'Hello there,' said Mex, and winked at Antony.

'Hi,' said Zara.

'Actually, we'd better be going,' said Antony. He stood up and held out a hand to help Zara, but she ignored it, rising to her feet from her cross-legged position in one seamless action. Xanthe giggled and he felt his hand shoot defensively up to his birthmark.

'Antony's always such a gentleman, isn't he?' said Xanthe, looking with bright, colluding eyes at Zara.

'Is he?' Zara spoke politely, defusing the joke. Xanthe flushed slightly, then decided to giggle again.

'I'm so pissed!' she said. She held out the bottle to Zara. 'Have some.'

'I don't drink,' said Zara. 'But thanks anyway.' She put her hands into her pockets and hunched her shoulders up again.

'We'd better go,' said Antony. 'Your mother might be back.'

'Your mother?' said Xanthe at once. 'Who's your mother?' Zara looked away.

'Fleur,' she said. She sounded suddenly weary. 'My mother's Fleur.'

As they walked back to The Maples, the sun disappeared behind a cloud, casting the road into shadow. Zara stared stonily ahead, quelling the feeling of tearfulness inside her with a frown which grew more severe with every step. It was always like this at first; she'd be OK in a day or two. Homesickness, the people

131

at school called it. But she couldn't really be feeling homesick, because she didn't have a home to be sick for. There was school, with its smell of polish and its hockey pitches and its lumpish, stupid girls, and there was Johnny and Felix's flat, where there wasn't really room for her, and then there was wherever Fleur was staying. And that was how it had always been, ever since she could remember.

She'd been at boarding school since she was five. Before that, they must have had some kind of home, she guessed, but she couldn't really remember, and Fleur claimed she couldn't remember either. So her first home had really been the Court School in Bayswater, a cosy house full of diplomats' children tucked into bed with expensive teddies. She'd loved it there, had loved all the teachers passionately, especially Mrs Burton, the headmistress.

And she'd loved Nat, her best friend, whom she'd met on her first day there. Nat's parents were working in Moscow and, he'd confided to her over bedtime hot chocolate, didn't love him at all, not one tiny bit.

'My mother doesn't love me either,' she'd said at once.

'I think my *mother* loves me,' Nat had said, eyes huge over the rim of his white china mug, 'but my father hates me.' Zara had thought for a moment.

'I don't know my father,' she'd confessed eventually, 'but he's American.' Nat had looked at her with respect.

'Is he a cowboy?'

'I think so,' Zara had replied. 'He wears a great big hat.'

The next day, Nat had drawn a picture of Zara's father wearing his hat, and their friendship had been sealed. They had sat next to each other in all their lessons and played together at breaktime and been each other's partners in the school crocodile and some-times – which was strictly forbidden – even crept into each other's bed at night and told each other stories.

And then, when she was seven, Zara had arrived back at school after a half-term of sipping strawberry milk shakes in a Kensington hotel suite, to find Nat's bed stripped and all his things gone from his cupboard. Mrs Burton had begun to explain kindly to her that Nat's parents had with no warning moved from Moscow to Washington and plucked him from the Court School to go and live with them – but before she could finish, Zara's screeches of grief were echoing all over the school. Nat had left her. His parents did love him after all. And he had gone to America, where her father was a cowboy, and he hadn't taken her.

For a week she wept every day, refusing to eat, refus-ing to write to Nat, refusing at first to speak at all, then only in her notion of an American accent. Eventually Fleur had been summoned to the school and Zara had begged her, hysterically, to please take her to live in America.

But instead, Fleur whipped her straight out of the Court School and sent her off to a nice healthy girls' preparatory school in Dorset, where farmers' daughters rode their own ponies and kept dogs and didn't form unnatural attachments to each other. Zara had arrived, the oddity from London, prone to tears and still cling-ing to her American accent. She had been the oddity ever since.

She was incredible, just like Fleur was incredible – but completely different. Antony walked silently beside Zara, his head buzzing with thoughts, his body filled with a faint excitement. The implications of Zara's arrival were only now beginning to take shape in his mind. If she stayed at The Maples for a bit then he'd have someone to hang out with. Someone to impress the others with. Xanthe's face had been something else when she saw Zara. Even Mex had looked impressed.

He suddenly found himself fervently hoping that his dad didn't do anything idiotic, like break up with Fleur. It was nice, having Fleur around. And it would be even nicer having Zara around the place. She wasn't exactly the friendliest person in the world but that didn't matter. And maybe she'd loosen up after a while. Surreptitiously, he glanced at Zara's face. Her forehead was furrowed and her jaw was tense and her eyes were glittering. Bolshy, thought Antony. She's probably pissed off that we got interrupted before she'd finished smoking her joint. Druggy people were always a bit funny.

Just then they turned a corner, and the evening sun fell on Zara's face. Antony's heart gave a little jolt. For in that brief glint of light her thin cheeks looked less harsh than wistful, and her eyes seemed to be glittering not with anger but with tears. And she suddenly seemed less like a druggy person and more like a lonely little girl.

By the time they arrived back at The Maples, Zara had been allocated a bedroom, and everyone was waiting for her.

'Darling!' said Fleur, as soon as she and Antony came in through the front door; before anyone else could speak. 'Let's go straight upstairs to your room, shall we?' She smiled at Richard. 'You don't mind if I have a few moments alone with my daughter?'

'Absolutely not! Take your time!' Richard smiled encouragingly at Zara. 'Just let me say how glad I am to welcome you, Zara. How glad we all are.'

Zara was silent as they walked up the stairs and along the corridor to her room. Then, as the door shut, she turned on Fleur.

'You didn't tell me where you were.'

'Didn't I? I meant to, poppet.' Fleur went over to the window and pushed it open. 'That's better.' She turned round. 'Don't look so cross, sweetheart. I knew Johnny would tell you where I was.'

'Johnny was away.' She spat each word out with a separate emphasis. 'Term broke up a week ago. I had to check into a hotel.'

'Oh yes?' said Fleur interestedly. 'Which one?' Zara's neck became rigid.

'It doesn't matter which one. You should have let me know where you were. You said you would.'

'I really did mean to, poppet. Anyway, you got here. That's the main thing.'

Zara sat down on a green upholstered dressing-table stool and looked at Fleur's reflection in the mirror.

'What happened to Sakis?' she said. Fleur shrugged.

'I moved on. These things happen.' She waved her hands vaguely in the air.

'No money, huh?' said Zara. 'He seemed loaded to me.' Fleur flushed in irritation.

'Be quiet!' she said. 'Someone might hear.' Zara shrugged. She pulled a piece of gum from her pocket and began to chew.

'So, who's this guy?' she said, gesturing around. 'Is he rich?'

'He's very nice,' said Fleur.

'Where d'you meet him? A funeral?'

'A memorial service.'

'Uh-huh.' Zara opened a drawer of the dressing table, looked at the lining paper for a moment, then closed it again. 'How long are you planning to stay here?'

'That all depends.'

'Uh-huh.' Zara chewed some more. 'Aren't you going to tell me any more?'

'You're a child,' said Fleur. 'You don't need to know everything.'

'I do!' retorted Zara. 'Of course I do!' Fleur flinched. 'Zara, keep your voice down!'

'Listen, Fleur,' hissed Zara angrily. 'I do need to know. I need to know what's going on. You used to tell me. Remember? You used to tell me where we were going and who the people were and what to say. Now you just expect me to . . . to just *find* you. Like, you could be staying anywhere, but I have to *find* you, and then I have to say all the right stuff, and not make any mistakes . . .'

'You don't have to say anything.'

'I'm not ten years old any more. People talk to me. They ask me questions. I can't just keep saying I don't know or I can't remember.'

'You're an intelligent girl. You can think on your feet.'

'Aren't you afraid I'll make a mistake?' Zara looked at Fleur with hostile, challenging eyes. 'Aren't you afraid I'll ruin everything for you?'

'No,' said Fleur, at once, 'I'm not. Because you know that if you do, you're in trouble as much as I am. School fees don't come out of thin air, you know, and neither does that dreadful stuff you smoke.' Zara's head jerked up. 'Johnny told me,' Fleur said. 'He was shocked.'

'Johnny can go screw himself.' A corner of Fleur's mouth twisted into a smile.

'That'll be a pound in Felix's swear box,' she said. In spite of herself, Zara grinned down at her hands. She chewed some more and looked at the huge silver ring on her left hand, the one Johnny had given her during

136

that awful week in between leaving the Court School and going to Heathland School for Girls. Whenever you're feeling low, he'd told her, just polish your ring and you'll see my reflection smiling back at you. And she'd believed him. She still half did.

'Johnny wants you to call him, by the way,' she said. 'It's very urgent.' Fleur sighed.

'What is it this time?' Zara shrugged.

'I don't know. He wouldn't tell me. Something important, I guess.'

'A funeral?'

'I don't know.' Zara's voice was patient. 'He wouldn't tell me. I already said that.'

Fleur sighed again, and examined her nails.

'Urgent. What does that mean? I expect he's choosing new wallpaper.'

'Or he's having a party and he doesn't know what to wear.'

'Maybe he's lost his dry-cleaning ticket again. Do you remember?' Fleur met Zara's eyes and for the first time since meeting they smiled at each other. This always happens, thought Zara. We get on best when we're talking about Johnny. The rest of the time, forget it.

'Well, I'll see you later,' said Fleur abruptly, standing up. 'And since you're so interested in fine details, perhaps I should tell you that Richard Favour's late wife was called Emily and she was a friend of mine long ago. But we don't talk about her very much.'

'No,' said Zara, spitting her gum into the bin. 'I'll bet you don't.'

At eight o'clock, Gillian brought a jug of Pimm's into the drawing room.

'Where's Daddy?' said Philippa, coming into the

room and looking around. 'I've hardly seen him today and we can't stay too late.'

'He's still working,' said Lambert. 'In his office.' He took the glass that Gillian offered and took several large swigs, feeling as though if he didn't get some alcohol inside him, he would simmer over with frustration. Since arriving back, he'd sidled along to the office as often as he could, but each time the door had been slightly open and the desk lamp had been on and the back of Richard's head had been just visible through the chink. The bastard hadn't budged. So it looked as though he'd missed his chance. He was going to have to go back to London no closer to sorting out his overdraft problem. Not to mention the deal with Briggs and Co., a deal which should have been signed and sealed by six o'clock. A feeling of suppressed fury burned in Lambert's chest. What a bloody disaster the day had turned out to be. And it was all the fault of that fucking woman, Fleur.

'Lambert, have you met Zara?' And there she was again, wearing a tight red dress that made her look like a whore, smiling as if she owned the place, shepherding her bloody daughter into the room.

'Hello Zara,' he said, staring at the curve of Fleur's breasts under her dress. Zara. What kind of bloody stupid name was that?

'Hello!' Philippa came rushing over to Zara with bright-eyed enthusiasm. Whilst walking back to the house, another idea had occurred to her. She could become friendly with Fleur's daughter. She would be an older sister figure. The two of them would talk about clothes and make-up and boyfriend troubles, and the younger girl would confide in her, and Philippa would issue kindly advice . . . 'I'm Philippa,' she said, smiling warmly at Zara. 'Antony's older sister.'

'Hi Philippa.' Zara's voice was flat and uninterested. There was a little silence.

'Would you like some lemonade, dear?' said Gillian.

'Water, thank you,' said Zara.

'We can eat soon,' said Gillian, looking at Philippa, 'if you have to get off. As soon as your father comes downstairs. Why don't you call him, and we'll all sit down.'

'OK,' said Philippa, loitering slightly. She looked again at Zara. She had never seen anyone, she thought, quite so thin. She could have been a model. Was she really only thirteen? She looked more like—

'Philippa!' Gillian's voice interrupted her thoughts.

'Oh, sorry,' said Philippa. 'Daydreaming again!' She tried to catch Zara's eye in a giggle, but Zara gazed stonily past her. Immediately Philippa felt slighted. Just who did this girl think she was?

Richard appeared at the door.

'Sorry to have kept you,' he said. 'There were a few things I had to think about.'

Philippa was aware of Lambert glancing up sharply, then looking away again. She nudged him gently, meaning to catch his eye and roll her eyes expressively in the direction of Zara. But Lambert ignored her. She gave a hurt little sniff. Everyone was ignoring her tonight, even her own husband.

'But now let's have a toast,' continued Richard. He took the glass which Gillian was holding out to him, and held it up. 'Welcome to Zara.'

'Welcome to Zara,' chorused the others obediently.

Philippa looked down into her drink. When was the last time anyone had toasted her? When was the last time anyone had welcomed her anywhere? Everyone ignored her, even her own family. She didn't have any friends. Gillian didn't care about her any more. No-one cared about her any more. Philippa blinked a few times, and squeezed hard on the few real emotions in her mind, until slowly a tear oozed out of her eye and onto her cheek. Now they've made me cry, she thought. I'm crying, and no-one's even noticing. Another tear oozed onto her cheek, and she sniffed again.

'Philippa!' Richard's alarmed voice interrupted the conversation. 'Are you all right, darling?'

Philippa looked up, with a trembling face.

'I'm OK,' she said. 'I was just thinking . . . about Mummy. I-I don't know why.'

'Oh, my darling.' Richard hurried over.

'Don't worry,' said Philippa. 'I'm fine, really.' She gave another sniff, and smiled at her father, and allowed him to put an arm round her shoulder and lead her out of the room. Everyone was silent; everyone was looking at her tear-stained face with concern. As she neared Zara, Philippa glanced up, ready to meet another sympathetic face, stare bravely ahead and then lower her eyes. But as soon as Zara's dispassionate gaze met hers, Philippa felt a shiver go through her and her expression begin to slip. In front of this girl she felt foolish and transparent, as though Zara somehow knew exactly what she was thinking.

'I'm sorry for you,' said Zara quietly.

'What do you mean?' said Philippa, feeling rattled.

Zara's expression didn't flicker.

'Losing your mother.'

'Oh. Thank you.' Philippa exhaled sharply, and tried to reform her features into the brave stare. But she didn't feel brave any more. Her tears had dried; no-one was looking at her; Lambert had started discussing the cricket with Antony. The moment was gone and it was Zara who had spoiled it all for her.

Chapter Nine

Two weeks later, Richard looked up from his copy of *The Times* and chortled.

'Look at that!' he said, pointing to a tiny item on the business pages entitled 'Accountant Suspended'. Fleur's eyes ran down the few lines of text and a smile appeared on her face.

'I told you!' she said. 'I knew those people were crooks.'

'What's happened?' said Gillian, coming into the room. Richard looked up delightedly.

'The people we played golf with the other week. Briggs & Co. One of them's been caught fiddling the books of another company. It's in the paper.'

'Gracious,' said Gillian confusedly. 'Is that a good thing?'

'No. The good thing is that we decided not to hire them. The good thing is that Fleur cottoned onto them.' Richard reached for Fleur's hand and squeezed it affectionately. 'Fleur's the good thing around here,' he said. 'As I think we all agree.' He glanced up at Gillian. 'You look nice.'

'I'm off to my bridge lesson,' said Gillian. She looked at Fleur. 'Are you sure you won't come?'

'Darling, I got quite lost last week. I still can't remember how many tricks in a suit. Or is it the other way round?' Fleur wrinkled her nose at Gillian, who laughed. 'And Tricia was very keen to find a partner. So off you go. Have a lovely time.'

'Well . . .' Gillian paused, smoothing her jacket down over her hips. It was a new, pale-blue linen jacket, bought during a shopping trip with Fleur the week before. She was wearing with it a long, cream-coloured skirt, also new, and the blue scarf which Fleur had given her. 'If you're really sure.'

'I'm positive,' said Fleur. 'And remember I'm doing the supper tonight. So no hurrying back.'

'All right, then.' A little smile came to Gillian's face. 'I am enjoying these lessons, you know. I never thought a card game could be so invigorating!'

'I always used to enjoy a game of bridge,' said Richard, 'but Emily was never keen.'

'You have to concentrate quite hard,' said Gillian, 'but that's what I enjoy about it.'

'I'm glad,' said Richard, smiling at her. 'It's nice to see you taking up a hobby.' Gillian flushed slightly.

'It's just a bit of fun,' she said. She looked at Fleur. 'I'll probably be back in time to get supper. There's no need for you to do it.'

'I want to do it!' said Fleur. 'Now go, or you'll be late!'

'All right,' said Gillian. She hovered for a moment more, then hitched up her bag and walked as far as the door. There she stopped, and looked back.

'Everything should be in the fridge, I think,' she began. Richard started to laugh.

'Gillian, just go!'

When she had finally managed to leave, they relapsed into a companionable silence.

'I'm surprised Lambert hasn't telephoned,' said Richard suddenly. 'He must have seen the papers this morning.'

'He's probably embarrassed,' said Fleur.

'He may well be,' said Richard, 'but he also owes you an apology.' He sighed and put down his paper. 'I'm afraid to confess that the better I know Lambert, the less I like him. I suppose Philippa must love him, but . . .' He tailed away and shrugged.

'Were you surprised when they got married?' said Fleur.

'Yes, I was,' said Richard. 'I thought possibly they were hurrying into it. But they seemed very keen on the idea. And Emily was terribly pleased. She didn't seem surprised at all.' He paused. 'A mother's intuition, I suppose.'

'What about a father's intuition?'

'Temporarily out of order, I should think.' He grinned. 'I mean, they seem very happy now. Don't you think?'

'Oh yes,' said Fleur. 'Very happy.' She paused, then added, 'But I agree with you about Lambert. I was quite taken aback at the way he seemed so hostile towards me. Almost . . . distrustful.' She looked at Richard with a hurt expression. 'I was only giving my opinion.'

'Of course you were!' said Richard hotly. 'And your opinion was absolutely spot on! That Lambert's got a lot to answer for. If it weren't for you—' He broke off and gazed across the table at Fleur with more love in his face than she'd ever seen there before.

Fleur stared at him for an instant, thinking quickly. Then suddenly she exclaimed, 'Oh no!' and clasped her hand to her mouth.

'What?'

'Nothing,' said Fleur. 'It doesn't matter.' She sighed. 'It's just my purse. You remember I lost it last week?'

'Did you?'

'Didn't I tell you? Yes, I lost it out shopping. I reported it to some policeman or other but you know what they're like . . .'

'I had no idea!' said Richard. 'Did you cancel your cards?'

'Oh yes,' said Fleur. 'In fact, that's the problem. I haven't got any replacements.'

'Do you need some money?' Richard began to feel in his pocket. 'Darling, you should have said!'

'The trouble is, the replacements will take a while,' said Fleur. She frowned. 'It's all a bit complicated. You know I bank in the Cayman Islands. And Switzerland, of course.'

'I didn't,' said Richard, 'but nothing surprises me about you any more.'

'They're very good generally,' said Fleur, 'but they're hopeless about issuing new cards.'

'You should try a normal bank, like the rest of us,' said Richard.

'I know,' said Fleur, 'but my accountants recommended I go offshore for some reason . . .' She spread her hands vaguely.

'Here's a hundred pounds,' said Richard, holding out some notes.

'I've got cash,' said Fleur distractedly. 'It's just that . . . I've only just remembered it's Zara's birthday next week. I'd completely forgotten!'

'Zara's birthday!' said Richard. 'I had no idea.'

'I really want to buy her something nice.' She tapped her nails urgently on the arm of her chair. 'What I really need is my replacement Gold Card. But quickly.'

'Let me give them a ring,' said Richard.

'I'm telling you,' said Fleur, 'they're hopeless.'

She tapped her nails on the chair a few more times. Then suddenly she looked up.

'Richard, you've got a Gold Card, haven't you? Could you get me on it quickly? In the next couple of days? Then I could whiz over to Guildford and get Zara something nice – and by then my replacements might just have come through. If I'm lucky.' She looked seriously at him. 'I know it's a lot to ask you . . .'

'Well,' said Richard, 'no, it's not. I'm only too happy to help. But I don't think we need to go to all the trouble of another Gold Card. Why don't I just lend you some money?'

'Cash?' Fleur shuddered. 'I never carry cash when I'm shopping. Never! It makes me feel as though I'm asking to be attacked.'

'Well, then, why don't I come shopping with you for Zara's presents? I'd enjoy doing that. You know,' Richard's face softened, 'I've become very fond of Zara. Although I do wish she'd eat more.'

'What?' Fleur stared at him, temporarily diverted.

'All these salads and glasses of water! Each time I watch her picking at her food like a little bird, I have an overwhelming urge to cook her a plate of bacon and eggs and force her to eat them!' Richard shrugged. 'I'm sure you're doing the right thing, not drawing attention to her eating habits. And I'm sure there isn't really a problem there. But she is so terribly thin.' He smiled. 'Knowing Zara, I don't suppose she'd take kindly to being told what to eat!'

'No,' said Fleur. 'I don't suppose she would.'

'But she'll have a birthday cake, at any rate!' Richard's eyes began to shine. 'We'll plan a party for her. Perhaps we could make it a surprise!'

'When can you get me on your Gold Card? By Saturday?'

'Fleur, I'm not sure about this Gold Card scheme.'

'Oh.' Fleur stared at him. 'Why not?'

'It's just . . . something I've never done. Put someone else on my card. It doesn't seem necessary.'

'Oh. I see.' Fleur thought for a moment. 'Wasn't Emily on your card?'

'No, she had her own. We always kept money affairs separate. It seemed sensible.'

'Separate?' Fleur stared at Richard with features which she hoped displayed surprise, rather than the irritation which had begun to spark inside her. How dared he balk at putting her on his Gold Card? she thought furiously. What was happening to her? Was she losing her touch? 'But that's not natural!' she said out loud. 'You were married! Didn't you want to . . . to share everything?' Richard rubbed his nose.

'I wanted to,' he said, 'at first. I liked the idea of a joint bank account. I wanted to pool everything. But Emily didn't. She wanted everything more cut and dried. So she had her own account and her own credit cards and—' He broke off and smiled sheepishly. 'I'm not sure how we got on to this subject. It's very boring.'

'Zara's birthday,' said Fleur.

'Oh yes,' said Richard. 'Don't worry – we'll give Zara a wonderful birthday.'

'And you don't think it would be more sensible for me to put my name on your card? Just to whiz round the shops with.'

'Not really,' said Richard. 'But, if you like, we can apply for one for you in your own name.'

'OK,' said Fleur lightly. Her jaw tightened imperceptibly and she stared at her nails. Richard turned to the sports section of *The Times*. For a few minutes there was silence. Then suddenly without looking up, Fleur said, 'I might be going to a funeral soon.'

'Oh dear!' Richard looked up.

'A friend in London has asked me to call him. We've

been expecting bad news for a while. I've got a feeling this might be it.'

'I know what it's like,' said Richard soberly. 'These things can drag on and on. You know, I sometimes think it's better—'

'Yes,' said Fleur, reaching for *The Times* and turning to the announcements column. 'Yes, so do I.'

'How long are you going to stay with us?' asked Antony. He was sitting with Zara in a secluded corner of the garden, idly plucking strawberries from the patch and eating them, while she pored intently over a thick, glossy magazine. Zara looked up at him. She was wearing opaque black sunglasses and he couldn't read her expression.

'I don't know,' she said, and looked down at her magazine again.

'It would be great if you were still here when Will gets back,' said Antony. He waited for Zara to ask who Will was or where he was. But all she did was chew a few times on her gum, and turn the page. Antony ate another strawberry and wondered why he didn't just go off and play golf or something. Zara didn't need looking after; she hardly ever said anything; she never smiled or laughed. It wasn't as if they were having a riotous time together. And yet something about her fascinated him. He would actually be quite happy, he admitted to himself, to sit staring at Zara all day and do nothing else. But at the same time it felt wrong, to sit alone with someone and not at least try to talk to them.

'Where do you normally live?' he said.

'We move around,' said Zara.

'But you must have a home.' Zara shrugged. Antony thought for a moment.

'Like . . . where were you last holidays?'

'Staying with a friend,' said Zara. 'On his yacht.'

'Oh right.' Antony shifted on the grass. Yachts were outside his experience. All he knew, from people at school, was that you had to be bloody rich to have one. He looked at Zara with new respect, wondering if she would elaborate. But her attention was still fixed on her magazine. Antony looked over her shoulder at the pictures. They were all of girls like Zara, thin and young, with bony shoulders and hollow chests, staring with huge sad eyes at the camera. None of them looked any older than Zara. He wondered if she recognized herself in the pictures or whether she was just looking at the clothes. Personally he thought every outfit more frightful than the one before.

'Do you like designer clothes?' he tried. He looked at the T-shirt she was wearing. Might that be by some famous designer? He couldn't tell. 'Your mother wears lovely clothes,' he added politely. An image popped into his mind of Fleur in her red dress, all curves and shiny hair and bubbling laughter. Zara couldn't have been more different from her mother if she'd tried. Then it occurred to him that perhaps she did try.

'What's your star sign?' Her raspy voice interrupted his thoughts.

'Oh. Aries.' Without looking up, she began to read aloud.

'"Planetary activity in Pluto is transforming your direction in life. After the 18th, you will enter a more purposeful phase".' She turned the page.

'Do you really believe in all that stuff?' said Antony, before she could continue.

'It depends what it says. When it's good, I believe it.' She glanced up at him and a little grin appeared at the corner of her mouth.

'So what does yours say? What are you?'

'Sagittarius.' She threw the magazine down. 'Mine says get a life and stop reading crappy horoscopes.' She threw her head back and breathed in deeply. Antony thought fast. Now was the moment to get a conversation going.

'Do you ever go out clubbing?' he said.

'Sure,' said Zara. 'When we're in London. When I have someone to go with.'

'Oh, right.' Antony thought again. 'Is London where your dad lives?'

'No. He lives in the States.'

'Oh right! Is he American?'

'Yes.'

'Cool! Whereabouts does he live?' This was great, thought Antony. They could start talking about where they'd been in the States. He could tell her about his school trip to California. Maybe he could even get out his photos.

'I don't know.' Zara looked away. 'I've never seen him. I don't even know his name.'

'What?' Antony, who had been poised to display his knowledge of San Francisco, found himself exhaling sharply instead. Had he heard her right? 'You don't know your dad's name?' he said, trying to sound interested rather than shaken.

'No.'

'Hasn't your . . .' Whatever he said, it was going to sound stupid. 'Hasn't your mother told you?'

'She says it doesn't matter what he's called.'

'Do you know anything about him?'

'Nope.'

'So how do you know he lives in the States?'

'That's the only thing she's ever told me. Ages ago, when I was a little kid.' She hunched her knees to her chest. 'I always used to think . . .' She raised her head

149

and sunlight flashed off her shades. 'I always used to think he was a cowboy.'

'Maybe he is,' said Antony. He stared at Zara, all scrunched up and bony, and imagined her relaxed and laughing, sitting on a horse, in front of a tanned, heroic cowboy. It seemed as likely as anything else.

'Why won't your mother tell you?' he said bluntly. 'Isn't that against the law or something?'

'Maybe,' said Zara. 'That wouldn't worry Fleur.' She sighed. 'She won't tell me because she doesn't want me trying to find him. It's like . . . he's her past, not mine.'

'But he's your father!'

'I know,' said Zara. 'He's my father.' She pushed her shades up, off her face and looked straight at Antony. 'Don't worry. I am going to find him,' she said.

'How?'

'When I'm sixteen,' said Zara. 'Then she's going to tell me who he is. She's promised.' Antony stared at her. Her eyes were faintly gleaming. 'Two and a half years to go. Then I'll be off to the States. She can't stop me.'

'I'll have left school by then,' said Antony eagerly. 'I could come with you!'

'OK,' said Zara. She met his eyes and, for the first time, she smiled properly at him. 'We'll both go.'

Later on, they both wandered in, hot and sunburned, to find Richard sitting alone in the kitchen, a glass of beer in front of him. It was quiet and still and the light of early evening streamed in through the window and across his face. Antony opened the fridge and got out a couple of cans.

'Did you play golf today?' he asked his father.

'No. Did you?'

'No.'

'I thought you guys were golf addicts,' said Zara. Richard smiled.

'Is that what your mother told you?'

'It's obvious,' said Zara. 'You live on a golf course, for Christ's sake.'

'Well, I do enjoy a game of golf,' said Richard. 'But it's not the only thing in the world.'

'Where's Fleur?' said Zara.

'I don't know,' said Richard. 'She must have popped out somewhere.'

Richard no longer winced when he heard Zara refer to her mother as 'Fleur'. Sometimes he even found it faintly endearing. He watched as Antony and Zara settled themselves on the windowseat with drinks; comfortably, like a pair of cats. Zara's was a low-calorie drink, he noticed – and he wondered again how much she weighed. Then he chided himself. She wasn't his daughter; he mustn't start behaving as though she were.

But still. Oliver Sterndale's words rang again through his mind. What would happen if you were, say, to remarry?

'What indeed?' said Richard aloud. Antony and Zara looked up. 'Don't mind me,' he added.

'Oh right,' said Antony politely. 'Do you mind if we have the telly on?'

'Not at all,' said Richard. 'Go ahead.'

As the kitchen filled with chattering sound, he took a sip of beer. The money was all still on deposit, waiting for him to make up his mind. A small fortune, to be split between his two children. It had seemed such an obvious step when he'd discussed it with Emily. The picture had seemed complete; the cast of players had seemed finite.

But now there were two more players in the scene.

There was Fleur. And there was little Zara. Richard leaned back and closed his eyes. Had Emily ever thought that he might marry after her death? Or had she, like him, believed that their love could never be supplanted? The possibility of remarriage had never, not once, crossed his mind. His grief had seemed too huge; his love too strong. And then he'd met Fleur, and everything had started to change.

Did he want to marry Fleur? He didn't know. At the moment he was still enjoying the fluid, day-to-day nature of their existence together. Nothing was defined, there were no outside pressures, the days were floating by agreeably.

But it was not in Richard's nature to float indefinitely; it was not in his nature to ignore problems in the hope that they would go away. Problems must be addressed. In particular, the problem of . . . the problem of . . . Richard squirmed awkwardly in his seat. As usual, his thoughts wanted to shy away from the subject. But this time he forced them back; this time he confronted the very word in his thoughts. Of sex. The problem of sex.

Fleur was an understanding woman, but she would not understand for ever. Why should she, when Richard didn't understand himself? He adored Fleur. She was beautiful and desirable and every other man envied him. Yet whenever he came to her bedroom and saw her lying in bed, staring at him with those mesmerizing eyes, inviting him in, a guilty fear came over him, subsuming his desire and leaving him pale and shaking with frustration.

He had thought until now that this factor alone would prove the obstacle to his marrying Fleur; had resigned himself to the fact that before long she would make her excuses and move off, like an exotic insect, to another, more fruitful flower. But she seemed in no hurry to leave. She almost seemed to know something he didn't. And so Richard had begun to wonder whether he weren't looking at the problem in the wrong way. He had been telling himself that the lack of sex came in the way of a marriage. But might it not be that the lack of a marriage was coming in the way of sex? Might it not be that until he fully committed himself to Fleur, he would feel unable to cast off the shadow of Emily? And had Fleur — perceptive Fleur — already realized this? Did she understand him better than he understood himself?

Taking another sip of his beer, Richard resolved to talk to Fleur about it that very night. He wouldn't make the mistake he had made with Emily, of leaving things unsaid until it was too late. With Fleur it would be different. With Fleur there would be no hidden thoughts. With Fleur, thought Richard, nothing was secret.

Chapter Ten

Fleur rarely dwelled on mistakes or misfortune. Striding swiftly along the paths of the Greyworth estate, blinking as the dazzling evening sunlight caught her in the eye, she did not allow herself to consider that the past few months with Richard Favour might all have been for no financial gain whatsoever. Instead, she focused her mind fully ahead. The next funeral, the next memorial service, the next conquest. Thinking positive was Fleur's speciality. She would call Johnny and fix herself up some more funerals and Richard Favour would become just another name from the past.

In fact, she rationalized, leaning against a tree to catch her breath, it had been no bad thing for her to stay at The Maples for a while, money or no money. After all, few of the men whose hospitality she had enjoyed in the past had allowed her to get away with doing so very little as Richard Favour did. The demands he made on her were practically zero. She wasn't required to exert herself in the bedroom. She wasn't required to exert herself in the kitchen. She wasn't expected to host elaborate functions, nor to remember people's names, nor to profess fondness for any small children or animals.

This time with Richard had been a recharging time. A rest-cure, practically. She would emerge refreshed and regenerated, ready for the next challenge. And it was unrealistic to suppose that she would leave The Maples with no money whatsoever. She would manage to mop up a couple of thousand before she left, maybe more. She wouldn't exactly steal it – breaking the law directly wasn't Fleur's style. But twisting the law to suit her own ends was exactly her style, as was judging exactly how much she could risk taking from a man without provoking a chase.

She had reached The Meadows – a remote corner of the Greyworth estate laid over to natural beauty which was rarely visited. Glancing around to check no-one was around to overhear, she took her mobile phone from her bag, switched it on, and dialled Johnny's number.

'Johnny.'

'Fleur! At last!'

'What do you mean, at last?' said Fleur, frowning slightly.

'Didn't Zara tell you to ring me?'

'Oh,' said Fleur, remembering. 'Yes, she did. She said you were in a tizz.'

'Yes, I am. And it's all your fault.'

'My fault? Johnny, what are you talking about?'

'It's not *what* I'm talking about,' said Johnny, in a voice laden with drama. 'It's *who* I'm talking about.' Fleur had a sudden mental picture of him standing by the mantelpiece in his Chelsea drawing room, sipping sherry, enjoying every moment of their conversation.

'All right, Johnny,' she said patiently. 'Who are you talking about?' There was a perfectly timed pause, then Johnny said,

'Hal Winters. That's who.'

'Oh, for God's sake.' Rattled, Fleur found herself snapping more loudly than she had meant to. 'Not that old story again. I've told you, Johnny . . .'

'He's in London.'

'What?' Fleur felt the colour drain from her cheeks. 'What's he doing in London?'

'Looking for you.'

'How can he be looking for me? He wouldn't know where to start.'

'He started with us.'

'I see.' Fleur stared ahead for a few seconds, as thoughts whirled round her mind. An evening breeze rustled the trees and blew through her hair, warm and soft. Here at Greyworth, London seemed another country. And yet it was under an hour away. Hal Winters was under an hour away.

'So what did you tell him?' she said at last. 'I hope you sent him away.'

'We stalled him,' said Johnny.

'Meaning?'

'Meaning in a few days' time, he's going to be back on our doorstep, wanting to know if we've got anywhere.'

'And you'll just tell him that you haven't,' said Fleur briskly.

'No we won't.'

'What?' Fleur stared at the receiver.

'Felix and I have discussed it. We think you should agree to see him.'

'Well you can both bugger off!'

'Fleur . . .'

'I know. A pound in the bloody swear box.'

'Fleur, listen to me.' Suddenly the drama was gone from Johnny's voice. 'You can't keep running away for ever.'

'I'm not running away!'

'What do you call your life, then?'

'I . . . What do you mean? Johnny, what is all this?'

'You can't treat Hal Winters like you treat all the others. You can't run away from him. It's not fair.'

'Who are you to tell me what's fair and what isn't?' said Fleur furiously. 'You've got nothing to do with it. And if you tell Hal Winters where I am . . .'

'I wouldn't do that without your permission,' said Johnny. 'But I'm asking you to change your mind. If you could have seen his face you'd understand. He's desperate.'

'Why should he be desperate to see me?' said Fleur sharply. 'It's not as though he knows.'

'But he does know!' said Johnny. 'That's the whole point! He does know!' Fleur felt her legs weaken beneath her.

'He knows?'

'He doesn't exactly know,' amended Johnny. 'But he's obviously found something out. And now he wants the whole story.'

'Well, he can bugger off too.'

'Fleur, grow up! He deserves to know the truth. You know he does. And Zara deserves to meet her father.'

Gillian arrived back from her bridge lesson to find Richard on his third glass of beer, Antony and Zara engrossed in the television, no sign of Fleur and no sign of supper.

'What's everyone been doing?' she said shortly, dumping her bag on the kitchen table and opening the fridge. All the dishes and packets that she had set aside for Fleur were still there, untouched.

'Nothing,' said Richard idly. 'Just sitting.' He glanced up and smiled at Gillian. She half-smiled back, but on her face was the beginnings of a frown. Richard looked past her at the fridge, and suddenly realized what had happened.

'Gillian! The supper! I'm so sorry. Quick, Antony, let's help Gillian.' He leapt to his feet, and Antony slowly followed suit.

'What's wrong?' he said, eyes still glued to the television, moving like a zombie across the kitchen.

'Well, Fleur . . .' Richard tailed away in discomfiture. 'Oh dear. Oh Gillian, I'm terribly sorry.'

'It doesn't matter,' said Gillian, staring gloomily down at the unassembled ingredients before her.

'Fleur promised to make supper, right?' Zara's voice cut harshly across the kitchen.

'Well, she did make some mention of it,' said Richard feebly. 'I've no idea where she's got to.' Zara rolled her eyes.

'What I would do,' she said, 'is order take-out and make her pay for it. Forget all this stuff.' She gestured at the table. 'Get something easy and expensive. You got a phone book?'

'It'll be just as quick for me to do it,' said Gillian, taking off her jacket with a sigh. 'And we've got everything out now.'

'Yeah, so we put it away again. And we make a phone call. And they deliver the food. How quick is that? Quicker than peeling a pile of carrots.' Zara shrugged. 'It's up to you. But I'd go for take-out. This stuff'll keep, right?'

'Well, yes,' said Gillian grudgingly. 'Most of it.'

'Which things won't? Tell us exactly, then we can keep those bits out and eat them. Is it like . . . salad-type stuff?' Zara grinned at Antony. 'You can tell I failed Home Ec.' She turned back to Gillian. 'What won't keep?'

'I'll . . . I'll have to have a look.'

Gillian moved away from Zara and prodded a packet of lettuce. It was ridiculous; the girl was only a child.

But Zara's easy analysis of the situation left her feeling suddenly unsure of herself. Inside, a familiar mass of resentment had already built up; grumbling phrases were on her lips; her face was poised to frown in martyred gloom. That was the role she knew; that was the role which everyone expected. Everyone but Zara.

'I should add that I can't stand Indian,' added Zara, taking a swig from her can. 'And we don't want some crummy pizza. Do you have a good Thai take-out place round here?'

'I have no idea,' said Richard, starting to laugh. 'We're not really "take-out" sort of people. Are we Gillian?'

'I don't know,' said Gillian. Weakly, she sat down. Antony was already putting her dishes and labelled plastic boxes back into the fridge. Zara was scanning the Yellow Pages. The moment for righteous indignation had gone; had dissipated. She felt strangely robbed, and at the same time, uplifted.

'I don't think I've ever had Thai food,' she said cautiously.

'Oh, then we absolutely have to have Thai,' said Zara at once. 'Thai food is just the best.' She looked up with an animated face. 'These friends of ours in London, they live right above a Thai food place. I practically live off the stuff when I'm staying with them. Antony, how does this stupid book work? Find me the Thai take-out page.'

'Oh, right.' Obediently, Antony trotted over to Zara's side and began to leaf through the pages. Richard caught Gillian's eye and she felt a sudden urge to giggle.

'OK,' said Zara. 'Let's try these.' She picked up the phone and dialled briskly. 'Hello? Could you please fax me your menu? I'll give you the number.'

'Gillian, why don't you have a drink,' said Richard in an undertone. His eyes were twinkling. 'Dinner seems to be well under control.'

'Cool,' said Zara, putting down the phone. 'The menu'll be here any minute. Shall I choose?'

'I'll help,' said Antony. 'Dad, can we have the key to your office? We need to get at the fax.'

'You don't mind if I order for everyone?' said Zara.

'You go ahead,' said Richard. He handed the office key to Antony and watched as he and Zara hurried out of the kitchen.

'I was beginning to worry about Zara's eating habits,' he remarked to Gillian when the two of them were out of earshot. 'I think I was worrying about nothing. I've never seen her look so sparky.'

He stood up, stretched, and went into the larder.

'But I am sorry, Gillian,' he said, returning with a bottle of wine. 'About Fleur, I mean. It's not like her to let people down.'

'I know it isn't,' said Gillian. 'I imagine something must have happened to hold her up.'

'I hope she's all right.' Richard frowned, and handed Gillian a glass of wine. 'Perhaps I'll ring the clubhouse in a minute. See if she went for a swim.'

'Good idea,' said Gillian. She took a deep breath. 'And there's no need to apologize. What does a meal matter? It's only food.'

'Well,' said Richard awkwardly. 'Even so.'

'I know I have a tendency to take these things too seriously.' Gillian bit her lip. 'I get . . . what would Antony say? Stressed out. By silly little things.' She sighed. 'I'm the one who should be sorry.'

'Nonsense!' said Richard. 'Goodness me, Gillian . . .' She ignored him.

'But I think I'm changing.' She sat back, took a sip of

wine and looked at Richard over the rim of her glass. 'Fleur's changing me.'

Richard gave a gallant little laugh.

'Changing our charming Gillian? I hope not!'

'Richard!' There was a blade of anger in Gillian's voice. 'Don't be polite to me, please. Tell me I'm changing for the better.' She took a deep sip of wine. 'I know you and I don't usually speak to each other on this . . . on this . . .'

'This level.' Richard's expression was suddenly serious.

'Exactly. This level.' She swallowed. 'But you must realize as well as I that since Fleur has been here things have been different. There's something about Fleur . . .' She tailed away and blinked a few times.

'I know,' agreed Richard. 'There is.'

'Fleur is kind to me in a way that my own sister never was,' said Gillian in a voice which trembled slightly.

'Emily?' Richard stared at her.

'Emily was a dear sister to me. But she had her faults. She did things that were thoughtless and unkind.' Gillian raised her head and looked straight at Richard. Her blue eyes were glistening. 'Perhaps I shouldn't be telling you this now,' she said. 'But it's the truth. Emily was unkind to me. And Fleur is kind. That's all.'

Fleur had arrived back at The Maples, gone straight upstairs and into her bedroom. Now she was seated in front of the mirror in her bedroom, wearing her black veiled hat, staring at her reflection. She had been sitting there for half an hour without moving, waiting for the unfamiliar feeling of disquiet to subside. But still her insides felt clenched and her brow was screwed up in wrinkles, and Johnny's voice rang in her ear, cross and pestering like a woodpecker. 'Why won't you see him? Why won't you face up to your past? When are you going to stop running?'

Never before had she heard Johnny so stern; so unbiddable.

'What do you expect me to do? Invite him to stay?' she'd said, trying to sound flippant. 'Introduce him to Richard? Come on, Johnny. Be serious.'

'I expect you to acknowledge his existence,' said Johnny. 'You could meet him in London.'

'I couldn't. I haven't got time.'

'You haven't got time.' Johnny's voice was scathing. 'Well, perhaps Zara has got time.'

'She can't meet her father yet! She . . . she isn't ready! She needs to be prepared!'

'And you're going to do that, are you?'

There was silence.

'OK, Fleur, have it your own way,' said Johnny at last. 'You let me know when Zara's ready to meet her father, and I'll keep putting him off for the moment. But that's all I'm doing.'

'Johnny, you're a doll . . .'

'No more funerals,' said Johnny. 'No more invitations. No more arriving out of the blue and expecting to use our spare room.'

'Johnny!'

'I'm not pleased with you, Fleur.'

And as she stared disbelievingly at the phone, he'd rung off, and a cold chunk of dismay had descended into her stomach. Everything was suddenly going wrong. Richard wouldn't give her a Gold Card; Johnny was cross with her; Hal Winters was in the country.

Hal Winters. The very name irritated her. He'd already caused enough trouble in her life; now here he was again, turning up out of the blue, threatening to ruin everything, turning her friends against her. Turning Johnny against her. A pang of alarm ran through Fleur. If she lost Johnny, who did she have? Who else was there for her?

Never before had Fleur realized quite how much she depended on Johnny and Felix. For twenty years, Johnny's flat had been at her disposal. For twenty years she had confided in him, gossiped with him, shopped with him. She had thought nothing of it. If asked, she would have described their friendship as casual. Now that it was under threat, it seemed suddenly far more than that. Fleur closed her eyes. She and Johnny had never disagreed before over anything more significant than the colour of a sofa. He had scolded her often enough in the past, but always with a twinkle in his eye. Never seriously, never like this. This, he was taking seriously. This time he meant business. And all because of a man named Hal Winters.

Fleur stared angrily at her reflection. She looked a sophisticated, elegant woman. She could be the consort of an ambassador. A prince. And Hal Winters was . . . what? A drugs salesman from Scottsdale, Arizona. A cheap drugs salesman who fourteen years ago had coupled nervously with her in the back of his Chevy and then brushed his hair carefully back into place so that his mother wouldn't notice anything awry. Who had asked her to keep her distance in public and please not blaspheme in front of his family.

Bitterly, Fleur wondered again how she could have been so stupid. How she could have mistaken that sulky diffidence for gauche charm. How she could have allowed him to invade her body; plant a piece of his second-rate self in her own. She had let him into her life once; never again. A man like Hal Winters could not be recognized as part of her existence. Could never be permitted to claim a piece of her life. And if that meant losing Johnny, then so it would have to be.

Fleur lifted her chin determinedly. Quickly she took off the veiled hat and replaced it with another. A black cloche; a smart, serious hat. She would find a memorial service to wear it to next week. So Johnny refused to feed her any suitable funerals. Well, what of it? She didn't need Johnny. She could survive very well on her own. On the dressing table in front of her were three newspaper clippings. Three London memorial services. Three chances for a fresh start. And this time, she wouldn't sit around for weeks, letting her life slip away. She would pounce at once. If Richard Favour wasn't going to make her a rich woman, then somebody was.

She bit her lip, and quickly reached for another hat; another distraction. This was made from black silk and sprinkled with tiny violets. A very pretty hat, thought Fleur, admiring the picture she made in the mirror. Almost too pretty for a funeral; almost a hat for a wedding.

As she turned her head from side to side, she heard a knock at the door.

'Hello?'

'Fleur! Can I come in?' It was Richard. He sounded flustered.

'Of course!' she called back. 'Come on in!'

The door burst open and in came Richard.

'I don't know what I was thinking of this morning,' he said in a flurry. 'Of course you can have a Gold Card. You have whatever you damn well like! My darling Fleur . . .' Suddenly he seemed to see her for the first time, and broke off. 'That . . . that hat,' he faltered.

'Forget the hat!' Fleur tore it off her head and threw it on the floor. 'Richard, you're a poppet!' She looked up, a dazzling smile on her face. He was standing completely still, staring at her as though he'd never seen her before in his life.

'Richard?' she said. 'Is something wrong?'

He really hadn't expected her to be in her bedroom. He had planned to go and see how the two young people were getting on with the food ordering, then ring the health club and ask whether Fleur was there. But as he'd passed her door, it had occurred to him, at the back of his troubled mind, that he might as well knock on the door, just to be sure. He'd done so perfunctorily, his thoughts elsewhere, swirling uneasily around this new, undigested fact about Emily.

Emily had been unkind to Gillian. He found it painful to frame the thought in his mind. His own, sweet timid Emily, unkind to her own sister. It was an astonishing accusation; one which he found it difficult to believe. But not – and it was this that troubled him the most – not impossible. For even as Gillian had told him there had been, amongst the immediate protestations and shouts of denial around his brain, a small, sober part of him that was not surprised; that perhaps had always known.

As he'd left the kitchen, a pain had begun to jab at his chest and he had felt a renewed grief for Emily – the Emily he had loved. A sweet, remote creature with hidden qualities. Qualities he had been desperate to unmask. Was unkindness one of those qualities? You wanted to find out, he told himself bitterly, as he walked up the stairs. And now you have found out. All the time, underneath that mild exterior had been a secret unkindness, from which Gillian had suffered in uncomplaining silence. He could hardly bear to think about it.

And suddenly he'd wanted, above anything else, to see Fleur. Warm, loving Fleur, with not an unkind bone in her body. Fleur, who made Gillian happy and him happy and everybody happy. When he'd heard her voice unexpectedly answer his knock he'd felt an almost tearful love rising through him; an enveloping emotion which propelled him through the door, forced speech from his lips.

And then he'd seen her, sitting in front of the dressing table in a hat. A hat just like Emily had worn on the day of their wedding; a hat just like the one she'd been unpinning as he discovered the first of the cold, steely gates that would forever lie between them. Part of him had expected Fleur to do the same as Emily had then. To unpin her hat, and lay it aside carefully, and look straight through him, and ask, 'What time's dinner?'

But instead, she'd thrown it aside in a whirl, as though contemptuous of anything which got in the way of them. The two of them. Him and Fleur. Now she was holding out her arms to him. Warm and open and loving.

'Fleur, I love you,' he found himself saying. 'I love you.' A tear fell from his eye. 'I love you.'

'And I love you.' She caught him up in an exuberant hug. 'You sweet man.'

Richard buried his head in Fleur's pale neck, feeling tears suddenly stream from his eyes. Tears that mourned the loss of his perfect Emily, the discovery of her fallibility; which marked the passing of his innocence. His mouth was wet and salty when he eventually raised it to Fleur's; began to pull her closer to him, suddenly wanting to feel her warm skin against his own, wanting to break down all barriers between them.

'Why did I wait?' he murmured as his hands feverishly roamed the body she had been offering him for weeks. 'Why on earth did I wait?'

Struggling out of his clothes, feeling her bare skin in patches against his, was an agony of frustration. As her hands ran lightly down his back, he began to shiver with a desperate anticipation, almost frightened that having pitched over the edge he would never make the other side.

'Come here.' Her voice was low and melodious in his ear; her fingers were warm and confident on his body. He felt unable to reciprocate, unable to do anything but shudder in a paralysis of delight. And then, slowly, she took him into her mouth, and he felt a disbelieving ecstasy which he couldn't begin to control; which he couldn't begin to measure; which made him whimper and cry out until he suddenly fell, spent and exhausted, into her arms.

'I . . .'

'Sssh.' She put a finger against his lips and he fell silent. He lay against her, listening to her heartbeat, and felt like a child, naked and vulnerable and accepting.

'I will give you anything,' he whispered at last. 'Anything you want.'

'All I want is you,' said Fleur softly. He felt her fingers twining in his hair. 'And I've got you, haven't I?'

Chapter Eleven

A few days later a package arrived for Fleur through the post. Inside was a shiny golden American Express card.

'Cool!' said Antony, as she opened it at breakfast. 'A Gold Card. Dad, why can't I have one of those? Some of the blokes at school have got them.'

'Then their parents are very stupid as well as very rich,' said Richard, grinning. 'Now, where's a pen? You should sign it straight away, Fleur. It wouldn't do if it fell into the wrong hands.'

'I'll be very careful,' said Fleur, smiling at him. She squeezed his hand. 'It's very good of you, Richard. Now I'll be able to get something really super for Zara.'

'Zara?' Antony looked up.

'It's Zara's birthday this week,' said Richard.

'Her birthday?' echoed Antony.

'On Wednesday. Is that right, Fleur?'

'Yes,' said Fleur, signing the Gold Card with a flourish. 'I'll go into Guildford this morning.'

'Would she like it if I made a cake, do you think?' enquired Gillian.

'I'm sure she would,' said Fleur, smiling warmly at Gillian.

'How old is she going to be?' said Antony.

'Fourteen,' said Fleur, after a moment's hesitation.

'Oh right.' Antony frowned slightly. 'Because I thought she wasn't fourteen for a while yet.'

'Lying about her age already!' said Fleur, and gave a peal of laughter. 'Antony, you should be flattered!' Antony coloured slightly, and looked down at his plate.

'What about . . .' Gillian hesitated, glanced at Richard, then continued. 'What about Zara's father? Will he want to . . . visit her?' She flushed. 'Perhaps I shouldn't have mentioned it. I just thought, if it's her birthday . . .'

'Gillian, you're very kind,' said Fleur. She took a sip of coffee. 'Unfortunately, Zara's father is dead.'

'Dead?' Antony's head jerked up. 'But I thought . . . I thought Zara's dad lived in America. She told me . . .'

Fleur shook her head sadly.

'Zara found it very difficult to come to terms with her father's death,' she said, and sipped again at her coffee. 'In her mind, he's still alive. She has many different fantasies about him. The current one is that he's living somewhere in America.' She sighed. 'I've been told that the best thing is just to play along with her.'

'But . . .'

'I blame myself,' said Fleur. 'I should have talked to her more about it. But it was a painful time for me, too.'

She broke off, and looked at Antony with wide, sympathetic eyes. Richard took her hand and squeezed it.

'I didn't realize,' said Antony feebly. 'I thought . . .'

'She's coming,' interrupted Gillian quickly. 'Hello Zara,' she exclaimed brightly as Zara entered the conservatory. 'We were just talking about your birthday.'

'My birthday,' echoed Zara, stopping still in the doorway. Her cautious gaze swept the scene and landed on the Gold Card, glinting among the paper packaging on the table. She looked up at Fleur, then back at the Gold Card. 'Sure,' she said. 'My birthday.'

'We want Wednesday to be a really special day for

you, darling,' said Fleur. 'With a cake, and candles, and . . .' she spread her hands vaguely.

'Party-poppers,' said Zara tonelessly.

'Party-poppers! What a good idea!'

'Yup,' said Zara.

'Well, that's settled,' said Richard. 'Now, I have some calls to make.' He got up.

'If you'd like a lift into Guildford,' said Gillian to Fleur, 'I could do with popping in myself.'

'Lovely,' said Fleur.

'And what will you two young things do?' said Richard to Antony.

'Dunno,' said Antony. Zara shrugged, and looked away.

'Well,' said Richard comfortably, 'I'm sure you'll think of something jolly.'

As Zara ate her breakfast, she stared straight downwards and avoided Antony's eyes. An angry disappointment was burning in her chest; she didn't trust herself not to burst into tears. Fleur had got hold of a Gold Card. Which meant they were going to move on. As soon as Fleur had cleaned up, they would be off.

It was just like bouncing a ball, Fleur had explained to her a couple of years before, as they sat in some airport restaurant, waiting for a plane.

'You take the Gold Card, and you cash some money, and the next day you put it back again. Then you cash some more, and put that back again. And you keep going, bouncing higher and higher until you're as high as you can go – then you scoop up all the money and disappear!' She'd laughed, and Zara had laughed too.

'Why don't you just scoop it all up at the beginning?' she'd asked.

'Too suspicious, darling,' Fleur had said. 'You have to work up gradually, so no-one notices.'

'And how do you know when you're as high as you can go?'

'You don't. You try to find out as much as you can before you start. Is he rich? Is he poor? How much can he afford to lose? But then you've just got to guess. And that's part of the game. Two thousand? Ten thousand? Fifty thousand? Who knows what the limit is?'

Fleur had laughed again, and so had Zara. Back then, it had seemed fun. A good game. Now the whole idea made Zara feel sick.

'Do you want to go swimming?' Antony's voice interrupted her thoughts.

'Oh.' With a huge effort, Zara raised her head to meet Antony's gaze. He was staring at her with a peculiar expression on his face, almost as though he could read her thoughts. Almost as though he knew what was going on.

A dart of panic raced through Zara; her face became guarded. In all these years of pretending, she had never yet slipped up. She couldn't allow herself to become careless. If she gave away the truth to Antony, Fleur would never forgive her. Fleur would never forgive her, and she would never get to meet her father.

'Sure,' she said, forcing a casual tone into her voice, shrugging her shoulders. 'Why not.'

'OK.' He was still staring at her weirdly. 'I'll get my stuff.'

'OK,' she said. And she looked down at her bowl of Honey Nut Loops and didn't look up again until he had gone.

* * *

Oliver Sterndale was in the office, his secretary informed Richard over the telephone, but he was about to leave on holiday.

'This won't take long,' said Richard cheerfully. As he waited for Oliver's voice, he looked around his dull, ordered office and wondered why he had never thought to have it redecorated. The walls were plain white, unrelieved by pictures, the carpet a functional slate grey. There was not one object in the room that could be described as beautiful.

Things like the colour of walls had never seemed to matter to him before. But now he looked at the world through Fleur's eyes. Now he saw possibility where before he had only seen fact. He wouldn't sit in this dull little box any longer. He would ask Fleur to redesign the office for him.

'Richard!' Oliver's voice made him jump. 'I'm just on my way.'

'I know. Off on holiday. This won't take long. I just wanted to tell you that I've made up my mind about the trust.'

'Oh yes?'

'I'm going to go ahead with it.'

'I see. And might I ask why?'

'I've realized that what I really want is to make Philippa and Antony financially independent,' said Richard. 'Beholden to no-one, not even . . .' He paused, and bit his lip. 'Not even a member of their own family. Above all, I want them to feel they have control of their own lives.' He frowned. 'I also want to . . . to close a chapter in my life. Start afresh.'

'Starting afresh usually means spending money,' said Oliver.

'I've got money,' said Richard impatiently. 'Plenty of money. Oliver, we've been over this.'

172

'All right. Well, it's your decision. But I can't do anything about it for a week.'

'There's no hurry. I just thought I'd let you know. I won't keep you. Have a good holiday. Where are you going?'

'Provence. Some friends have a house there.'

'Lovely,' said Richard automatically. 'Beautiful countryside in that part of the—'

'Yes, yes,' interrupted Oliver impatiently. 'Look, Richard.'

'Yes?'

'Listen. This starting afresh of yours. Does it involve marrying your friend Fleur?'

'I very much hope so,' said Richard, smiling at the receiver. Oliver sighed.

'Richard, please be cautious.'

'Oliver, not again . . .'

'Just think about the implications of marriage for a moment. I gather, for instance, that Fleur has a daughter of school age.'

'Zara.'

'Zara. Indeed. Now, does her mother have the money to support Zara? Or will that be a role which you're expected to take on?'

'Fleur has the money to send her to Heathland School for Girls,' said Richard drily. 'Is that support enough for you?'

'Well, all right – but you're sure that she pays the fees herself? You're sure that they don't come from some sort of income which will stop if she remarries?'

'No, I'm not sure,' replied Richard testily. 'I haven't had the impertinence to ask.'

'Well, if I were you, I should ask. Just to get an idea.'

'Oliver, you're being ridiculous! What does it matter? You know perfectly well I could afford to send a whole orphanage to public school if I wanted to. Trust or no trust.'

'It's the principle of the thing,' said Oliver testily. 'First it's school fees, then it's failing business ventures, and before you know it . . .'

'Oliver!'

'I'm only trying to safeguard your interests, Richard. Marriage is a very serious matter.'

'Did you ask Helen all these questions before you asked her to marry you?' retorted Richard. 'Lucky girl.' Oliver laughed.

'*Touché*. Look, Richard, I really must go. But we'll talk again when I get back.'

'Have a good time.'

'*Au revoir, mon ami*. And do think about what I've said.'

Zara and Antony walked along in silence, swimming things thrown over their shoulders. Zara stared stonily ahead; Antony was frowning perplexedly. Eventually he said, in a burst,

'Why didn't you tell me it was your birthday this week?'

'I don't have to tell you everything.'

'Didn't you want me to know how old you were?' He risked a little smile.

'I'm thirteen,' said Zara flatly. 'Next birthday, I'll be fourteen.'

'This Wednesday, you'll be fourteen,' corrected Antony.

'Whatever.'

'So, what do you want as a present?'

'Nothing.'

'Come on. There must be something.'

'Nope.' Antony sighed.

'Zara, most people look forward to their birthday.'

'Well I don't.' There was a short silence. Antony peered at Zara's face, trying to elicit some response. There was none. He felt as though he had been catapulted back to the beginning again: that he didn't really know Zara at all.

Then it occurred to him that this silent treatment might all be tied up with her dad and . . . and all that business. He swallowed, feeling suddenly mature and understanding.

'If you ever want to talk,' he said, 'about your dad. I'm here.' He stopped, and felt foolish. Of course he was here – where else could he be? 'I'm here for you,' he amended.

'What's there to talk about?'

'Well, you know . . .'

'I don't. That's the problem. I don't know anything about him.'

Antony sighed.

'Zara, you have to face up to the truth.'

'What truth? You think I won't find him?'

'Zara . . .' She turned her head, finally, and looked at him.

'What? Why are you looking at me like that?'

'Your mother told us.'

'Told you what?'

'That your father's dead.'

'What!' Her screech rose high into the wood; a crow flapped noisily out of the treetops. Antony stared at her in alarm. Her face was white, her nostrils flared, her chin taut and disbelieving. 'Fleur said what?'

'She just told us about your father. Zara, I'm really sorry. I know what it's like when—'

'He isn't dead!'

175

'Oh God. Look, I shouldn't have said anything.'

'He's not dead, all right?' To Antony's dismay, a tear sprang from Zara's eye.

'Zara! I didn't mean . . .'

'I know you didn't.' She stared down at the ground. 'Look, it's not your fault. This is just something that . . . I have to deal with.'

'Right,' said Antony uncertainly. He didn't feel mature and understanding any more. On the contrary, he felt as though he'd cocked things up completely.

Fleur arrived back from Guildford laden with presents not only for Zara, but also for Richard, Antony and Gillian.

'Zara has to wait until Wednesday,' she said gaily to Richard, pulling out a flamboyant silk tie. 'But you don't. Put it on! See how it looks. I spent quite a lot,' she added, as Richard put the tie around his neck. 'I hope your card can take it. Some credit companies get jumpy whenever you spend more than fifty pounds.'

'I wouldn't worry,' said Richard, knotting the tie. 'That's beautiful, Fleur! Thank you.' He glanced at the plastic bags littering the hall. 'So, a successful trip, I take it?'

'Wonderful,' beamed Fleur. 'I got a present for the whole family, too.' She pointed to a box which had been carried in by the taxi driver. 'It's a video camera.'

'Fleur! How extraordinarily generous of you!'

'That's why I asked about the credit card,' said Fleur, grinning at him. 'It cost quite a lot.'

'I bet it did,' said Richard. 'Goodness me . . .'

'But don't worry. I've already asked my bank in the Cayman Islands to transfer some funds to your account. They can do that overnight, apparently, even though sending me a chequebook seems beyond their capabilities.' Fleur rolled her eyes, then grinned. 'Won't we have fun with this? I've never used a video camera before.' She began to rip at the packaging.

'Neither have I,' replied Richard, watching her. 'I haven't the first idea how to use one.'

'Antony will know. Or Zara.'

'I expect you're right.' Richard frowned slightly. 'Fleur, we've never talked about money, have we?'

'No,' said Fleur. 'We haven't. Which reminds me.' She glanced up at him. 'Would you mind terribly if I made a credit payment to your Gold Card account? I've got some money coming through, and believe it or not, for me at the moment, that would be the most convenient place to deposit it.' She rolled her eyes, then tugged some more at the wrapping of the video camera.

'Oh,' said Richard. 'No. Of course I wouldn't mind. How much?'

'Not very much,' said Fleur carelessly. 'About twenty thousand pounds. I don't know if your card is used to transactions like that.'

'Well, not every day of the week,' said Richard, starting to laugh. 'But I think it could probably cope. Are you sure you don't have somewhere else more orthodox?'

'It would just be for a bit,' said Fleur. 'While I sort out my banking arrangements generally. You don't mind, do you?' She gave a final tug, and lifted the video camera out of its box. 'Oh my God, look at all these buttons! They told me it was easy to use!'

'Perhaps it's easier than it looks. Where are the instructions?'

'They must be in here somewhere. The thing is,'

she added, starting to root through the packaging, 'this money's come through rather unexpectedly. From a trust. You know what these family trusts are like.'

'I'm learning,' said Richard.

'And I haven't decided what to use it for yet. I could pay a load of Zara's school fees in advance, in which case I want to keep it ready. Or I could do something else. Invest it, maybe. Here we are! User's Manual.' They both stared at the thick, glossy paperback. 'And this is the 'Upgrade Supplement,' added Fleur, picking up a further volume. She began to giggle.

'I think I was imagining more of a leaflet,' said Richard. 'A slim pamphlet.' He reached for the manual and flipped through it a couple of times. 'So you pay Zara's school fees yourself?'

'But of course,' said Fleur. 'Who else did you think might pay them?'

'I thought perhaps Zara's father's family might have offered . . .'

'No,' said Fleur. 'We don't really speak.'

'Oh dear. I didn't realize.'

'But I have some money of my own. Enough for Zara and me.'

She looked at him with luminous eyes, and suddenly Richard felt as though he were trespassing on very private ground. What right did he have to quiz her on matters of money, when he hadn't yet proposed marriage to her? What could she think of him?

'Forgive my curiosity,' he said hastily. 'It's none of my business.'

'Look!' Fleur beamed back at him. 'I think I've found the zoom!'

*   *   *

Antony and Zara arrived back from swimming to find Fleur and Richard still sitting in the hall, poring over the instructions.

'Excellent,' Antony said immediately. 'We've got one of these at school. Shall I have a go?' He picked the video up, took a few steps back and pointed it at the others. 'Now smile. Smile, Dad! Smile, Zara!'

'I don't feel like smiling,' she said, and stumped up the stairs.

'I think she's a bit upset,' Antony said apologetically to Fleur, 'about her dad.'

'I see,' said Fleur. 'Maybe I'd better go up and have a little talk with her.'

'OK,' said Antony, already peering through the viewfinder again. 'Dad, you've got to look *natural*.'

Zara was in her room, sitting on the bed, with her arms clasped round her knees.

'So my father's dead, is he?' she said as Fleur entered the room. 'Fleur, you're a bitch.'

'Don't talk to me like that!'

'Or what?'

Fleur stared at her for a moment. Then, unexpectedly, she gave Zara a sympathetic smile.

'I know things are difficult for you at the moment, darling. It's perfectly normal to be a little moody at your age.'

'I'm not moody! And it's not my fucking birthday on Wednesday, either.'

'Surely you're not going to complain about that! Extra presents, a party . . . It's not even as if it's the first time.' Fleur peered at her reflection in the mirror and smoothed an eyebrow with her thumb. 'You didn't complain when you were ten twice.'

'That's because I was ten,' said Zara. 'I was young. I was dumb. I didn't think it mattered.'

'It doesn't.'

'It does! I just want a regular birthday like everyone else.'

'Yes, well, we all want things we can't have, I'm afraid.'

'And what do you want?' Zara's voice was dry and hostile. She met Fleur's eyes in the mirror. 'What do you want, Fleur? A big house? A big car?'

'Darling . . .'

'Because what I want is for us to stay here. With Richard and Gillian and Antony. I want to stay.' Her voice cracked slightly. 'Why can't we stay?'

'It's all very complex, poppet.' Fleur took out a lipstick and began to apply it carefully.

'No it's not! We could stay here if you wanted to! Richard loves you. I know he does. You two could get married.'

'You're such a child still.' Fleur put down the lipstick and smiled at Zara affectionately. 'I know you've always wanted to be a bridesmaid. When was it that we bought that sweet pink dress for you?'

'It was when I was nine! Jesus!' Zara sprang to her feet in frustration.

'Darling, keep your voice down.'

'Don't you understand?' Suddenly two fat tears sprang onto Zara's cheeks, and she brushed them away impatiently. 'Now I just want . . . I just want a house where I live. You know, like when people say "Where do you live?" And I always have to say "Sometimes in London and sometimes in other places."'

'What's wrong with that? It sounds very glamorous!'

'No-one else lives in "other places". They all have a home!'

'Poppet, I know it's hard for you.'

'It's hard for me because you make it hard!' cried

Zara. 'If you wanted to, we could just stay somewhere. We could have a home.'

'One day we will, darling. I promise. When we're really comfortably off, we'll set up home somewhere, just the two of us.'

'No we won't,' said Zara bitterly. 'You told me we'd be settled by the time I was ten. And look, now I'm thirteen — oops, sorry, fourteen. And we still live with whoever you happen to be fucking.'

'That's enough!' hissed Fleur angrily. 'Now you just listen to me! Quite apart from your atrocious language, which we'll ignore for now, might I point out that you are still a very young girl who doesn't know what's best for her? That I am your mother? That life hasn't been easy for me, either? And that as far as I'm concerned, you've had a wonderful life, full of opportunities and excitements which most girls your age would kill for?'

'Fuck your opportunities!' cried Zara. More tears began to stream down her face. 'I want to stay here. And I don't want you telling people my father's dead!'

'That was unfortunate,' said Fleur, frowning slightly. 'I am sorry about that.'

'But not about the rest,' shuddered Zara. 'You're not sorry about the rest.'

'Darling.' Fleur came over and tenderly wiped away Zara's tears. 'Come on, little one! How about you and I have lunch tomorrow? And have manicures? Just the two of us. We'll have fun.'

Zara gave a silent, shaking shrug. Tears were now coursing down her face onto her neck, dripping in spots onto her T-shirt.

'I can't believe you're really a teenager,' said Fleur fondly. 'Sometimes you only look about ten years old.' She pulled Zara close and kissed the top of her head.

'Don't you worry, poppet. It'll all come right in the end. We'll sort our lives out.' A fresh stream of tears ran down Zara's face; she was struggling to speak.

'You're tired,' said Fleur. 'You've probably been overdoing it. I think the best thing is if I leave you to get some rest. Have a nice hot bath, and I'll see you downstairs later.' Affectionately she took one of Zara's long blond tresses in her fingers, held it up to the light and let it drop again. Then, without giving Zara another glance, she picked up her lipstick, glanced at her reflection, and left the room.

Chapter Twelve

Philippa was becoming worried about Lambert. Over the last few weeks he had seemed permanently in a sullen mood; permanently irritated with her. And now his mood was descending from surliness to a snappish anger. Nothing she said was right; nothing she did could please him.

It had all begun with the Briggs & Co. fiasco. The day of the golf game had been bad enough. Then his friend had been exposed in the press as a crook, and Lambert had exploded with a savage anger which seemed primarily directed at Fleur. Philippa suspected that her father had probably had a few words with Lambert at work, which couldn't have helped matters. And now he greeted every morning with a miserable gloom, arrived home from work each evening frowning, and snarled at her if she tried to cheer him up.

To begin with, she hadn't minded. She'd almost welcomed the challenge of Helping her Husband through a Difficult Time. 'For better for worse, for richer for poorer', she'd muttered to herself several times a day. 'To love and to cherish.' Except that Lambert didn't particularly seem to want her love or her cherishing. He didn't seem to want her around at all.

She'd consulted magazine articles on the subject of relationships, and leafed through books at the library, then tried to implement some of the suggestions. She'd tried new recipes for dinner, she'd tried suggesting that the two of them took up a new hobby together, she'd tried asking him seriously if he'd like to discuss things, she'd tried instigating sex. And to each of her attempts she'd received the same frown of displeasure.

There was no-one she could talk to about it. The girls at work talked freely enough about their husbands and boyfriends, but Philippa had always refrained from joining in. For one thing, she had a natural modesty which stopped her from confiding bedroom secrets over the coffee machine. For another – and if she were honest, this was the real reason – Lambert seemed so different from everyone else's husband that she felt embarrassed to tell the others the truth. They all seemed to be married to cheery chaps who liked football, the pub and sex; who appeared at office parties and, even if complete strangers to each other, immediately found a common, joky blokes' footing. But Lambert wasn't like that. He didn't follow the football, nor did he go to the pub. Sometimes he liked sex; sometimes it almost seemed to disgust him. And at office functions he always sat apart from everyone else, smoking a cigar, looking bored. Afterwards, in the car, he would mock the accents of everyone she worked with, and Philippa would find herself sadly abandoning her scheme of inviting a few nice couples home for dinner.

They hadn't been back to The Maples since the day of the golf débâcle. Every time she suggested it, Lambert scowled and said he hadn't got time. And although she could have gone home on her own, she didn't want to. She didn't want anyone guessing anything was wrong. And so she sat in with Lambert, night after night, watching the television and reading novels. At the weekends, when every other couple seemed to have plans, she and Lambert had none. They got up, and Lambert went to his study and read the paper, and then it was lunchtime, and then sometimes Philippa went out and wandered round the shops. And every day she felt more lonely.

Then, with no warning whatsoever, Fleur rang Philippa up.

'Philippa, it's Fleur. I'm up in London on Friday for a memorial service. How about a spot of lunch?'

'Lunch? Gosh!' Philippa felt herself blushing and her heart beginning to thud, as though she were being asked on a date. 'I'd love to!'

'I know you'll be at work,' Fleur said, 'otherwise I'd suggest meeting earlier and doing some shopping.'

'I'll take the day off,' Philippa found herself saying. 'I've loads of spare holiday.'

'Lucky you! Well, why don't you meet my train? I'll let you know which one. And we can take it from there.'

As Philippa rang off, she was filled with elated lightness. Fleur wanted to be her friend. Immediately a picture came into her mind of the two of them, giggling together as they ordered a meal in an expensive restaurant; daring one another to try on outlandish outfits. Arranging another meeting. Philippa hugged herself with excitement. Fleur was her friend!

'I'm having lunch with Fleur on Friday,' she called to Lambert, trying to sound casual. 'She's up in London.'

'Bully for her.'

'She's going to a memorial service,' said Philippa, unable to stop a flow of happy words from spilling out of her. 'I wonder whose? Someone from her family, I expect. Or a friend maybe. She'll probably look quite smart. I wonder what I should wear? Shall I buy something new?'

* * *

As Philippa's voice babbled on, Lambert's mind was elsewhere. In front of him was another tightly worded letter from the bank, requiring solid assurance that he was going to be able to pay off his substantial, unapproved overdraft. He had to lay his hands on some money and soon. Which meant going down to The Maples again and getting into Richard's office. But it was risky. Particularly since he wasn't in Richard's good books at the moment. Lambert scowled. The old fool had called him into his office at work and ticked him off for insulting Fleur. Ticked him off! Never mind that Fleur had completely fucked up their game; that she had no idea how to behave on a golf course. But of course there was no point talking sense to Richard at the moment. He'd fallen under the spell of Fleur and there was nothing to be done about it except wait for it to pass and, preferably, avoid The Maples until Richard had snapped out of it.

'What I really need is some shorts,' Philippa was saying, next door, as though she thought he was still listening. 'For the weekends. Kind of tailored, but not too smart . . .'

The problem was that he couldn't wait until Richard had snapped out of it. He needed money quickly. Lambert took a sip of beer from the heavy silver tankard on his desk and stared at the letter again. Fifty thousand would keep the bank quiet. He was sure it would. And it was waiting for him at The Maples. If he could be certain that he wouldn't cock things up; that he wouldn't be discovered . . . A sudden unwanted memory came to him of Fleur's voice behind him, startling him as he leafed through Richard's files, and he felt again a prickling of cold sweat on the back of his neck. Of course she hadn't suspected anything, why should she? But if that had been Richard . . .

Suddenly Philippa's voice pierced his consciousness.

'Apparently Daddy'll be away at a meeting that day,' she was saying, 'and Gillian's got her bridge lesson.' Lambert's head twitched up. 'Otherwise Fleur would have suggested they came along too. But I think it's quite nice, don't you? Just the two of us? Like a kind of, you know, bonding thing?'

Lambert stood up and stalked into the next room.

'What did you say? Your father's got a meeting on Friday?'

'Yes. He's got to go to Newcastle, apparently.'

'First I've heard of it.'

'Oh dear. Hasn't he asked you to go, too?' Philippa bit her lip. 'You could come to lunch with Fleur and me,' she said doubtfully. 'If you want to.'

'Don't be stupid. Me have lunch with a pair of gigglers like you?'

Philippa tittered, pleased by the notion of herself and Fleur as a pair of gigglers. Feeling suddenly generous, Lambert grinned back at her.

'You two ladies have your lunch together,' he said. 'I've more important things to do that day.'

Wednesday dawned bright and hot and blue. By the time Zara arrived downstairs, the breakfast table had been laid in the garden. A huge posy of flowers was arranged beside her place, a silver helium balloon rose shimmering from the back of her chair, and her plate was covered in cards and packages.

'Happy birthday!' cried Antony as soon as he saw her stepping out of the conservatory. 'Gillian, Zara's here! Get the buck's fizz! That was my idea,' he said to Zara. 'Buck's fizz for breakfast. And pancakes.'

Zara said nothing. She was staring at the decorated table as though she'd never seen anything like it before.

'Is this all for me?' she said at last, in a husky voice.

'Well, of course it is! It's your birthday! Sit yourself down, he added, in a host-like voice. 'Have some strawberries.'

Fleur appeared on the lawn holding a cafetière, and smiled prettily at Zara.

'Happy birthday, darling. Would you like some coffee?'

'No,' said Zara.

'Suit yourself.' Fleur shrugged.

'You must have a strawberry, though,' insisted Antony. 'They're delicious.'

Zara sat down and looked at the cards piled on her plate. She seemed slightly dazed.

'Cool balloon, huh?' said Antony happily. 'It's from Xanthe and Mex.'

'What?' She looked up to see if he was joking.

'They heard it was your birthday. I think there's a card from them, too. And I said we might meet them for a drink later. But it depends what you want to do.'

'They sent me a balloon,' said Zara in stupefaction. She tugged at the string and watched it float back up. 'But I hardly know them.' She looked up at him. 'And I thought you hated them.'

'Xanthe's not so bad.' Antony grinned sheepishly at her. 'Now, go on, open some of your presents.'

'Wait!' called Richard from the conservatory. 'I want to get this on video!'

'Oh for God's sake,' said Antony. 'We'll be here all day.'

Gillian arrived in the garden, bearing a tray of glasses filled with orange juice and champagne bubbles.

'Happy birthday, Zara!' she exclaimed. 'What a lovely day!'

'Thank you,' muttered Zara.

'OK?' called Richard. 'I'm filming. You can start opening your presents.'

'Open mine first,' said Antony excitedly. 'That red stripy one.'

Zara picked up the parcel and looked at it for a few moments without saying anything.

'That looks lovely,' said Fleur gaily. Zara's gaze shot towards Fleur and away again. Then, biting her lip, she began to tug at the wrapping. Onto her lap fell a small framed print.

'It's America,' said Antony. 'It's a map of America. For when you . . . when you go there.' Zara looked up at him. Her chin was shaking.

'Thank you Antony,' she said, and burst into tears.

'Zara!'

'What's wrong, poppet?'

'Don't you like it?' asked Antony anxiously.

'I love it,' whispered Zara. 'I'm sorry. It's just . . .'

'It's just that you need a good sip of buck's fizz and some pancakes inside you,' said Gillian briskly. 'You know, it's not easy, turning fourteen. I remember it well. Come on Zara.' She patted Zara's bare, thin shoulder. 'You come and help me bring out the breakfast, and we'll have the rest of the presents in a little while.'

'Aren't you enjoying your birthday, then?' asked Antony later on. They were sitting at the bottom of the garden in a hidden sun-trap, listening to the pounding of Zara's new portable ghetto blaster.

'Sure.'

'You don't look very happy.'

'I'm fine, all right?' she snapped.

Antony waited for a few minutes. Then he said, casually, 'Zara, what's your star sign?'

'Sagi—' she began, then stopped. 'I don't believe in all that phooey.'

'Yes you do. You were reading your horoscope the other day.'

'That doesn't mean I believe it. Jesus, if every time you read a horoscope—'

'You still know what your sign is though, don't you?' he interrupted. 'It isn't Sagittarius. It can't be. So what is it?'

'Why do you want to know?' She sat up, knocking her diet lemonade onto her jacket. 'Fuck,' she said. 'I'll go and get a cloth.'

'No you won't! Don't change the subject! Zara, what's your star sign?'

'Look, you asshole, my jacket's drenched.'

'So what? You drenched it on purpose. God, you must think I'm really stupid.' She began to move, and he shot out a strong hand, pinning her wrist to the ground. 'Zara, what's your star sign? Tell me!'

'For Christ's sake!' She gave him a scornful look and tossed back her hair. 'OK,' she said. 'It's Scorpio.'

'Wrong.' He leaned back. 'It's Leo.'

'So what?' snapped Zara. 'Scorpio, Leo. Who gives a shit?'

'Zara, what's going on?'

'Don't ask me. You're the one behaving like an asshole.'

'It's not really your birthday today is it?'

'Of course it is.' She looked away and took a piece of gum from her pocket.

'It's not! Your birthday is between the 22nd of November and the 21st of December. I looked up Sagittarius.' He shuffled round on the grass until he could see her face, and gazed pleadingly at her. 'Zara, what's going on? Whatever it is, I won't tell anyone, I promise. Zara, I'm your friend, aren't I?'

She shrugged silently and put the gum in her mouth.

Antony looked at her for a while. Then he said, 'I don't think your father's dead, either.' He spoke slowly, not taking his eyes from her face. 'I think he's still alive. I think your mother was lying about that, too.'

Zara was chewing quickly, almost desperately, staring away from him at the trees.

'Tell me,' begged Antony. 'I won't tell anyone. Who would I tell, anyway? I don't know anyone to tell.'

Zara gave a short laugh.

'You know plenty of people to tell,' she said. 'Your father . . . Gillian . . .'

'But I wouldn't!' exclaimed Antony. He lowered his voice. 'Whatever it is, I won't tell them. But I want to know the truth. I want to know when your real birthday is. And why you're pretending it's today. And . . . and everything.'

There was a long pause. Then Zara turned to him.

'OK, listen,' she said in a low voice. 'If you tell anyone else what I'm about to tell you, I'll say that you tried to rape me.'

'What?' Antony stared at her in horror.

'I'll say you asked me to come down to the bottom of the garden and you held me to the ground. By the wrists.' She stopped and looked at Antony's hand – the hand which, a few minutes before, had pinned her down on the grass. A fiery red colour came to his cheeks. 'And then I'll say you tried to rape me.'

'You little . . .'

'They probably won't press charges. But they'll interview you. That won't be nice. And some people will think you did it. Some people always do.'

'I just don't believe . . .' He was staring at her, panting slightly.

'You see, I mean it,' said Zara deliberately. 'You're not allowed to tell. If you say anything to your father or Gillian, or anyone – I'll go to the police. And you'll be in shit.' She spat her gum out. 'Now, do you want to know or don't you?'

Richard felt as though his life was finally falling into place. He sat in his chair watching Fleur leaf through a book of wallpaper patterns, and wondered how he could have mistaken what he had with Emily for true love. He could hardly bear to think of all the wasted years; years spent living in sombre shades of charcoal. Now he was living in bright, solid colour; in splashes of vibrant hues that jumped off the page and took the eye by surprise.

'You'll have to decide if you want painted walls or wallpaper in your office,' said Fleur. She looked at him over her sunglasses. 'And give me a budget.'

'I'll give you whatever you like,' said Richard. He met her eye and she gave him a delicious, secretive smile. In response, he felt his skin tingle slightly under his shirt, as though in anticipation of another night of pleasure.

Fleur no longer occupied her own bedroom. She now slept with him every night, her body curving up against his, her hair falling across his pillow. Every morning her smile was waiting for him; every morning his heart gave a leap as he saw her again. And they talked more now than they had ever done, and Richard felt happier than he had ever done, and Fleur's eyes sparkled even more than they had before. She seemed to glow with happiness and excitement at the moment, thought Richard, and there was a spring in her step which hadn't been there before. A spring — his mouth twisted into a small, embarrassed smile — which he had put there.

And when he asked her to marry him, everything would be complete. When Oliver had returned from holiday, when he had sorted out the trust, when he had finally closed the chapter on Emily. He would choose a suitable moment, a suitable place, a suitable ring . . . A quiet, suitable wedding. And then an exuberant, noisy, joyful honeymoon. The honeymoon he'd been waiting for all his life.

When Zara had finished telling him, Antony flopped down onto the grass and stared up at the blue sky.

'I don't believe it,' he said. 'She goes to all that trouble just to get hold of a Gold Card?'

'You can do a lot of damage with a Gold Card,' said Zara.

'But I mean . . .' He broke off, and frowned. 'I don't understand. How does your dad being dead fit into it?'

'She told your father she was a widow. I guess she thought it made her seem more appealing.'

For a few moments Antony was silent. Then he said slowly, 'So all the time, she's just been after him for his money.' He sat up. 'It's crazy! I mean, we're not that rich.'

'Maybe she made a mistake. Or maybe you're richer than you think.'

'God, poor Dad. And he hasn't got a clue! Zara, I've got to tell him.'

'Then he pinned me down on the grass, Your Honour,' Zara started to recite tonelessly. 'I tried to struggle, but he was stronger than me.'

'All right!' said Antony irritably. 'I won't say

anything. But I mean, bloody hell! My dad can't afford to lose loads of money!'

'Think of it as payment,' said Zara. 'Fleur always does.'

'What, so she's done this before?' Antony stared at Zara. 'Gone out with men just for their money?'

Zara shrugged, and looked away. It had been easy to feed Antony a limited, edited version of the truth, a truth which, even if he did blab, wouldn't ruin everything for Fleur. She'd painted Fleur as a silly spendthrift, who was desperate for a Gold Card, who would fritter Richard's money on high heels and haircuts. And he was shocked by that. What would happen if she told him the real facts? Told him that her mother was a cynical, heartless confidence trickster? Who entered people's lives because of their vulnerability and desperation; who escaped freely because of their embarrassment and wounded pride?

The truth was there, inside her; she felt as though there was only a thin curtain hiding it from the rest of the world. If he stretched out a hand and tugged, the thin material would come tumbling down and he would see all the deceits, the ugly lies and stories, curled up in her brain like snakes. But he wouldn't stretch out his hand. He thought he'd prised the truth out of her already. It would never occur to him that there was more.

'So basically, she's just a prostitute!' he was saying.

'She takes what she's worth,' snapped back Zara. 'Hasn't your dad had a good time over the last few months?' Antony stared at her.

'But he really thinks she loves him. I did too. I thought she loved him!'

'Well, maybe she does.'

'People who love each other aren't interested in money!'

'Of course they are,' said Zara scornfully. 'Wouldn't you rather have a girlfriend who could buy you a Porsche? And if you say no, you're lying.'

'Yeah, but real love is different!' protested Antony. 'It's about the person inside.'

'It's about everything,' retorted Zara. 'It's about money first, looks second, and personality if you're desperate.'

'God you're twisted! Money doesn't come into it! I mean . . . suppose you marry someone really rich and there's a stockmarket crash and they lose all their money?'

'Suppose you marry someone really nice and there's a car crash and they lose all their personality? What's the difference?'

'It isn't the same! You know it's not the same.' He peered at her. 'Why are you defending your mother?'

'I don't know!' cried Zara jerkily. 'Because she's my mother, I guess! I've never talked to anyone about her before. I never realized—' She broke off. 'Oh, for God's sake! I wish I'd never told you!'

'So do I! What a bloody mess.'

They stared at each other in fury.

'Look,' said Zara eventually. 'Your dad's not stupid. He's not going to let her rip him off completely, is he?' She forced herself to meet his eye unwaveringly.

'No,' said Antony. He exhaled slowly. 'I suppose not.'

'And you like having her around, don't you?'

'Of course I do! I love having her around. And I like . . . I like having you around.'

'Good,' said Zara. She slowly smiled at him. ''Cause I like being around.'

Later on they wandered back up to the house to find Fleur and Richard arguing good-humouredly about wallpaper.

'Antony!' exclaimed Fleur. 'Talk some sense into your father. First he gives me *carte blanche* to redecorate his office, then he says he won't have anything but stripes or fleur-de-lis.'

'I don't know what fleur-de-lis is,' said Antony. He stared at Fleur. His image of her in his mind had changed now that he knew the truth; as they'd walked towards her he'd honestly expected that she would look different. More . . . monster-like. He'd found himself dreading the moment of meeting her eye. But there she was, just the same, warm and pretty and friendly. And now she was smiling at him, and he was grinning back, and suddenly he found himself wondering if everything Zara had said about her could really be true.

'Tell you what,' said Richard to Fleur. 'Why not get some more wallpaper books when you're in London? I'm sure we can reach a compromise. Just remember, I'm the one who has to sit in the room and try to work.' He grinned at Antony and Zara. 'Fleur is very keen on orange walls.'

'Not orange. Terracotta.'

'When are you going to London?' asked Zara.

'On Friday,' said Fleur. 'The day after tomorrow.'

'Your mother has to go to a memorial service,' said Richard.

Zara froze; her face turned pale.

'You're going to a memorial service?' she said.

'That's right,' said Fleur.

'A memorial service?' repeated Zara disbelievingly. 'You're going to a *memorial* service?'

'Yes darling,' said Fleur impatiently. 'And please stop making such a fuss.' Her eyes bored into Zara's. 'I'll only be gone a day. It's for poor Hattie Fairbrother,' she added casually. 'You remember Hattie, don't you darling?' Zara flinched, and turned away.

'Zara!' They were interrupted by Gillian. 'You've got a phone call. Someone called Johnny.'

'Johnny?' Zara's head shot up. 'Johnny's on the phone? OK, I'm coming! I'm coming! Don't let him hang up!' And without looking back, she bounded into the house.

'Do you want a Diet Coke?' Antony called, but she wasn't listening. 'I'll just . . . see if she wants a Diet Coke,' he said to the others, and disappeared after her.

Richard looked at Fleur.

'Zara seemed very upset at the idea of you going to a memorial service,' he said.

'I know,' said Fleur. 'Ever since her father passed away, anything to do with death upsets her.' She looked sad. 'I try not to press the point.'

'Of course,' said Gillian. 'It's perfectly understandable.'

'Poor little thing,' said Richard. His eyes twinkled slightly. 'And who's Johnny? A special friend of Zara's?'

'A friend of us both,' said Fleur. Her face closed up slightly. 'I've known him for years.'

'You should ask him to stay,' suggested Richard. 'I'd like to meet some of your friends.'

'Maybe,' said Fleur, and changed the subject.

Zara had disappeared into the tiny room off the hall that contained nothing but a telephone, a chair and a little table for messages. As she came out, Antony was waiting for her. He stared at her: her eyes were sparkling; she looked suddenly cheerful again.

'So, who's Johnny?' he said, before he could stop himself. 'Your boyfriend?'

'Don't be dumb!' said Zara. 'I haven't got a boyfriend. Johnny's just a friend. A really good friend.'

'Oh yeah?' said Antony, trying to sound lighthearted and teasing. 'I've heard that one before.'

'Antony, Johnny's fifty-six!'

'Oh,' said Antony, feeling foolish.

'And he's gay!' added Zara.

'Gay?' He stared at her.

'Yes, gay!' She giggled. 'Satisfied now?' She started to head into the garden.

'Where are you going?' called Antony, running after her.

'I have a message for Fleur from Johnny.'

They arrived on the lawn together, panting.

'OK, Johnny says he hopes you've changed your mind and will you give him a call if you have,' announced Zara.

'About what?' said Fleur.

'He said you knew what he was talking about. And . . . he also said he might take me to New York! As a special fourteenth birthday treat!' She darted a triumphant glance at Fleur.

'New York!' exclaimed Antony. 'Fantastic!'

'How nice,' said Fleur acidly.

'Anyway, that's the message.' Zara took a piece of gum from her pocket and happily began to chew. 'So, are you gonna call him?'

'No,' said Fleur, snapping the wallpaper book shut. 'I'm not.'

Chapter Thirteen

On Friday morning, Richard left early for his meeting, and Fleur breathed a sigh of relief. She was finding his continual presence a little oppressive. As the weather reached summer perfection, he was taking great swaths of time off work – days of long-owed holiday, he'd explained – and spending them all at home. The first time he'd used the word 'holiday', Fleur had smiled prettily, and wondered whether she could persuade him to take her to Barbados. But Richard didn't want to go away. Like a love-struck adolescent, all he wanted was to be with her. He was in her bed all night; he was at her side all day; she couldn't escape him. The day before, she'd actually found herself suggesting that the two of them play golf together. Anything, to break up the monotony. We'll have to be careful, she found herself thinking as she drank the last of her breakfast coffee, or we'll fall into a rut.

Then, abruptly, she pulled herself up. She wasn't going to fall into a rut with Richard because she wasn't going to stay with Richard. By three o'clock that afternoon, she would be at the memorial service of Hattie Fairbrother, wife of the retired business magnate Edward Fairbrother; by the time the reception was over she might have new plans entirely.

She stood up, checking her black suit for creases, and went upstairs. As she passed the office door, she lingered. She still hadn't had a chance to explore

Richard's affairs. Now that she was officially decorating the office, it should have been easy. She could wander in whenever she chose, poke around, open drawers and close them again, find out everything she wanted to about Richard's business affairs, and no-one would suspect anything. And yet with Richard in constant adoration at her side, it was harder than she had imagined to find a moment when she could be alone in there. Besides which, she was almost sure that he was not quite in the league she had hoped. Johnny had got it wrong. Richard Favour was no more than a moderately well-off man, whose Gold Card would net her perhaps fifteen, perhaps twenty thousand pounds. It was almost not worth bothering to look through his dull little books.

But force of habit drew her towards the office door. Her taxi would be arriving in a few minutes, to take her to the station, but there was time to have a quick glance through his most recent correspondence. And she was, after all, supposed to be decorating the place. She let herself into the office with the duplicate key he'd given her, looked around at the bleak walls and shuddered. Her eye fell on the large window behind the desk; in her mind she saw it curtained in a large, dramatic swag of deep green. She would match the curtains with a dark green carpet. And on the walls, a set of antique golfing prints. She would pick some up for him at auction, perhaps.

Except of course she wouldn't do anything of the sort. Biting her lip, Fleur sat down on Richard's chair and swivelled round idly. Out of the window she could just see the garden: the lawn, the pear tree, the badminton net which Antony and Zara had left up the night before. They were familiar sights. Too familiar. It would be surprisingly difficult to leave them.

And, if she were honest with herself, it would be surprisingly difficult to leave Richard.

But then, life was surprisingly difficult. Fleur's chin tightened and she tapped her fingernails on the polished wood of the desk, impatient with herself. She hadn't yet achieved her goal. She wasn't yet a rich woman. Therefore she would have to move on; she had no choice. And there was no point hanging around here endlessly for the last dribs and drabs. Richard wasn't the sort who would suddenly splash out on a last-minute couture dress or diamond bracelet. As soon as she had worked out how much he could afford to lose, she would bounce his Gold Card up to the limit, take the cash and go. If she got the amount just right – as she would – then he would quietly pay it off, say nothing, lick his wounds in private and put the whole affair down to experience. They always did. And by that time, she would be in another family, another home, perhaps even another country.

Sighing, she pulled Richard's in-tray towards her and began to flip through his most recent correspondence. Her fingers felt slow and reluctant; her mind was only half-concentrating. What she was looking for she hardly knew. The thrill of pursuit seemed to have evaporated inside her; her drive had lost its edge. Once she would have scanned each letter urgently, searching for clues; seeking opportunities for financial gain. Now her eyes fell dully on each page, taking in a few words here, a few words there, then moving on. There was a short letter about the lease on Richard's London flat. There was a request for donations from a children's charity. There was a bank statement.

As she pulled it from its envelope, Fleur felt a small quickening inside her. At least this should prove interesting. She unfolded the single sheet and her gaze flicked automatically to the final balance, already estimating in her mind what sort of figure she might expect to see. And then, as her eyes focused, and she realized what she was looking at, she felt a shock jolt round her body. Her fingers felt suddenly clammy; her throat was dry; she couldn't breathe.

No, she thought, trying to keep control of herself. That couldn't be right. It simply couldn't be right. Could it? She felt dizzy with astonishment. Was she reading the figures correctly? She closed her eyes, swallowed, took a deep breath and opened them again. The same number sat, ludicrously, in the credit column. She gazed at it, devouring it with her mind. Could it possibly be correct? Was she really looking at—

'Fleur!' called Gillian from downstairs. Fleur jumped; her eyes darted towards the door. 'Your taxi's here!'

'Thank you!' called back Fleur. Her voice felt high and unnatural; suddenly she realized that her hand was shaking. She looked at the figure again, feeling slightly faint. What the hell was going on? No-one, but *no-one* kept a sum like that just sitting in a bank account. Not unless they were very stupid – which Richard wasn't – or unless they were very, very rich indeed . . .

'Fleur! You'll miss your train!'

'I'm coming!' Quickly, before Gillian decided to come and fetch her, Fleur put the bank statement back where she had found it. She had to think about this. She had to think very carefully indeed.

Philippa had bought an entirely new outfit for her day out with Fleur. She stood by the ticket barrier at Waterloo station, feeling conspicuous in her pale pink suit, and wondering whether she should have gone for something more casual. But as soon as she saw Fleur her heart gave a relieved bounce. Fleur looked even more dressed up than she did. She was wearing the same black suit she'd been wearing when Philippa had first seen her at the memorial service, topped with a glorious black hat, covered in tiny purple flowers. People were staring as she made her way along the concourse, and Philippa felt a glow of pride. This groomed, elegant beauty was her friend. Her friend!

'Darling!' Fleur's kiss was more showy than warm, but Philippa didn't mind. She imagined, with a rush of exhilaration, the picture the two of them made standing in their suits – one pink, one black. Two glamorous women, meeting for lunch. If, yesterday, she'd seen such a sight, she would have been filled with wistful envy; today she *was* the sight. She *was* one of those glamorous women.

'Where shall we go first?' asked Fleur. 'I've booked a table at Harvey Nichols for twelve-thirty, but we could begin somewhere else. Where would you like to shop?'

'I don't know!' exclaimed Philippa excitedly. 'Let's look on the map. I've got a tube pass . . .'

'I was thinking more of a taxi,' interrupted Fleur kindly. 'I never travel by tube if I can help it.' Philippa looked up, and felt an embarrassed crimson staining her cheeks. For a horrible moment she felt as though the day might have been spoiled already. But suddenly Fleur laughed, and put her arm through Philippa's.

'I shouldn't be so fussy,' she said. 'I expect you travel on the tube all the time, don't you, Philippa?'

'Every day,' said Philippa. She forced herself to flash a smile at Fleur. 'But I'm willing to break the habit.'

Fleur laughed. 'That's my girl.' They began to walk

towards the taxi rank, and Philippa allowed her arm to stay in Fleur's. She felt almost dizzy with excitement, as though she were embarking on some sort of love affair.

In the taxi, Philippa turned to Fleur expectantly, waiting for the start of some hilarious, intimate gossip. She could feel a laugh bubbling up at the back of her throat; even had an affectionate gesture prepared. 'Oh Fleur!' she would exclaim, at an appropriate moment, 'You're just too much!' And she would squeeze Fleur's arm, just like an old established friend. The taxi driver would look at them in the mirror and think they were lifelong chums. Or maybe even sisters.

But Fleur was gazing silently out of the window at the traffic. Her forehead was creased in a slight frown and she was biting her lip and she looked, thought Philippa uneasily, as though she didn't want to be disturbed. As if she were thinking about something; as if she didn't really want to be there at all.

Then, suddenly, she turned towards Philippa.

'Tell me, are you and Lambert happy together?' she said. Philippa gave a startled jump. She didn't want to think about Lambert today. But Fleur was waiting for an answer.

'Oh yes,' she said, and gave Fleur a bright smile. 'We have a very happy marriage.'

'A happy marriage,' echoed Fleur. 'What exactly makes a happy marriage?'

'Well,' said Philippa doubtfully. 'You know.'

'Do I?' said Fleur. 'I'm not sure I do.'

'But you were married, weren't you?' said Philippa. 'To Zara's father.'

'Oh yes,' said Fleur vaguely. 'Of course I was. But not happily.'

'Really? I didn't know that,' said Philippa. She

looked at Fleur uneasily, wondering if she wanted to talk about her unhappy marriage. But Fleur gave an impatient wave of the hand.

'What I really mean is, why does one get married in the first place?' She gazed at Philippa. 'What made you decide to get married to Lambert?'

A tremor of alarm went through Philippa, as though she were being questioned on the wrong special subject. Swift, positive images of herself and Lambert passed through her mind: the two of them on their wedding day; their honeymoon in the Maldives; Lambert tanned and affectionate; afternoons of sex underneath a mosquito net.

'Well, I love Lambert,' she found herself saying. 'He's strong, and he looks after me . . .' She glanced at Fleur.

'And?' said Fleur.

'And we have fun together,' said Philippa hesitantly.

'But how did you know he was the right man for you?' persisted Fleur. 'How did you know it was the right time to stop looking and . . . and settle down for good?'

Philippa felt a flush come to her cheeks.

'I just knew,' she said, in a voice which was too high and defensive.

And suddenly into her mind flashed a memory of her mother; a memory she thought she'd quashed for ever. Her mother, sitting up in bed, fixing Philippa with her ice-blue stare, saying, 'You say yes to Lambert, Philippa, and be grateful. What other man is going to want a girl like you?'

'Jim wanted me,' Philippa had quavered.

'Jim?' her mother had snapped. 'Your father despises Jim! He'd never let you marry Jim. You'd better accept Lambert.'

'But . . .'

'But nothing. This is your only chance. Look at you! You're not pretty, you're not charming, you're not even a virgin. What other man will want you?'

As she'd listened, Philippa had felt sick, as though she were physically being torn apart. Now suddenly, she felt sick again.

'"You just knew".' Fleur sounded dissatisfied. 'But I just knew this was the hat for me.' She gestured at her head. 'And then, when I'd bought it, I saw an even better one.'

'It's a lovely hat,' said Philippa feebly.

'The thing is,' said Fleur, 'you can have more than one hat. You can have twenty hats. But you can't have twenty husbands. Don't you ever worry that you chose too soon?'

'No!' said Philippa at once. 'I don't. Lambert's perfect for me.'

'Well, good,' said Fleur. She smiled at Philippa. 'I'm glad for you.'

Philippa stared at Fleur, and felt her bright happy smile start to fade away, and suddenly wished, for the first time in her life, that she'd been more honest. She could have confided in Fleur; she could have shared her worries and asked for advice. But her foremost instinct had been to paint a rosy, romantic picture of herself; a picture that Fleur would appreciate and, quite possibly, envy. And now her chance to tell the truth was gone.

Lambert arrived at The Maples shortly after Gillian had left for her bridge class. He parked the car, let himself into the house and stood in the hall, listening for voices. But the house was silent, as he'd expected it to be. The night before he'd rung up and casually mentioned to Gillian that he might drop by between meetings.

'But no-one will be here,' she'd said. 'Richard's going to Newcastle, I'll be playing bridge, and Antony will probably be out with Zara, practising for the Club Cup.'

'I'll pop in anyway,' Lambert had replied casually, 'since I'm passing.'

Now, without hesitating, he headed for Richard's office. It would be a simple matter to find the information he needed, then, when he got back home, transfer an appropriate sum of money into his own account. He would be able to have a cheque ready for the bank within a week, which would buy him a few months. And then, by Christmas, Philippa would be twenty-nine and the trust money would be even nearer and his inconvenient financial problems would be over for ever.

As he entered the office he found himself, ludicrously, bending down to check under the desk. As if he didn't know that Fleur was in London, with his own wife. Attending another memorial service. Didn't the woman have anything better to do with her time than go to bloody memorial services? He frowned at the dusty carpet, then stood up and strode over to the filing cabinet and pulled open the third drawer; the drawer which he hadn't reached last time. And there, like a reward, were files and files of Richard's bank statements.

'Bingo,' he muttered softly under his breath. He knelt down and, at random, pulled out a file marked 'Household'. The statements were neatly clipped together; as he fanned through them, he began to feel a sense of anticipation. Here was Richard's financial life, laid out for him to see. The wealth that, one day, would be his and Philippa's. Except that in this account, there was little evidence of wealth. The balance never seemed to rise above three thousand pounds. What bloody good was that?

Impatiently he replaced it, and pulled out another, rather tattered, marked 'Children'. Pocket money, thought Lambert contemptuously, and threw it down on the floor, where it fell open. His hand was outstretched towards another file as he glanced casually down at it. What he saw made him freeze in shock. The top statement was dated the previous month, and the balance was approaching ten million pounds.

'How many courses shall we have?' said Philippa, squinting at the menu. 'Three?'

'Ten million,' said Fleur absently.

'What?' Philippa looked up.

'Oh, nothing.' Fleur smiled. 'Sorry, I was miles away.' She began to take off her hat and shake back her red-gold hair. In the corner of the restaurant, a young waiter watched admiringly.

'Ten million miles away,' said Philippa, and laughed heartily. The day had, so far, more than lived up to her expectations. She and Fleur had sauntered from shop to shop, trying on clothes, squirting scent on one another and laughing merrily, attracting attention like two birds of paradise. The magazines were wrong, thought Philippa. They all said that the Way to Get your Man was to go around with someone uglier than yourself. But it wasn't true. Fleur was much prettier than her, even if she was much older – but today, instead of feeling inadequate, Philippa had felt elevated to Fleur's status. And people had treated her differently. They had smiled at her, and men had opened the door for her, and young office girls rushing past had looked at her with envy in their eyes. And Philippa had relished every moment.

'Oh, I don't know,' said Fleur suddenly. 'It's all so difficult. Why can't life be straightforward?' She sighed. 'Let's have a cocktail.' She beckoned to the young waiter, who came striding over.

'A Manhattan,' said Fleur, smiling at him.

'Two,' said Philippa. The waiter grinned back at her. He was, thought Philippa, extraordinarily good-looking. In fact, everybody who worked in expensive shops seemed to be good-looking.

'Excuse me, ladies.' Another waiter was approaching their table. He was holding a silver tray, on which reposed a bottle of champagne. 'This has been ordered and pre-paid for you.'

'No!' Fleur burst into peals of laughter. 'Champagne!' She looked at the bottle. 'Very good champagne, in fact. Who ordered it for us?' She looked around. 'Are we allowed to know?'

'It's just like a film,' said Philippa excitedly.

'I have a message card for a Mrs Daxeny,' said the head waiter.

'Aha!' said Fleur. 'So they know our names!'

'Read it!' said Philippa.

Fleur ripped open the little card.

'"Have a lovely lunch, my sweethearts,"' she read, '"and I wish I could be there with you. Richard".' Fleur looked up. 'It's from your father,' she said. She sounded astonished. 'Your father sent us champagne.'

'I thought it was from an anonymous prince,' said Philippa disappointedly. 'How did Daddy know where we'd be?'

'I must have told him,' said Fleur slowly. 'And he must have remembered, and ordered this for us over the phone, and hoped that we wouldn't change our lunch plans. And all the time he said nothing about it.'

'Shall I open it?' said the head waiter.

'Ooh yes!' said Philippa.

'Yes please,' said Fleur. She picked up the little card and gazed at it for a few seconds. 'What an extraordinarily thoughtful man your father is.'

'Actually, I think I'll still have my Manhattan,' said Philippa. 'And then go on to champagne. After all, I'm not driving anywhere!' She glanced up brightly at Fleur. 'Are you OK?'

'I'm fine,' said Fleur, frowning slightly. 'I was just . . . thinking.'

They both watched as, with the tiniest of whispered pops, the head waiter opened the champagne and poured out a single glass. He handed it ceremonially to Fleur.

'You know, men don't usually manage to take me by surprise,' she said, as though to herself. 'But today . . .' she took a sip. 'This is delicious.'

'Today you've been taken by surprise,' said Philippa triumphantly.

'Today I've been taken by surprise,' agreed Fleur. She took another sip and looked thoughtfully at her glass. 'Twice.'

The sound of the cleaner's key in the front door made Lambert give a startled jump. With fumbling hands he replaced all the bank statements in the filing cabinet, hurried out of the office, and sauntered down the stairs. He gave the cleaner a cheery smile as he passed her in the hall, but his heart was beating hard and shock was still needling down his back.

Ten million liquid assets. That had to be the money for the trust. But it wasn't in trust, it was still in

Richard's account. What was going on? He reached his car and paused, panting slightly, trying not to let panic overwhelm him. The money wasn't in trust. Which meant Philippa wasn't the millionairess he'd thought she was. And he had an enormous overdraft and no means of paying it off except her.

He opened the car door, got in, and rested his clammy head on the steering wheel. It didn't make sense. Had Emily been *lying* to him? She'd promised him that Philippa was going to be rich. She'd told him they were going to sort it out straight away. She'd said the money would be put in Philippa's name; that as soon as she turned thirty it would be hers. And instead, where was it? It was still in Richard's name. From the look of things, Richard had been liquidizing his assets for months. He was obviously planning to do something with the money. But what? Give it to Philippa? Or throw it to the fucking birds? Nothing would have surprised Lambert any more. And the worst thing was, there was absolutely nothing he could do about it.

As the puddings arrived, Philippa leaned across the table and looked Fleur in the eye. Fleur looked back at her. Philippa had drunk two Manhattans and at least her share of the champagne and had become more and more garrulous and less and less distinct. Her cheeks were flushed and her hair was dishevelled and she seemed to have something important to say.

'I lied to you.' Her words came tumbling out, and Fleur peered at her in surprise.

'I'm sorry?'

'No, *I'm* sorry. I mean, you're my best friend, and I lied to you. You're my best friend,' repeated Philippa with a swaying emphasis. 'And I lied to you.' She reached for Fleur's hand and blinked back a couple of tears. 'About Lambert.'

'Really? What did you tell me about Lambert?' Fleur disentangled her hand and reached for her spoon. 'Eat your pudding.'

Obediently, Philippa picked up her spoon and cracked the surface of her *crème brûlée*. Then she looked up.

'I told you I loved him.'

Fleur unhurriedly finished her mouthful of chocolate mousse.

'You don't love Lambert?'

'Sometimes I think I do – but,' Philippa shuddered. 'I don't really.'

'I don't blame you.'

'I'm trapped in a loveless marriage.' Philippa gazed at Fleur with bloodshot eyes.

'Well then leave it.' Fleur took another spoonful of chocolate mousse.

'You think I should leave Lambert?'

'If he doesn't make you happy, then leave him.'

'You don't think maybe I should have an affair?' said Philippa hopefully.

'No,' replied Fleur firmly. 'Definitely not.' Philippa took a spoonful of *crème brûlée*, munched half-heartedly, then took another one. A tear rolled down her cheek.

'But what if I leave Lambert and then . . . and then I realize I do love him really?'

'Well, then, you'll know.'

'But what if he won't have me back? I'll be on my own!'

Fleur shrugged.

'So what?'

'So what? I couldn't stand to be on my own!'

Philippa's voice rose above the clamour of the restaurant. 'Do you know how difficult it is to meet people these days?'

'I do,' said Fleur. She allowed herself a tiny smile. 'You have to look in the right places.'

'I couldn't stand to be on my own,' repeated Philippa doggedly. Fleur sighed impatiently.

'Well then, stay with him. Philippa, you've had a lot to drink . . .'

'No, you're right,' interrupted Philippa. 'I'm going to leave him.' She shuddered. 'He's disgusting.'

'I have to agree with you there,' said Fleur.

'I didn't want to marry him,' said Philippa. A fresh flurry of tears fell onto the table.

'And now you're going to leave him,' said Fleur, stifling a yawn. 'So that's all right. Shall we get the bill?'

'And you'll help me through it?'

'Of course.' Fleur raised her hand and two waiters with identical blond haircuts immediately descended.

'Our bill, please,' she said. Philippa looked at her watch.

'You've got to go to your service, haven't you?' she said blearily. 'Your memorial service.'

'Well, you know, I may not go to the memorial service, after all,' said Fleur slowly. 'I'm not sure . . .' She paused. 'Hattie wasn't such a great friend to me. And I'm not really in the mood for it. It's . . . a bit of a difficult situation.'

Philippa wasn't listening.

'Fleur?' she said, wiping her eyes, 'I really like you.'

'Do you, darling?' Fleur smiled kindly at her. How on earth, she wondered, could someone like Richard have produced such a characterless lump of self-pity?

'Are you going to marry Daddy?' sniffed Philippa.

'He hasn't asked me,' replied Fleur swiftly, giving Philippa a dazzling smile.

The bill arrived in a leather folder; without looking at it, Fleur placed Richard's Gold Card inside it. They both watched silently as it was borne away by one of the identical waiters.

'But if he does ask you,' said Philippa. 'If he does. Will you?'

'Well,' said Fleur slowly. She leaned back in her chair. Ten million, she thought. The idea ran round her mind like a big shiny ball-bearing. Ten million pounds. A fortune by any standards. 'Who knows?' she said at last, and drained her glass.

'So, do you reckon your mother will marry my father?' asked Antony, flopping down on the immaculate green turf of the putting green.

'I don't know,' said Zara irritably. 'Stop asking me that. I can't concentrate.' She screwed up her nose, took a deep breath, and jabbed at the golf ball with her putter. It trickled a few inches towards the hole, then stopped. 'There. Look what you made me do. That was crap.'

'No it wasn't,' said Antony. 'You're picking it up really well.'

'I'm not. It's a stupid game.' She banged her putter crossly on the ground, and Antony looked around nervously to check no-one had seen her. But few people were about. They were on the junior putting green, an out of the way practice area shielded by pine trees and usually empty. Antony had spent half the morning practising his putting in preparation for the Club Cup, the major golfing event of the summer. The other half he'd spent retrieving the golf balls which Zara seemed unable to prevent flying over the hedge every few minutes.

'Putting's supposed to be, like, really controlled,' he said. 'You should just imagine . . .'

'There's nothing to imagine,' snapped Zara. 'I know what I've got to do. Get the fucking ball into the hole. It's just I can't do it.' She threw her putter down on the ground, and sat down beside Antony. 'I don't know how you can play this dumb game. You don't even burn off any calories.'

'You kind of get hooked on it,' said Antony. 'Anyway, you don't need to lose weight.' Zara ignored him and hunched her shoulders up. For a few moments neither of them said anything.

'So, come on,' said Antony at last. 'How come you're in such a bad mood?'

'I'm not.'

'Yes you are. You've been in a terrible mood all day. Ever since your mum left this morning.' He paused. 'Is it because . . .' He broke off awkwardly.

'What?'

'Well. I just wondered if maybe you knew the person whose memorial service she's going to. And maybe that was why you were a bit—'

'No,' interrupted Zara. 'No, that's not it.' She turned away from him slightly; her face looked fiercer than ever.

'It'll be great when you go to New York,' said Antony brightly.

'If I go.'

'Of course you'll go! Your friend Johnny's going to take you!'

Zara shrugged.

'I don't see it happening somehow.'

'Why not?' She shrugged again.

'I just don't.'

'You're just feeling a bit miserable,' said Antony understandingly.

'I'm not *miserable*. I'd just like . . .'

'What?' said Antony eagerly. 'What would you like?'

'I'd like to know what's going to happen. OK? I'd just like to know.'

'Between your mum and my dad?'

'Yeah.' Her mutter was almost imperceptible.

'I think they're going to get married.' Antony's voice bubbled over with enthusiasm. 'I bet Dad asks her really soon. And then all that stuff with the Gold Card . . .' He lowered his voice slightly. 'Well, it won't matter any more, will it? I mean, she'll be his wife! They'll share all their worldly goods anyway!' Zara looked at him.

'You've got it all neatly sorted out in your mind, haven't you?'

'Well.' He coloured slightly and plucked at the close-shorn grass.

'Antony, you're so fucking *decent*.'

'I'm not!' he retorted angrily. Zara gave a sudden laugh.

'It's not a *bad* thing to be.'

'You make me sound really square,' he protested. 'But I'm not. I've done loads of . . . stuff.'

'What have you done?' said Zara teasingly. 'Shop-lifting?'

'No. Of course not!'

'Gambling, then?' said Zara. 'What about sex?' Antony flushed and Zara moved closer to him. 'Have you ever had sex, Antony?'

'Have you?' he parried.

'Don't be dumb. I'm only thirteen years old.'

Antony felt a sudden swoosh of relief.

'Well, how am I supposed to know?' he said

truculently. 'You might have done. I mean, you smoke dope, don't you?'

'That's different,' said Zara. 'Anyway,' she added, 'if you have sex too young you get cervical cancer.'

'So-vital cancer?' said Antony, mishearing. 'What's that?'

'Cer-vi-cal, dummy! Cancer of the cervix. You know what the cervix is? It's right here.' She pointed to a spot at the top of her jeans fly-buttons. 'Right up inside.' Antony followed her finger with his gaze; as he did so he felt blood start to rush to his head. His hand shot up confusedly to his birthmark.

'Don't cover it up,' said Zara.

'What?' His voice felt strangled.

'Your birthmark. I like it. Don't cover it up.'

'You like it?'

'Sure. Don't you?' Antony looked away, not knowing quite what to say. No-one ever mentioned his birthmark; he'd got used to pretending he thought it wasn't there.

'It's sexy.' Her voice fell, soft and raspy on his ears. Antony felt his breathing quicken. No-one had ever called him sexy before.

'My mother hated it,' he said, without meaning to.

'I bet she didn't,' said Zara encouragingly.

'She did! She . . .' He broke off. 'It doesn't matter.'

'Sure it matters.'

For a few silent moments Antony stared downwards. Years of loyalty to his mother battled with a sudden, desperate yearning to unburden himself.

'She wanted me to wear an eyepatch, to hide it,' he said, suddenly.

'An eyepatch?'

Antony swivelled round to meet Zara's incredulous gaze.

'When I was about seven. She asked me if I didn't think it would be fun to wear an eyepatch. Like a pirate, she said. And she pulled out this . . . this horrible black plastic thing, on elastic.'

'What did you do?'

Antony closed his eyes and remembered his mother, staring at him with that look of distaste, half masked by a bright, fake smile. A pain grabbed him in the chest and he took a deep, shuddering breath.

'I just sort of stared at it, and said, But I won't be able to see if I wear an eyepatch. And then she laughed, and pretended she was just joking. But . . .' He swallowed. 'I knew she wasn't. Even then, I knew. She wanted me to cover my eye up so no-one could see my birthmark.'

'Jesus. What a bitch.'

'She wasn't a bitch!' Antony's voice cracked. 'She was just . . .' He bit his lip.

'Well, you know what? I think it's sexy.' Zara moved closer still. 'Very sexy.' There was an infinitesimal pause. Zara met his eyes.

'Does . . . does kissing give you cervical cancer?' asked Antony eventually. His voice sounded husky to his own ears; his heart was pulsing loudly in his chest.

'I don't think so,' said Zara.

'Good,' said Antony.

Slowly, self-consciously, he put an arm round her skinny shoulders and pulled her towards him. Her lips tasted of mint and Diet Coke; her tongue found his immediately. She's been kissed before, he thought hazily. She's been kissed lots. More than me, probably. And as they drew apart he looked at her cautiously, half expecting her to be giggling at him; half expecting her to humiliate him with some barbed, experienced comment.

But to his horrified surprise, she was gazing into the

distance and a tear was running down her cheek. Visions of accusations and useless denials raced terrifyingly through his mind.

'Zara, I'm sorry!' he gasped. 'I didn't mean . . .'

'Don't worry,' she said in a low voice. 'It's not you. It's nothing to do with you.'

'So you didn't mind . . .' He stared at her, panting slightly.

'Of course I didn't mind,' she said. 'I wanted you to kiss me. You knew that.' She wiped away the tear, looked up at him and smiled. 'And you know what? Now I want you to kiss me again.'

By the time she arrived home, Philippa had a throbbing headache. After Fleur had left in a taxi for Waterloo, she had continued shopping by herself, wandering into the cheaper shops which Fleur had ignored but which she secretly preferred. Now her shoes felt too tight, and her hair was falling out of shape, and she felt raw and grimy from the London streets. But as she let herself in, she heard an unfamiliar voice in the study, and her heart quickened. Perhaps Lambert had invited guests over. Perhaps they would have an impromptu supper party. What a good thing she was wearing her pink suit; they'd think she wore clothes like this every day. She hurried down the hall, checking her reflection in the mirror, adopting a sophisticated yet welcoming expression, and threw open the door of the study.

But Lambert was alone. He was slumped in the armchair by the fire, listening to a message on the answer machine. A woman's voice which Philippa didn't recognize was saying, 'It is absolutely *imperative* that we meet without delay to discuss your situation.'

'What situation?' said Philippa.

'Nothing,' snapped Lambert. Philippa looked at the machine's red light.

'Is she on the line now? Why don't you just pick up and speak to her?'

'Why don't you just shut up?' snarled Lambert.

Philippa looked at him. As the afternoon had worn on, she'd begun to think that perhaps her marriage was not the loveless shell she had described; that perhaps there was hope in it. Her determination to leave Lambert had melted away, leaving behind only a familiar, faded disappointment that life had not turned out quite the way she had imagined.

But now, suddenly she felt her resolve return. She took a deep breath, and clenched her fists.

'You're always so bloody rude to me!' she exclaimed.

'What?' Lambert's head moved round slowly until he was looking at her in what seemed genuine astonishment.

'I'm sick of it!' Philippa advanced into the room, realized she was still holding two carrier bags, and put them down. 'I'm sick of the way you treat me. Like a skivvy! Like an imbecile! I want some respect!' She stamped her foot triumphantly and wished she had a bit more of an audience. Phrases were springing plentifully to her lips; scenes of confrontation from a thousand novels were filling her mind. She felt like a romantic, feisty heroine. 'I married you for love, Lambert,' she continued, lowering her voice to a tremble. 'I wanted to share your life. Your hopes, your dreams. And yet you cut me out; you ignore me . . .'

'I don't ignore you!' said Lambert. 'What are you talking about?'

'You treat me like shit,' said Philippa, tossing her hair back. 'Well, I've just about had enough. I want out.'

'You what?' Lambert's voice rose in an astonished squawk. 'Philippa, what the fuck's wrong with you?'

'Ask yourself the same question,' said Philippa. 'I'm going to leave you, Lambert.' She lifted her chin high, picked up her carrier bags and headed for the door. 'I'm going to leave you, and there's nothing you can do about it.'

Chapter Fourteen

Fleur arrived back from London to find Geoffrey Forrester, captain of Greyworth Golf Club, shaking hands with Richard in the hall.

'Aha!' said Geoffrey, as he saw Fleur. 'You're just in time to hear the good news. Shall I tell Fleur, Richard, or do you want to?'

'What is it?' said Fleur.

'Geoffrey's just informed me that, if I'm willing, I'm to be nominated as captain of the club,' said Richard. Fleur looked at him. He was obviously trying to keep his face sober but his mouth had twisted into a smile, and his eyes were shining with delight.

'As I told Richard, the committee voted unanimously in favour of him,' said Geoffrey. 'Which doesn't always happen, I can tell you.'

'Well done, darling!' said Fleur. 'I'm so pleased.'

'Anyway, I'd better shoot off,' said Geoffrey, looking at his watch. 'So, Richard, you'll let me know your decision in the morning?'

'Absolutely,' said Richard. 'Good night, Geoffrey.'

'And I hope we'll be seeing the two of you up at the Club Cup?' said Geoffrey. 'No excuses now, Richard!' He gave Fleur a jovial grin. 'Tell you what, Fleur, isn't it about time you took up the game yourself?'

'I'm not sure I'm really a golfer,' said Fleur, smiling back at him.

'It's never too late to start!' Geoffrey chuckled. 'We'll get you yet, Fleur! Won't we Richard?'

'I hope so,' said Richard. He reached for Fleur's hand and gave it a squeeze. 'I certainly hope so.'

They watched as his car roared out of the drive, then walked back inside the house.

'What decision was he talking about?' said Fleur.

'I told Geoffrey that I couldn't agree to being nominated until I'd consulted you first,' said Richard.

'What?' Fleur stared at him. 'But why? You want to be captain, don't you?' Richard sighed.

'Of course I want to – on one level. But it's not as simple as that. Being captain is, as well as being a huge honour, a huge commitment.' He lifted a strand of Fleur's hair and brushed it against his lips. 'If I take it on, I'll have to spend far more time at the club than I have been doing recently. I'll have to play more, get my game up to form again, attend meetings . . .' He spread his hands. 'There's a lot to it. And all of that will mean I have less time to spend with you.'

'But you'll be captain! Isn't that worth it?' Fleur narrowed her eyes. 'Isn't being captain of Greyworth what you've always wanted?'

'It's funny,' said Richard. 'I've thought for years that it was exactly what I wanted. Being captain of Greyworth was – well, it was my goal. And now I've got my goal within my grasp, I can't quite remember what I wanted it for. The goal posts have shifted.' His nose began to twitch. 'Or should I perhaps say, the eighteenth flag has shifted.' He gave a little snuffle of laughter, but Fleur was frowning distractedly.

'You can't just abandon your goal,' she said suddenly. 'If it's something you've been aiming for all your life.'

'I don't see why not. The question is, why was I

aiming for it?' said Richard. 'And what happens if I don't particularly value what it has to offer any more?' He shrugged. 'What if I'd prefer to spend my time with you, rather than going round the course with some bore from a neighbouring golf club?'

'Richard, you can't just cop out!' exclaimed Fleur. 'You can't just settle for . . . a nice quiet life! You've always wanted to be captain of Greyworth and now here's your chance. People should grasp the opportunities they're given in life. Even if it means—' She broke off, breathing hard.

'Even if it means they're unhappy?' Richard laughed.

'Maybe, yes! Better to take the opportunity and be unhappy than pass it up and always regret it.'

'Fleur.' He took both her hands and kissed them. 'You're extraordinary; absolutely extraordinary! I can't imagine a more encouraging, supportive wife . . .'

There was a sharp silence.

'Except I'm not your wife,' said Fleur slowly. Richard looked down. He took a deep breath, then looked up, straight at her.

'Fleur,' he began.

'Richard, I have to go and shower,' said Fleur, before he could continue. 'I'm absolutely filthy from London.' She disentangled herself from his grasp and headed quickly for the stairs.

'Of course,' said Richard quietly. Then he smiled up at her. 'You must be exhausted. And I haven't even asked you how the memorial service went.'

'I didn't go in the end,' said Fleur. 'I was too busy having fun with Philippa.'

'Oh good! I'm very glad you two are making friends.'

'And thank you for the champagne!' added Fleur, from halfway up the stairs. 'We were so surprised.'

'Yes,' said Richard. 'I hoped you would be.'

Fleur headed straight for the bathroom, turned both bath taps on and locked the door. Her mind felt fuddled; she needed to think. Sighing, she sat down on the bathroom seat – a hideous upholstered affair – and stared at her reflection in the mirror.

What was her own goal in life? The answer came immediately, without her even thinking. Her goal was to acquire a large amount of money. What was a large amount of money? Ten million pounds was a large amount of money. If she married Richard, she would have a large amount of money.

'But not on my own terms,' said Fleur aloud to her reflection. She sighed, and pushed her shoes off. Her feet were aching very slightly from the London streets, despite the soft, expensive leather of her shoes; despite the many taxis.

Could she stand to become Richard's wife? Mrs Richard Favour, of Greyworth. Fleur shuddered slightly; the very thought stifled her. Men changed after marriage. Richard would buy her tartan trousers and expect her to take up golf. He would give her an allowance. He would be there every morning when she woke up, smiling at her with that eager, innocent smile. If she planned a trip abroad, he would come too.

But at the same time . . . Fleur bit her lip. At the same time, he had a lot of money. He was an opportunity that might not come her way again. She tore off her jacket and tossed it over the towel rail. The sight of the black silk suddenly reminded her of the memorial service she'd missed that afternoon. A chance passed up. Who might have been at that service? What fortunate meeting might have occurred if she'd gone?

'Make up your mind,' said Fleur to her reflection,

stepping out of her skirt, undoing her bra. 'Either you take what's going, or you leave.'

She ripped her stockings off, padded over to the bath and swung her feet over the side. As she lowered them into the hot, foamy water she felt her whole body start to relax and her mind blank out.

A knock at the door made her jump.

'It's me!' came Richard's voice. 'I've brought you up a glass of wine.'

'Thanks, darling!' called back Fleur. 'I'll get it in a second.'

'And Philippa's on the phone. She wants to speak to you.' Fleur rolled her eyes. She'd had enough of Philippa for one day.

'Tell her I'll call her back.'

'Right you are. I'm leaving the glass here,' came Richard's voice again. 'Just outside the door.'

She imagined him stooping down, carefully placing the glass on the carpet outside the bathroom door; looking at it, wondering whether she might not knock it over by mistake, then bending down again and moving it a few inches further back before tiptoeing away. A careful prudent man. Would he let her spend all his money? Quite possibly not. And then she would have married him for nothing.

Philippa put the telephone receiver down and bit her lip. A fresh flood of tears poured down her red, raw face; she felt as though her insides were being wrenched apart. There was no-one else she could phone. No-one else she could confide in. She had to talk to Fleur, and Fleur was in the bath.

'Oh God,' she said aloud. 'Oh God help me.'

She sank off the sofa onto the floor and began to weep frenziedly, clutching her stomach, rocking back and forwards. Her pink suit was crumpled and tear-stained but she didn't care what she looked like; there was no-one to see her. No-one to hear her.

Lambert had slammed the door half an hour before, leaving her sitting in numb, silent mortification. For a while she'd crouched on the sofa, unable to move without a pain hitting her in the stomach and tears springing to her eyes. Then, as her breathing calmed, she'd somehow managed to get to the phone and dial the number of The Maples and ask for Fleur in a voice that sounded normal. Fleur, she'd thought desperately. Fleur. If only I can talk to Fleur.

But Fleur was in the bath and couldn't talk to her. And as she'd said goodbye to her father, the tears had once more started to pour down her face, and she'd sunk to the floor, and wondered why a day that had started off so perfectly should have ended up in a mess of humiliation.

He'd laughed at her. To begin with, Lambert had laughed at her. A nasty, mocking laugh which had made her throw her shoulders back and look him in the eyes and say, in an even more feisty voice than before, 'I'm leaving you!' A zingy adrenalin had begun to pump round her body, a smile had come to her lips, and it had occurred to her that she should have done this ages ago. 'I expect I'll go to my father's house,' she'd added in a businesslike way. 'Until I get settled in my own place.' And Lambert had looked up and said,

'Philippa, shut up, will you?'

'Lambert, don't you understand? I'm leaving you!'

'No you're not.'

'Yes I am!'

'No you're bloody not.'

'I am! You don't love me, so what's the point in carrying on together?'

'The point is, we're fucking married. All right?'

'Well maybe I don't want to be fucking married any more!' she'd cried.

'Well maybe I do!'

And Lambert had got to his feet, come over and taken her wrist. 'You're not leaving me, Philippa,' he'd said, in a voice she hardly recognized; a voice which almost frightened her. He was bright red and trembling; he looked as though he was possessed. 'You're not fucking leaving me, all right?'

And she'd felt flattered. She'd gazed up at his desperate face and thought, that's love. He really does love me. She was about to succumb, to caress his chin and call him darling. When he moved towards her, she'd felt a smile creep across her face and prepared herself for a passionate, reuniting embrace. But suddenly his hands were grasping her roughly about the throat.

'You won't leave me!' he hissed. 'You won't ever leave me!' And his hands had tightened around her neck until she was hardly able to breathe, until she felt she would retch against the pressure on her throat.

'Tell me you won't leave me! Say it!'

'I won't leave you,' Philippa had managed in a hoarse voice.

'That's more like it.'

Suddenly he'd let her go, dropping her down onto the sofa like a child dropping an unwanted toy. She hadn't looked up as he'd left; hadn't asked him where he was going. Her entire body was riveted to the spot in misery. When she'd heard the door slamming, she'd felt tears of relief pouring down her face. Eventually she'd made her way shakily to the phone, jabbed in the number of The Maples and asked for the only person she could possibly tell about this. Somehow she'd managed to talk to her father in the semblance of a normal voice, giving away nothing. Somehow she'd managed to say that of course it didn't matter, cheerio Daddy, see you soon. But as soon as she'd put the phone down, she'd collapsed onto the carpet, a soggy mess of misery. Because Fleur was unavailable, and there was no-one else she could turn to.

Richard put down the receiver and gazed affectionately at it. He found it rather pleasing that Philippa had phoned wanting to speak to Fleur rather than him. It just showed, he thought, that Fleur was becoming more and more a member of the family: attached not simply to himself, but to all of them. Gillian was certainly very fond of Fleur. Antony seemed to enjoy her company well enough, and — Richard grinned to himself — he certainly liked young Zara.

In the space of a summer, Fleur had become so much part of all their lives that he found it difficult to remember how they'd existed before her. At the beginning she'd seemed a foreign, exotic creature, full of strange ideas, completely at odds with the life he led; with the life they all led. But now . . . Richard frowned. Now she seemed entirely normal. She was just Fleur. Whether she'd changed, or whether they'd changed, he wasn't entirely sure.

And it wasn't just within the family that the transformation had taken place, thought Richard, pouring himself a glass of wine. All those looks of disapproval in the clubhouse had, somewhere along the line, vanished. All the gossip had melted away. Now Fleur was as well respected at Greyworth as he was himself. His nomination as captain honoured her as much as it did him.

Richard bit his lip. It was time for him to honour her

too. It was time for him to get his affairs in order; time for him to buy an engagement ring; time for him to ask Fleur – properly – to be his wife.

By lunchtime the next day, Fleur had not yet found a moment to call Philippa back.

'She phoned again,' said Gillian, slicing tomatoes for lunch in the kitchen. 'While you were out having your fitness assessment. She sounded very upset that she'd missed you for the third time.'

'I've got very good stamina,' said Fleur, staring at the sheet of paper in her hand. 'But my lung capacity is terrible.' She looked up. 'Why should that be, I wonder?'

'Too much smoking,' said Zara.

'I don't smoke!'

'No, but you used to.'

'Only very briefly,' retorted Fleur. 'And I lived in the Swiss Alps for six months. That should have repaired any lung damage, shouldn't it?'

'You also had another phone call from your friend Johnny,' said Gillian, glancing at the pad of paper by the kitchen phone. 'You know, that's the fourth time he's phoned this week.'

'Jesus!' said Zara. 'Haven't you two made it up yet?'

'He was quite adamant that he needed to speak to you,' added Gillian. 'I did promise I'd try to persuade you to phone him.'

'I'm not in the mood for Johnny,' said Fleur, frowning. 'I'll call him later.'

'Call him now!' exclaimed Zara. 'If he wants you to call, he must have a good reason. What if it's urgent?'

'Nothing in Johnny's life is urgent,' said Fleur scathingly. 'He hasn't a care in the world.'

'And I suppose you have?' shot back Zara.

'Zara,' interrupted Gillian diplomatically, 'why don't you go and pick me some strawberries from the garden?' There was a short silence. Zara glared at Fleur.

'OK,' she said at last, and got to her feet.

'And maybe I'll find time to phone Johnny later,' said Fleur, examining her nails. 'But only maybe.'

Lambert was nearing crisis point. He sat in his office, shredding paper between his fingers, staring out of the window, unable to concentrate. Over the last few days he had received no fewer than three messages from Erica Fortescue at First Bank, exhorting him to contact her urgently. So far he'd managed to avoid speaking to her. But he couldn't run away for ever. What if she came into his office? What if she called Richard?

His overdraft now stood at three hundred and thirty thousand pounds. Lambert felt a cold sweat steal over his forehead. How had it become so large? How had he spent so much? What did he have to show for it? He had a car, some clothes, some watches. He had some friends; chaps and their wives whom he'd bought with bottles of brandy at his club, tickets to the opera, boxes at the cricket. He'd always pretended he was doling out freebies; his friends had always believed him. If they'd ever thought he was paying for everything out of his own pocket they would have been embarrassed; would probably have laughed at him. Now Lambert's cheeks flushed with an angry humiliation. Who were these friends? Mindless idiots whose names he could barely remember. And it was to show them a good time that he'd got himself into this trouble.

What had Emily been playing at, telling him he was going to be a rich man? What the fuck had she been playing at? A cold fury rose through Lambert and he cursed her for being dead, cursed her for having flitted out of the world leaving loose ends floating in the wind. What was the truth? Was Philippa going to be rich? Was that money going to be hers? Or had Richard changed his mind? Had the whole trust story been an invention of Emily's? He wouldn't have put it past her, the manipulative bitch. She'd encouraged him to think he was rich; encouraged him to start spending more than he had done before. And now he was in debt and all her hints and promises had come to nothing.

Except – Lambert bit his lip – he couldn't be sure that they would come to nothing. It was still tantalizingly possible that Richard would deliver. Maybe he was still going to put some of that money into trust for Philippa. Maybe when she turned thirty she would become a millionairess, just as Emily had promised. Or maybe Richard had now decided to wait a bit longer – until she was thirty-five, perhaps, or forty.

It was torturous, not knowing. And he had no way of finding out. Richard was a secretive bastard – he would never tell Lambert anything – and of course Philippa knew nothing. Philippa knew nothing about anything. A sudden memory came into Lambert's mind of Philippa's red, contorted face the night before. She'd been sobbing on the sofa when he'd stormed out of the house; he hadn't seen her since then.

He'd over-reacted to her feeble threat of leaving him; he realized that now. Of course, she hadn't meant it; Philippa would never leave him. But at the time, she'd rattled him. He'd felt white-hot panic flashing through his body and a conviction that he must, at all costs, stop her. He had to remain married to Philippa; he had to keep things ticking over, at least until he knew where he stood. And so he'd lashed out. Maybe he'd overdone it a bit, maybe he'd upset her a bit too much.

But at least that would keep her quiet for a while; give him time to sort himself out.

The phone rang, and he felt a spasm of fear zip through him. Perhaps this was Erica Fortescue from First Bank, he thought, ridiculously. She was down in reception; she was on the way up . . .

It rang again, and he snatched it up.

'Yes?' he barked, trying to conceal his nerves.

'Lambert?' It was his secretary, Lucy. 'Just to say, I've rearranged that meeting for you.'

'Good,' said Lambert, and put the phone down. He couldn't face any meetings at the moment; couldn't face anyone. He had to have some time to think what to do.

Should he just go to Richard, explain the situation and ask for a bail-out? Would Richard willingly hand over that kind of money? The total sum sprang into his mind again, and he shuddered. The figure which had seemed so reasonable when viewed against the mountain of Philippa's future fortune now seemed outlandish. He closed his eyes and imagined telling Richard; asking humbly for assistance; sitting silently while Richard lectured him. His life would be a misery. What a fucking nightmare.

This was all Larry Collins's fault, Lambert thought suddenly. Larry, his chum at the bank. Larry, who had *invited* Lambert to take out an overdraft. He'd been impressed by Lambert's assurances that soon Philippa would be coming into millions. He'd told Lambert he was a valued customer. He'd said the paperwork didn't matter; he'd upped the limit without question. If he hadn't been such an irresponsible moron; if his bosses hadn't been so fucking *blind* – then Lambert would never have had such a big overdraft limit in the first place and the whole problem would never have arisen.

But no-one had thought to check up, Lambert's overdraft had risen like the sun – and only then had Larry been fired. Larry was safely out of the picture, thanks very much, and it was Lambert who'd been left to pick up the pieces.

What was he to do? If he kept to his original plan – took fifty thousand from the ten million account and threw it at the bank to keep them happy – then he'd have to find a way of paying Richard back before the end of the year. He couldn't just leave it; Richard would notice a deficit of fifty thousand. So he'd need another overdraft. But who would authorize another overdraft now that Larry was gone? Who would authorize another overdraft for him without any proof that Philippa's trust fund was established? Lambert clenched his fists in frustration. If only he had proof. Some little corroborating piece of evidence. Something that would convince some fool somewhere to let him keep his overdraft. A document, or a letter. Something signed by Richard. Anything would do.

Chapter Fifteen

Two weeks later Richard sat in Oliver Sterndale's office, signing his name repeatedly on different pieces of paper. After the last signature he replaced the cap on Oliver's fountain pen, looked at his old friend and smiled.

'There,' he said. 'All done.'

'All gone, more like,' said Oliver tetchily. 'You do realize that you're now practically a pauper?'

Richard laughed.

'Oliver, for someone who has just signed away ten million pounds, I have an indecently large amount of money left to call my own. As well you know.'

'I know nothing of the sort,' said Oliver. His eyes met Richard's and suddenly twinkled. 'However, since you have been so consistently wedded to this little scheme, may I offer my congratulations on its successful completion?'

'You may.'

'Well then, congratulations.'

They both looked at the contracts, lying in thick piles on the desk.

'They're going to be two very rich young people,' said Oliver. 'Have you decided when to tell them?'

'Not yet,' said Richard. 'There's still plenty of time.'

'There's a fair amount of time,' said Oliver. 'But you do need to give them some warning. Especially

Philippa. You don't want to find it's the eve of her thirtieth birthday, and you're suddenly trying to find the words to tell her she's about to become a multi-millionairess. These announcements have a nasty habit of backfiring.'

'Oh, I'm aware of that,' said Richard. 'In fact, I thought I might bring both Philippa and Antony in here, say in a few weeks' time, and we could both explain it to them. Since you're the trustee of the fund.'

'Good idea,' said Oliver. 'Splendid idea.'

'You know, I feel liberated,' said Richard suddenly. 'This has been hanging over me more than I'd realized. Now I feel able to—' He broke off, and coloured slightly.

'To pursue your fresh start?'

'Exactly.'

Oliver cleared his throat delicately.

'Richard, is there anything which – as your lawyer – I should know?'

'I don't believe so.'

'But you would let me know if there were . . . anything.'

'Naturally I would.' A small smile played about Richard's lips, and Oliver gazed at him severely.

'And by that I don't mean a fax from Las Vegas saying "Guess what, I'm hitched".' Richard burst into laughter.

'Oliver, who do you think I am?'

'I think you're a decent man and a good friend.' Oliver's eyes bored into Richard's. 'And I think you may need protection.'

'From whom, may I ask?'

'From yourself. From your own generosity.'

'Oliver, just what are you saying?'

'I'm saying nothing. Just promise me you won't

get married without telling me first. Please.'

'Honestly, Oliver, I wouldn't dream of it. And anyway, who says I'm getting married?'

Oliver gave him a wry smile.

'Do you really want me to answer that? I can give you a list of names, if you like. Beginning with my own wife.'

'Perhaps you'd better not.' Richard chuckled. 'You know, I really don't care who says what about me any more. Let them gossip all they like.'

'Did you use to care?'

Richard thought for a minute.

'I'm not sure I did. But Emily used to worry terribly. And so of course I always used to worry too, on her behalf.'

'Yes,' said Oliver. 'I can imagine.' He grinned at Richard. 'You've certainly changed, haven't you?'

'Have I?' said Richard innocently.

'You know you have.' Oliver paused. 'And quite seriously, I'm glad things are working out so well for you. You deserve it.'

'I'm not sure I do,' said Richard. 'But thank you anyway, Oliver.' For a moment the two men's eyes met; then Richard looked away. 'And thanks for coming in on a Saturday morning,' he said lightly. 'On Club Cup morning, too!'

'It was no trouble.' Oliver leaned back comfortably in his chair. 'I'm not teeing off until twelve. What about you?'

'Half-past. Just enough time to get in some putting practice. I certainly need it. You know, I've barely played this summer.'

'I know,' said Oliver. 'That's what I said. You've changed.'

*　　*　　*

237

By eleven o'clock, Philippa was finally ready to leave the flat. She peered at herself in the mirror and gave her hair one last tug.

'Come on,' said Lambert. 'I tee off at one, remember.'

'There's plenty of time,' said Philippa tonelessly. Without meeting his eye, she followed him down the stairs.

How had it happened? she wondered for the hundredth time, as they both got into the car. How had she let Lambert back into her life without a protest; without so much as a question mark? He had arrived back at the flat, three days after the row, holding a bottle of wine and some flowers.

'These are for you,' he'd said gracelessly at the door of the sitting room, and her head had jerked round from the television in shock. She'd thought she would never see Lambert again. At one point, she'd considered changing the locks of the flat; then she'd discovered how much it cost and decided to spend the money on a crate of Baileys instead. By the time Lambert arrived back, she was on the fourth bottle.

The alcohol must have dimmed her faculties, she thought. Because as she'd looked at him, standing in the doorway, not sneering or swaggering but not looking particularly penitent either, she'd found herself entirely devoid of emotion. She'd tried as hard as she could to conjure up the anger and hatred which she knew should be burning inside her; tried to think of some appropriate insult to hiss at him. But nothing came to mind except 'You bastard.' And when she said it, it was in such lacklustre tones that she might as well not have bothered.

He'd given her the flowers, and she'd found herself looking at them and thinking they were rather nice. Then he'd opened the wine and poured it into a glass for her, and although she was feeling slightly sick, she'd drunk it. And once she'd taken his flowers and drunk his wine, it had seemed to be tacitly agreed between them that he was back, that he was forgiven, that the rift between them was healed.

It was as though the whole thing had never happened. As though she'd never threatened to leave him; he'd never touched her. As though none of the shouting and sobbing had occurred. He never referred to it and neither did she. Whenever she opened her mouth to speak about it, she began to feel sick and her heart began to pound, and it seemed so much easier to say nothing. And the more days that passed, the more remote and shadowy the whole thing seemed, and the less convinced she felt of her ability to tackle him on the subject.

Yet she wanted to. Part of her wanted to shout at him again; to work herself up into a frenzy and scream at him until he crumpled in guilt. Part of her wanted to relive the entire confrontation, this time as the heroine, the victor. And part of her wanted to find the energy to let the world know what had happened.

Because no-one knew. Fleur didn't know; her father didn't know; none of her friends knew. She had been through the worst crisis of her life, had come through it somehow, and no-one knew. Fleur still had not phoned her back. It had been over two weeks and she still hadn't phoned back.

Philippa felt angry tears spring to her eyes, and she looked out of the car window. At first, she'd kept ringing The Maples, frantic to talk to Fleur; desperate for some help and advice. Then Lambert had arrived back, and the two of them had seemed to patch things up – and Philippa had found herself wanting to relay her story to Fleur not so much for help as for the shocked admiration that it would surely provoke. Every time the phone had rung, she'd jumped to answer, thinking it was Fleur, ready to tell in low tones what had been happening to her; ready to savour the reaction at the other end. But Fleur hadn't called back and hadn't called back, and eventually Philippa had given up expecting her to. Perhaps Fleur was just hopeless with phones, she'd rationalized to herself. Perhaps she hadn't received any of Philippa's messages. Perhaps she'd always tried ringing just when Philippa was on the line to someone else.

But today was different; today they didn't need phones. She would have Fleur all to herself, and she would tell her the whole story. At the thought, Philippa felt an exhilarating anticipation begin to fizz inside her. She would tell Fleur every detail of what had happened. And Fleur would be astounded that Philippa had got through such a trauma on her own; astounded, and consumed with guilt.

'I had no-one,' Philippa heard herself saying to Fleur, in matter-of-fact tones. 'When you didn't call back . . .' She would give a little shrug. 'I was desperate. Of course, I turned to the bottle.'

'Oh darling. You didn't. I feel terrible!' Fleur would grasp her hands pleadingly; Philippa would simply give another little shrug.

'I got through it,' she would say carelessly. 'Somehow I got through it. Jesus, it was hard, though.'

'What?' said Lambert suddenly. 'Are you talking to me?'

'Oh!' said Philippa, and felt her cheeks turn red. 'No, I'm not.'

'Muttering away to yourself,' said Lambert. 'No wonder everyone thinks you're mad.'

'They don't think I'm mad,' said Philippa.

'Whatever,' said Lambert. Philippa looked crossly at him and tried to think of a clever retort. But her mind felt stultified in the real world; her words mismatched and fell apart in her mouth. Already she was flying happily back to Fleur, who would listen to her story, and gasp, and take Philippa's hand, and vow never to let her down again.

'Cool,' said Zara, as she and Antony approached the clubhouse. 'Look at all those flaggy things.'

'Bunting.'

'What?'

'Bunting. It's what they're called.' Zara gazed at him sceptically for a moment. 'Well anyway, they always decorate the clubhouse on Club Cup day,' continued Antony. 'And there's a band in the garden. It's quite fun. We'll get a cream tea later on.'

'But we have to go round the golf course first?'

'That's kind of the point.'

Zara gave a melodramatic sigh and collapsed onto the clubhouse steps.

'Look,' said Antony anxiously, sitting down beside her. 'I'll understand if you don't want to caddy for me after all. I mean it's a hot day, and everything.'

'Are you trying to fire me?'

'No! Of course not!'

'Well, OK then.' Zara squinted at Antony. 'You nervous?'

'Not really.'

'Who's going to do better? You, or your father?'

'Dad, I expect. He always does.'

'But he hasn't been practising all week like you have.' Antony shrugged awkwardly.

'Still. He's a bloody good golfer.' They sat in silence for a while.

'And you're a bloody good kisser,' said Zara suddenly. Antony's head jerked up in astonishment.

'What?'

'You heard.' She grinned. 'Should I say it again?'

'No! Someone might hear!'

'So what? It's the truth.' Antony flushed scarlet. A group of chattering women was coming up the clubhouse steps, and he turned his face away from them.

'And you're . . .' he began. 'I mean . . .'

'Don't feel you have to compliment me in return,' said Zara. 'I know I'm good. I was taught by an expert.'

'Who?' said Antony, feeling jealous.

'Cara.'

'Who the hell's Cara?'

'This Italian girl. Didn't I tell you about her? We were living in her house last summer. She had a rich daddy too. In the Mafia, I think.'

'A girl?' Antony goggled at her.

'Sure. But much older. She was seventeen. She'd kissed, like, loads of people.'

'How did she teach you?'

'How do you think?' Zara grinned at him.

'Jesus.' Antony's face grew even redder.

'She had a younger brother,' said Zara. 'But he was only interested in his dumb computer. Want some gum?' She looked up at Antony's face and laughed.

'You're shocked, aren't you?'

'Well, I mean . . . You were only twelve!' Zara shrugged.

'I guess they start early over there.' She unwrapped her gum and began to chew. Antony watched her silently for a few minutes.

'So what happened?' he asked eventually.

'What do you mean, what happened?'

'Why didn't you stay living with them?'

Zara looked away.

'We just didn't.'

'Did your mother and the Italian guy have a fight?'

'Not exactly,' said Zara. She looked around, and lowered her voice. 'Fleur got tired of living in Italy. So one night we just scooted.'

'What, just left?'

'Yup. Packed our bags and left.'

Antony stared at her for a moment, thinking.

'You're not . . .' He swallowed, and rubbed his shoe along the step. 'You're not going to scoot this time, are you?'

There was a long silence.

'I hope not,' said Zara eventually. 'I really hope not.' She hunched her shoulders and looked away. 'But with Fleur, you never know.'

Fleur was sitting in the clubhouse bar, watching as the competitors and their wives milled about, greeting one another, joshing each other on their form, breaking off mid-conversation to shriek to new arrivals. She felt at home here, she thought comfortably, leaning back and sipping her drink. The ambience here reminded her of her childhood; of the expatriate club in Dubai. These shrieking Surrey women could equally well have been the expat wives who had sat in clusters at the bar, drinking gin and admiring one another's shoes and complaining in low voices about their husbands' bosses. Those jovial chaps with their pints of beer could equally well have been the business acquaintances of her father: successful, tanned, obsessively competitive. In Dubai the golf courses had been sand-coloured, not green, but that was the only difference. That was the atmosphere in which she'd grown up; that was the atmosphere which felt, to her, most like home.

'Fleur!' A voice interrupted her thoughts, and she looked up to see Philippa. She was dressed in a white trouser suit and was gazing at Fleur with an intense, almost frightening expression.

'Philippa,' said Fleur lightly. 'How nice to see you again. Is Lambert playing in the Club Cup?'

'Yes, he is.' Philippa began to fiddle with her bag, tugging awkwardly at the zip until it stuck. 'And I wanted to talk to you.'

'Good,' said Fleur. 'That will be nice. But first let me get you a drink.'

'Drink!' said Philippa obscurely. 'My God, if you knew.' She sat down with a huge sigh. 'If you only knew.'

'Yes,' said Fleur doubtfully. 'Well, you just sit there, and I'll be back in a second.'

At the bar she found Lambert pushing his way to the head of the queue.

'Oh, hello,' he said unenthusiastically.

'I've come to buy your wife a drink,' said Fleur. 'Or perhaps you were planning to buy her one yourself?' Lambert sighed.

'What does she want?'

'I've no idea. A glass of white wine, I should think. Or a Manhattan.'

'She can have wine.'

'Good.' Fleur glanced back at Philippa, who was frantically searching through her handbag for something; a tissue, judging by the redness of her nose. Could the girl not invest in some decent face-powder? Fleur gave a little shudder and turned back to the bar. Suddenly it occurred to her that if she returned to Philippa's table she would probably be stuck with her all afternoon.

'Right,' she said slowly. 'Well, I think I'll go and find

Richard, to wish him good luck. Philippa's over there by the window.'

She waited for Lambert to grunt in response, then swiftly moved off, threading her way through the throng, keeping her head firmly averted from Philippa's until she was safely out of the bar.

On the steps of the clubhouse she found Richard, Antony and Zara.

'All set?' she said cheerfully. 'Who tees off first?'

'Dad,' said Antony. 'And I'm soon after.'

'*We're* soon after,' corrected Zara. 'I'm Antony's caddy,' she informed Richard. 'I tell him which club to use. The big one or the little one.'

'Yeah, right,' said Antony. 'You don't even know what the clubs are called.'

'Sure I do!'

Richard met Fleur's eye and smiled.

'And tonight we have a nice celebration supper,' he said.

'There may not be anything to celebrate,' said Antony.

'Oh, I hope there will,' said Richard.

'So do I,' said Zara, looking at Antony. 'I don't want to hang around with a loser.' Fleur laughed.

'That's my girl.'

'Right,' said Richard. 'Well, I'd better start getting ready.'

'Who's that?' said Antony, interrupting him. 'That man. He's waving at us!'

'Where?' said Fleur.

'He's just come in through the gate. I've no idea who he is.'

'Is he a member?' said Richard, and they all turned to look, squinting in the sunshine.

The man was dapper and tanned and had nut-brown

hair. He was dressed in immaculate pale linen and gazing with slight dismay at the pink culottes of the woman who was striding along in front of him. As they stared at him, he looked up and waved again. Fleur and Zara gasped in unison. Then Zara gave a huge whoop and began running towards him.

'Who on earth is it?' exclaimed Richard, watching as the strange man caught Zara in a huge hug. 'Is it a friend of yours?'

'I don't believe it,' said Fleur in a faint voice. 'It's Johnny.'

Chapter Sixteen

'I should have called,' said Fleur. She stretched her legs down the grassy bank on which she and Johnny were sitting. In the distance was the fourteenth hole; a man in a red shirt was lining up to putt. 'I'm sorry. I thought you were still cross with me.'

'I was. And I'm even crosser with you now!' exclaimed Johnny. 'Do you know what an effort it's been for me to come down here? You know I never leave London if I can help it.'

'I know,' said Fleur. 'But you're here now. I'm so glad we're still friends . . .'

'I had to *battle* to find out what time the train left. Then I realized I didn't know which station I should catch it from and I had to ring up again and the person I'd spoken to before had gone on a tea-break!' Johnny shook his head. 'The inefficiency of the system! And as for the train itself . . .'

'Well, it's lovely to see you,' said Fleur soothingly. 'How long are you staying?'

'I'm not staying! Good God, there are limits!'

'That'll be a pound in the swear box,' said Fleur idly. She lay back and felt the sun beat down on her face. It would be nice to be back in London with Johnny and Felix, she thought. Shopping, gossiping, the odd funeral . . .

'You seem very at home here,' said Johnny, looking

around. 'Quite the little Surrey wife. Have you taken up golf?'

'Of course not.'

'I'm glad to hear it. Such a deeply suburban game.'

'It's not so bad,' said Fleur defensively. 'Zara's been learning to play, you know.'

'Ah well,' said Johnny fondly. 'Zara never did have any taste.'

'It's a shame she had to go off and caddy.'

'Well, it's you I wanted to speak to,' said Johnny. 'That's why I've come down here. Since you wouldn't return my calls, you left me no other choice.'

'What do you want to speak to me about?' asked Fleur. Johnny was silent. Fleur abruptly sat up. 'Johnny, this isn't going to be about Hal Winters, is it?'

'Yes it is.'

'But you were going to get rid of him for me!'

'No I wasn't! Fleur, he's not some sort of household pest. He's your daughter's father. You told me you would prepare her for meeting him. Which you clearly haven't.'

'Zara doesn't need a father,' said Fleur sulkily.

'Of course she does.'

'She's got you.'

'Darling, it's hardly the same,' said Johnny, 'is it?' Fleur gave a little shrug, feeling her mouth twitching into a smile, in spite of herself.

'Perhaps not,' she said.

'Zara deserves the real thing,' said Johnny. 'And I can tell you, she's going to get it.'

'What do you mean?'

'Hal Winters is coming down here next Saturday. To meet Zara, ready or not.'

'What?' Fleur felt her face pale in shock. 'He's what?'

'It's all fixed up.'

'How dare you fix it up! It's got nothing to do with you!'

'It's got everything to do with us! If you abdicate responsibility, someone has to take over. I'll tell you, Felix was all for bringing him straight down in a taxi! But I said no, it's only fair to warn Fleur.' Johnny took a handkerchief from his pocket and mopped his brow. 'Believe it or not, I'm on your side, Fleur.'

'Well thanks very much!' spat Fleur. She felt slightly panicky and out of control. 'I don't want to see him!' she found herself saying. 'I don't want to see him.'

'You needn't see him. This is between him and Zara.'

'What, and I have nothing to do with it?'

'Of course you do. But you don't need him. Zara does.'

'She's fine!'

'She's not fine. She's on the telephone to me constantly about America; about her father. Fleur, she's obsessed!'

For a moment, Fleur stared at him, her face taut; her mouth thin. Then suddenly she relaxed.

'OK,' she said. 'Fine. You're absolutely right. Bring Mr Winters down next Saturday. But don't tell Zara yet. I'll prepare her myself.'

'Fleur . . .'

'I promise! This time I really will.' Johnny looked at her suspiciously.

'And you'll make sure she's here to meet him?'

'Of course I will darling,' said Fleur lightly, and, closing her eyes, she leaned back again in the sun.

Philippa was sitting alone at a table in the garden. In front of her was a pot of tea, several huge scones, and a bottle of wine which she'd won on the tombola. In the corner of the garden, the band was playing 'Strangers in the Night', and several children were attempting to dance with each other in front of the bandstand. A tear fell from Philippa's eye into her tea. She was all alone. Fleur had completely deserted her; Gillian was on the other side of the garden, chatting merrily to some woman Philippa had never met before. No-one had even asked her how she was, or why she looked so pale; no-one was interested in her. She took a sip of tea and looked wanly around. But everybody was laughing or talking or enjoying the music.

Suddenly she saw Zara and Antony coming towards her table. She gazed into the middle distance and pushed the plate of scones very slightly away from her to indicate her loss of appetite.

'Hi Philippa!' Antony's voice was exuberant. 'Is there enough tea for us?'

'Plenty,' whispered Philippa.

'Cool,' said Zara. She beamed at Philippa. 'You won't guess how well Antony played. Tell her, Antony.'

'I went round in sixty-eight,' said Antony, blushing red. A huge smile spread across his face.

'Sixty-eight!' echoed Zara.

'Is that good?' said Philippa dully.

'Of course it's good! It's the best!'

'Because of my handicap,' put in Antony quickly. 'My handicap's still pretty high, so I should do quite well.'

'You should win, you mean,' said Zara. 'Antony's the champion!'

'Sssh!' said Antony awkwardly. 'I'm not! Not yet.'

'Wait till we see your dad! You did better than him, you know!'

'I know,' said Antony. 'I feel a bit bad about that.'

Zara rolled her eyes.

'That's so typical. If I could ever beat Fleur at anything, I'd never let her forget it.'

'Where is Fleur?' said Philippa in a high-pitched voice.

'With Johnny, I guess.'

'Johnny?'

'This friend of ours,' said Zara casually. 'He came down on a surprise visit. He's, like, her closest friend.'

'I see,' said Philippa.

'Oh, and guess what,' said Antony. 'Xanthe Forrester's asked us to her parents' cottage in Cornwall. Just for a few days. D'you think Dad'll let us go?'

'I've no idea,' said Philippa dully. Jealousy was rising sickeningly inside her. Fleur's closest friend was a man named Johnny; a man Philippa had never heard of. She had rushed off to be with him and she hadn't given Philippa another thought.

'I bloody well hope he does,' said Antony. He looked at Zara. 'Shall we have a quick look at the scoreboard?'

'Absolutely,' said Zara, grinning at him. 'Let's look at all those other losers' scores and gloat.'

'No!' protested Antony. 'Just look.'

'You can just look if you like,' said Zara. 'I'm going to gloat.'

By six o'clock the final scores were in, and Antony was officially declared the winner of the Club Cup. As the result was announced, a cheer went up and Antony blushed bright scarlet.

'Well done!' exclaimed Richard. 'Antony, I'm so proud of you!' He patted Antony on the shoulder, and Antony blushed even deeper.

'I knew he was going to win!' said Zara to Richard. 'I just knew it!'

'So did I,' said Gillian, beaming. 'I made pavlova especially.'

'Cool,' said Antony.

'How lovely this all is,' said Fleur. 'Have I said well done yet? Say well done, Johnny.'

'Congratulations, young man,' said Johnny. 'I despise the game of golf and everything associated with it, but congratulations nevertheless.'

'Are you staying for supper?' said Gillian.

'Alas, no,' said Johnny. 'London calls. But I do hope to visit again in a week's time. You'll be back from Cornwall by then?' he said to Zara.

'Sure.'

'Good,' said Johnny. 'Because I'm going to bring you a present.'

Philippa and Lambert joined the group, and a slight pall fell over the atmosphere.

'You're starting early, Lambert,' said Fleur brightly, looking at the brandy glass in Lambert's hand.

'Well played, Antony,' said Lambert, ignoring Fleur and shaking Antony's hand a little too firmly. 'I played like shit.' He took a swig from his glass. 'Like complete shit.'

'I had no idea you were any good at golf, Antony,' said Philippa feebly. She tried to move closer to Fleur. 'Did you know, Fleur?'

'Of course I knew,' said Fleur warmly.

'Well, of course, I've been a bit distracted lately,' began Philippa, in a low voice. But she was interrupted by Johnny.

'My train! It leaves in fifteen minutes! I must call a taxi.'

'Someone will drive you,' said Fleur. 'Who's got a car? Lambert. Would you mind driving Johnny to the station?'

'I don't suppose so,' said Lambert grudgingly.

'Yes, you drive him, Lambert,' said Philippa at once. 'We'll see you back at the house.'

'Excellent,' said Fleur. 'And there'll be room for me too, in your nice big car.' Before Philippa could say anything the three of them rushed off. She stared after them in dismay, and felt a hurt anger growing in her chest. Fleur was behaving as though she wasn't there. As though she just didn't exist; as though she didn't matter.

'Are you all right, Philippa?' said Gillian.

'I'm fine,' snapped Philippa, and turned away. She didn't want Gillian's attention; Gillian was no good. She had to have Fleur.

As the others walked back to The Maples, Zara fell into step with Richard.

'Antony played so well today,' she said. 'You should be really proud of him.'

'I am,' said Richard, smiling at her.

'He was really . . .' Zara screwed up her face to think of the word. 'He was really confident,' she said eventually. 'Really masterful. You should have seen him.'

'He's come on a lot this summer,' said Richard.

'And it's like, he forgot all that birthmark stuff. He just played.'

'What did you say?' Richard frowned at her.

'You know. All that grief with the birthmark.'

'What exactly do you mean?' said Richard carefully. Zara lowered her voice.

'He told me how his mother hated it.' She shrugged. 'You know, the thing with the eyepatch and everything. But I guess he's put it behind him. And I think it really made a difference.'

'Zara, what—' Richard could barely speak. He

swallowed, and took a deep breath. 'What thing with the eyepatch?'

'Oh.' Zara looked up at him and bit her lip. 'You don't know? I guess neither of them ever told you.'

In the car, on the way back from the station, Fleur took out a compact. Ignoring Lambert, she began to paint her lips with a long golden brush. Out of the corner of his eye Lambert watched, mesmerized, as she smoothed on the deep glossy colour. With his eyes off the road, he swerved erratically a couple of times into the next lane, and the car behind hooted angrily.

'Lambert!' exclaimed Fleur. 'Are you all right to drive?' She leaned towards him, and sniffed. 'How many brandies did you have at the club?'

'I'm fine,' said Lambert shortly. He pulled up at a set of traffic lights and the car began to throb gently. He could smell Fleur's scent; could see her legs, stretched out in front of him. Long, pale, expensive legs.

'So, Fleur,' he said. 'You're enjoying living with Richard, are you?'

'Of course,' said Fleur. 'Richard's such a wonderful man.'

'A wealthy man, too,' said Lambert.

'Really?' said Fleur innocently.

'He's a fucking wealthy man,' said Lambert. He turned to look at Fleur, and she gave a slight shrug. 'Don't tell me you didn't know he was wealthy,' he said, scowling.

'I hadn't really thought about it.'

'Oh come on!'

'Lambert, let's just get home, shall we?'

'Home,' said Lambert mockingly. 'Yes, I suppose it is your home now, isn't it. Lady consort of Mr Filthy Fucking Rich.'

'Lambert,' said Fleur, in steely tones, 'you're drunk. You shouldn't be driving.'

'Crap.'

The lights turned to amber and Lambert thrust his foot down on the accelerator.

'So you're not interested in money, is that it?' he said, above the noise of the engine. 'You must be the only person in the whole fucking world who isn't.'

'You are a sordid man, aren't you?' said Fleur quietly.

'What's that?'

'You're sordid! A nasty, sordid man!'

'I live in the real world, all right?' Lambert was breathing heavily; his face was growing pink.

'We all live in the real world.'

'What, you? Don't make me laugh! What kind of real world do you live in? No job, no worries, just lie back and take the money.'

Fleur's jaw tightened; she said nothing.

'I suppose you thought Richard was a good bet, did you?' continued Lambert, in slurred tones. 'Spotted him from a mile off. Probably came to his wife's memorial service on purpose to catch him.'

'We're nearly home,' said Fleur. 'Thank God.' She looked at Lambert. 'You could have killed us both. And Johnny.'

'I wish I had. One less poofter on the face of the earth.' There was a short silence.

'I won't hit you,' said Fleur in a trembling voice, 'because you're driving and I don't want to cause an accident. But if you ever say anything like that again . . .'

'You'll beat me up? Well I'm terrified.'

'I won't beat you up,' said Fleur. 'Some of Johnny's friends might.' They pulled into the drive of The

Maples, and immediately Fleur opened the door. She looked at Lambert witheringly.

'You make me sick,' she said, and slammed it.

Lambert stared after her, feeling the blood pounding round his head and a slight confusion in his brain. Did he despise her or did he fancy her? She was bloody pissed off with him, at any rate.

He took out his hip flask and swigged some brandy. Sordid, was he? She should try having an overdraft of fucking three hundred thousand pounds. A familiar feeling of panic stole over him, and he took another swig of brandy. He had to do something about that overdraft. He had to get going now, before everyone started assembling for supper and wondering where he was. He looked at the front door, slightly ajar. Fleur had probably run straight off to Richard, to complain about him. Just like a woman. Lambert grinned to himself. Let her complain; let her say what she liked. At least it would keep Richard out of the way for a while.

When they got back to the house, Richard paused.

'I think,' he said to Zara, 'I'd like to have a moment alone with Antony. If you don't mind.'

'Of course not,' said Zara. 'I think he'll be in the garden. We were going to play badminton.' She looked up at Richard, face screwed up uncertainly. 'You don't mind that I told you about the eyepatch, do you?'

'No!' Richard swallowed. 'Of course I don't mind. You did just the right thing.'

He found Antony standing by the badminton post, patiently unwinding the net. For a moment he just stared at his son; his tall, kind, talented son. His perfect son.

'Come here,' he said, as Antony looked up. 'Let me congratulate you properly.'

He pulled Antony towards him and hugged him tightly. 'My boy,' he murmured against Antony's hair, and suddenly found himself trying to fight back tears. 'My boy.' He blinked a few times, then released Antony.

'I'm desperately proud of you,' he said.

'It's quite cool,' said Antony, giving an unwilling grin. He looked down at the badminton net. 'So you don't . . . you don't mind that I beat you, do you?'

'Mind?' Richard gazed at him. 'Of course I don't mind! It's time for you to start beating me. You're a man now!' A pink, embarrassed tinge spread slowly up Antony's neck, and Richard smiled to himself.

'But, Antony, it's not just your talent at golf that I'm proud of,' he continued. 'I'm proud of all of you. Every single little bit of you.' He paused. 'And I know that Mummy was proud of you too.'

Antony said nothing. His hands clenched tightly around the tangled strings of the badminton net.

'She may not always have shown it,' said Richard slowly. 'It was . . . difficult for her sometimes. But she was very proud of you. And she loved you more than anything in the world.'

'Really?' said Antony in a shaky voice, without looking up.

'She loved you more than anything in the world,' repeated Richard. For a few minutes there was silence. Richard watched as Antony's face slowly relaxed; as his hands loosened around the net. A small smile appeared on the boy's face and suddenly he took a huge breath, almost as though to begin life again.

You believe me, thought Richard; you believe me without question. Thank God for your trusting soul.

Zara had elected to join Gillian in the kitchen, unstacking the dishwasher while Gillian tipped salad leaves out of their plastic packets into a huge wooden bowl. She listened patiently while Gillian chattered away about some trip she was planning, all the time wondering what Antony's dad was saying to him.

'Such a coincidence!' Gillian was saying happily. 'Eleanor's always wanted to go to Egypt too. Apparently Geoffrey refuses to go on holiday anywhere that doesn't have a golf course.'

'So, will you see the Pyramids?'

'Of course! And we'll take a cruise up the Nile.'

'Then you'll get murdered,' said Zara. 'Like in Agatha Christie.' Gillian laughed.

'Do you know, that's just what Eleanor said.'

'I guess it's what everyone says.' Zara picked up a pan and looked at it. 'What the hell's this?'

'It's an asparagus steamer,' said Gillian tartly. 'And don't swear.' Zara rolled her eyes.

'You're as bad as Felix. He makes you put a pound in the swear box.'

'A jolly good idea. We had the same thing at school.'

'Yes well,' said Zara. 'This is the nineties, or hadn't you noticed?'

'I had noticed,' said Gillian. 'But thank you for pointing it out.' She picked up two bottles of salad dressing. 'Shall we have basil or garlic?'

'Both,' suggested Zara. 'Just kind of mix them together.'

'All right,' said Gillian. 'But if it goes wrong, I'm blaming you.'

They both looked up as Fleur came into the kitchen.

'Oh hi,' said Zara. 'Did Johnny make his train all right?'

'Just about,' said Fleur. 'Thank God we weren't both killed. Lambert was drunk! He was swerving about all over the place!'

'Jesus!' said Zara. She glanced at Gillian. 'I mean, goodness me!'

'Sit down,' said Gillian, hurrying over to Fleur. 'You poor thing!' She frowned. 'You know, it's not the first time this has happened. That Lambert should be prosecuted!'

'Let's call the cops,' said Zara eagerly.

'Put the kettle on, Zara,' said Gillian, 'and make your mother a nice cup of tea.'

'No thanks,' said Fleur. 'I think I'll go upstairs and have a bath.'

'Try on a few hats,' said Zara. 'That should cheer you up.'

'That's enough, Zara,' said Gillian. She looked at Fleur. 'Has Richard heard about this?'

'Not yet.'

'Well, he should.'

'Yes,' said Fleur. 'He will.'

She went out into the hall and began to climb the stairs. As she did so, a voice rang out from below.

'Fleur! There you are! I've been trying to find you all day!'

Fleur looked round. Philippa was hurrying towards her, red-faced, panting slightly.

'Fleur, we need to have a talk,' she was saying. 'I've got so much to tell you. About—' She swallowed, and wiped a tear from her eye. 'About me and Lambert. You just won't believe—'

'Philippa,' interrupted Fleur sharply, 'not now, darling. I'm really not in the mood. And if you want to know why, you can ask your husband.' And before Philippa could reply, she hurried upstairs.

Philippa gazed after Fleur, feeling hurt, disbelieving tears coming to her eyes. Fleur didn't want to talk to her. Fleur had abandoned her. She felt sick with misery and anger. Now she had no friends; no audience; no-one to tell her story to. And it was all because of Lambert. Lambert had somehow made Fleur angry. He spoiled everything. Philippa clenched her fists and felt her heart begin to beat more quickly. Lambert had ruined her life, she thought furiously. He'd ruined her entire life, and no-one even knew about it. He deserved punishment. He deserved for everyone to know what he was really like. He deserved revenge.

Chapter Seventeen

Half an hour later, supper was ready.

'Where on earth is everybody?' said Gillian, looking up from the oven. 'Where's Philippa?'

'Haven't seen her,' said Antony, opening a bottle of wine.

'And Lambert?'

'Who cares about him?' said Zara. 'Let's just start eating anyway.'

'Actually, I think I saw Philippa in the garden,' said Antony. 'When we were playing badminton.'

'I'll go and fetch her,' said Gillian. 'And can you please tell everybody else that supper's ready?'

'OK,' said Antony.

When Gillian had gone, he went to the door of the kitchen and called, 'Supper's ready!' Then he looked back at Zara and shrugged. 'It's not my fault if they can't hear.' He poured himself a glass of wine and took a sip.

'Hey,' said Zara. 'What about me? Don't I get some?' Antony looked up in surprise.

'You never drink wine!'

'There's always a first time,' said Zara, reaching for his glass. She took a cautious sip and wrinkled her nose. 'I guess it's an acquired taste. I think I'll stick to Diet Coke.'

'There's some in the larder,' said Antony. He looked at Zara and got to his feet.

'There's some in the fridge, too,' said Zara, giggling. But she got up and followed him into the larder. Antony closed the door behind them and put his arms around Zara. Their mouths met with accustomed ease; the door creaked slightly as they leaned against it.

'You're bloody sexy,' said Antony in blurred tones as they separated.

'So are you,' murmured Zara. Encouraged, his hand began to trace a cautious route down her spine.

'I don't suppose there's any chance . . .'

'No,' said Zara cheerfully. 'Absolutely none.'

Lambert heard Antony's voice calling out downstairs and felt a spasm of panic rush through him. He had to hurry; had to get out of Richard's office before everyone started to wonder where he was. Frowning, he started typing again, glancing every few seconds towards the door, trying frantically to formulate the right words in his mind.

He'd found a sheaf of Richard's personal writing paper and an old typewriter. He had the details of Richard's bank account in front of him, and the name of his lawyer and a copy of his signature. It should have been easy to knock off a quick all-purpose letter, proving that Richard was in the process of making his daughter – and therefore Lambert – seriously wealthy.

It should have been easy. But Lambert's eyes kept blurring over; his mind felt slow and ponderous; his thoughts were distracted every so often by a sudden memory of Fleur's legs. He jabbed at the typewriter viciously, trying to hurry, cursing every time he made a mistake. He'd already ruined five sheets of paper; torn them out and thrown them on the floor. The whole thing was a nightmare.

He took a swig of brandy and tried to focus his mind.

He just needed to concentrate; to hurry up and finish the bloody thing, then get downstairs; behave normally. And then he'd wait for First Bank to phone. 'Oh, you want a guarantee, do you?' he'd say, in tones of surprise. 'You should have said. How's a letter of instruction to Mr Favour's lawyer?' That would stop them in their tracks. They weren't going to question Richard fucking Favour, were they?

'Sum,' he said aloud, hitting each key very carefully, 'of f-i-v-e million. Full stop.'

Five million. God, if it were true, thought Lambert hazily, if it were only true . . .

'Lambert?' A voice interrupted his thoughts, and Lambert's heart stopped beating. Slowly he raised his head. Richard was standing at the door, gazing at him incredulously. 'Just what do you think you're doing?'

Gillian's mind was happily drifting through imagined pictures of Egypt as she wandered out into the garden. There was a lightness inside her; a lightness which gave energy to her feet, which caused her to smile to herself and hum ill-remembered snatches of popular songs. A holiday with Eleanor Forrester. With Eleanor Forrester of all people! Once upon a time she would have said 'No' automatically; would have thought the scheme quite out of the question. But now she thought, why not? Why should she not at last travel to an exotic, faraway land? Why should she not give Eleanor a chance as a travelling companion? She pictured herself wandering along dusty, sandy paths, gazing up with awe at the remains of a distant, fascinating civilization. Feeling the sun of a different continent beating down on her shoulders; listening to the babbling sounds of an unfamiliar language. Bartering for presents at a colourful street market.

Suddenly, a cracking sound underfoot brought her back to the real world. She looked down at the grass. A glass jar had been left out on the lawn.

'Dangerous!' said Gillian aloud, picking it up. She peered at it. It was an aspirin bottle and it was empty. Somebody must have left it outside without meaning to. There would be some commonsense explanation for its presence in the grass. Nevertheless, a twinge of alarm went through her and without meaning to, she increased her pace.

'Philippa!' she called. 'Supper's ready. Are you in the garden?'

There was a silence. Then suddenly Gillian heard a little groan.

'Philippa!' she called again, sharply. 'Is that you?' She began to walk towards the sound; she found herself running.

Behind the rose bushes at the bottom of the garden, Philippa was lying on the grass, her arms thrown out and her chin stained with vomit. Pinned to her chest was a neatly written letter beginning 'To Everyone I Know'. And beside her on the ground was a second empty aspirin bottle.

'You'd better explain yourself,' said Richard quietly. He looked at the sheet of paper in his hand. 'If this is what I think it is, then you have a lot of explaining to do.'

'It . . . it was a prank,' said Lambert. He stared desperately at Richard, trying to breathe calmly; trying to quell the terrified pounding in his head. He swallowed; his throat felt like sandpaper. 'A jape.'

'No, Lambert,' said Richard. 'This isn't a jape. This is fraud.'

Lambert licked his lips.

'Look, Richard,' he said. 'All it is is a letter. I mean
. . . I wasn't going to use it.'

'Oh really,' said Richard at once. 'And for what purpose were you not going to use it?'

'You don't understand!' Lambert tried a little laugh.

'No, I don't understand!' Richard's voice snapped
through the air. 'I don't understand how you could
possibly think it permissible to enter this office without my consent, to look through my private affairs and
to write a letter purporting to be from myself to my
solicitor. As for the content of the letter . . .' He flicked
it with his hand. 'I find that the most perplexing of all.'

'You mean . . .' Lambert stared at Richard and felt
sick. So Emily had lied to him. She'd been playing
games with him. That money wasn't coming to
Philippa after all. A white-hot fury swept through his
body, obliterating caution; wiping out fear.

'It's all right for you!' he suddenly found himself
shouting. 'You've got millions!'

'Lambert, you're forgetting yourself.'

'Emily told me I'd be a rich man! Emily said
Philippa was coming into a trust. She said I'd be able
to afford anything I wanted! But she was bloody lying,
wasn't she?'

Richard stared at him, unable to speak.

'Emily said that?' he said at last, in a voice which
shook slightly.

'She said I'd married a millionairess. And I believed
her!'

Richard stared at him in sudden comprehension.

'You owe money, is that it?'

'Of course that's it. I owe money. Just like everyone
else in the world. Everyone except you, of course.'
Lambert scowled. 'I've got an overdraft of three
hundred thousand pounds.' He looked up and met

Richard's incredulous eyes. 'Nothing compared to ten million, is it? You could pay it off tomorrow.'

Richard gazed at Lambert, trying to control his revulsion; reminding himself that Lambert was still his son-in-law.

'Does Philippa know about this?' he asked eventually.

'Of course not.'

'Thank God,' muttered Richard. He looked again at the paper in his hand. 'And what precisely were you planning to do with this?'

'Show it to the bank,' Lambert said. 'I thought it would keep them quiet for a while.'

'So you're brainless as well as dishonest!'

Lambert shrugged. For a few minutes they stared at each other in mutual dislike.

'I'm . . . I'm going to have to think about this,' said Richard at last. 'In the meantime, can I ask you not to mention it to Philippa. Or . . . anyone else.'

'Fine by me,' said Lambert, and he grinned cockily at Richard. Something inside Richard snapped.

'Don't you dare smile at me!' he shouted. 'You've got nothing to smile about! You're a dishonest, unprincipled . . . fraudster! My God, how did Philippa manage to fall in love with you?'

'My natural charm, I suppose,' said Lambert, running a hand through his hair.

'Just get out!' said Richard, shaking with rage. 'Get out of my office, before I . . . before I . . .' He stopped, struggling for words, and Lambert's mouth twisted into a sneer.

But before either of them could say anything else, they were interrupted by Gillian's voice, shrieking from the hall downstairs.

'Richard! Come quickly please! It's Philippa!'

Gillian had dragged Philippa into the house and dialled for an ambulance. By the time the two men arrived downstairs, Philippa was sitting up and moaning faintly.

'I think she's brought most of the pills back up again,' said Gillian. She frowned, and wiped a tear brusquely away from her eye. 'The silly, silly girl!'

Richard stared in speechless shock at his daughter; at her ungainly, unhappy form.

'Surely she didn't really want to . . .' he began, then stopped, unable to form the words in his mouth.

'Of course not,' said Gillian. 'It was a . . .' her voice faltered, 'a cry for help.'

'But she always seemed—' said Richard, and halted. He'd been about to say Philippa had always seemed happy. But suddenly he realized it wasn't true. It came to him that since she'd grown up, he'd rarely seen Philippa looking positively happy. She'd always seemed anxious, or sulky; when she was in high spirits there was always a slightly hysterical edge to her mood.

But he'd assumed she was more or less all right. Now a miserable guilt plunged through his body. I should have brought happiness to her life, he found himself thinking. I should have made sure she was happy and stable and content. But I left it to her mother and then I left it to her husband. And they failed her. We all failed her.

'Philippa,' said Lambert, bending down. 'Can you hear me?'

Philippa's eyes opened and she gave a louder moan.

'Lambert,' said Gillian. 'I think you should keep away from her.'

'Why?' said Lambert truculently. 'I'm her husband.'

'There was a note,' said Gillian. She passed it to Richard; as he skimmed it with his eyes his face darkened. A vein began to beat in his forehead.

'Give it to me,' said Lambert. 'I've got every right . . .'

'You have no rights!' spat Richard. 'No rights at all!'

'The ambulance is here,' said Gillian suddenly, looking out of the window. 'Who's going to go with her?'

'I will,' said Lambert.

'No,' said Richard at once, 'you won't. I will.'

On the way to the hospital, Richard gazed down at his daughter's face; held her head as she retched into a cardboard dish and smoothed her hair back.

'I didn't want to marry him,' she muttered, and tears coursed down her swollen face. 'He makes me sick!'

'All right, sweetheart,' said Richard gently. 'We'll be there soon. You'll be all right.'

'It was Mummy,' cried Philippa. 'She made me marry Lambert! She said I was ugly and I wasn't a . . .' She broke off and gazed at him with red-rimmed eyes. 'Did you really hate Jim?'

'Who's Jim?' asked Richard helplessly. But Philippa was vomiting again. Richard stared at her in silence. A heavy, bleak depression was creeping through him; he felt as though his happy family of shining jewels was being turned over one by one to reveal a swarm of ugly maggots. What else didn't he know? What else wasn't he being told?

'Where's Fleur?' said Philippa, as soon as she was able to sit up again. 'Does she know?'

'I'm not sure,' said Richard soothingly. 'We needn't tell her if you don't want us to.'

'But I do want her to know!' cried Philippa hysterically. 'I want her to be with me!'

'Yes, darling,' said Richard, feeling suddenly close to tears. 'Yes, so do I.'

Much later Richard arrived home, weary and depressed, to find everyone waiting in the hall for him.

'What happened?' asked Fleur. She hurried over and took his hand. 'Darling, I was so shocked when I heard about it.'

'They're keeping her in overnight,' said Richard. 'They don't think any damage has been done. They're going to . . .' He swallowed. 'They're going to set up some counselling for her.'

'Can we, like, go and visit her?' said Antony uncertainly. Richard looked at him, sitting on the stairs with Zara, and smiled. 'She'll be home tomorrow. Honestly, there's nothing to worry about. It was just a silly scare.'

'But why did she do it?' said Antony. 'I mean, didn't she realize? Didn't she think how frightened we'd all be?'

'I don't think she thought very hard about it at all,' said Richard gently. 'She's a bit confused at the moment.' Suddenly he looked around sharply. 'Where's Lambert?'

'Gone,' said Gillian. 'I packed him off to a hotel for the night.' Her mouth tightened. 'He was too drunk to drive.'

'Well done, Gillian.' Richard's eyes met hers. 'And thank you. If you hadn't gone looking for Philippa . . .'

'Yes, well.' Gillian looked away. 'Let's not think about that.' She glanced at her watch. 'It's late. Time for bed. Antony, Zara, off you go.'

'OK,' said Antony in a subdued voice. 'Well, good night everyone.'

'Good night,' said Zara.

'Antony, I'm sorry we didn't get to celebrate your win properly,' said Richard, suddenly remembering. 'But we will. Another time.'

'Sure, Dad. G'night.'

'I think I'll turn in, too,' said Gillian. She looked at Richard. 'Are you hungry?'

'No,' said Richard. 'Not hungry.' He looked at Fleur. 'But I think I could do with a glass of whisky.' She smiled.

'I'll pour you one,' she said, and disappeared into the drawing room. Richard looked at Gillian.

'Gillian,' he said quietly. 'Did you have any idea that this was on the cards? Did you realize Philippa was so unhappy?'

'No,' said Gillian. 'I had no idea.' She bit her lip. 'And yet when I look back, I wonder whether it wasn't obvious all along. Whether I should have noticed something.'

'Exactly,' said Richard. 'That's exactly how I feel.'

'I feel I let her down,' said Gillian.

'You didn't,' said Richard in suddenly fierce tones. 'You didn't let her down! If anyone let her down, it was her mother.'

'What?' Gillian stared at him.

'Emily let her down! Emily was a . . .' He broke off, breathing hard, and Gillian stared at him in dismay. For a few moments neither said anything.

'I was always convinced that there was a hidden side to Emily,' said Richard. 'I was desperate to find out more about her character.' He looked up bleakly. 'And now it seems that the sweet, innocent Emily I knew was only a . . . a façade! I didn't know the true Emily! I wouldn't have *wanted* to know the true Emily!'

'Oh Richard.' Tears glittered in Gillian's eyes. 'Emily wasn't all bad, you know.'

'I know she wasn't.' Richard rubbed his face. 'But I'd always thought she was perfect.'

'No-one's perfect,' said Gillian quietly. 'No-one in the world is perfect.'

'I know,' said Richard. 'I was a fool. A gullible fool.'

'You're no fool,' said Gillian. She got to her feet. 'Go and drink your whisky. And forget about Emily.' She met his eyes. 'It's time to move on.'

'Yes,' said Richard slowly. 'It is, isn't it?'

Fleur was sitting on the sofa in the drawing room, two tumblers of whisky at her side.

'You poor thing,' she murmured as Richard entered the room. 'What a horrendous evening.'

'You don't know the half of it,' said Richard. He picked up his glass of whisky and drained it. 'Sometimes, Fleur, I wonder if there are any decent people left in the world.'

'What do you mean?' said Fleur, getting up and replenishing his glass. 'Did something else happen tonight?'

'It's almost too sordid to recount,' said Richard. 'You'll be disgusted when you hear.'

'What?' She sat back down on the sofa and looked expectantly at Richard. He sighed and kicked off his shoes.

'Earlier this evening, I found Lambert in my office, attempting to forge a letter from me to my solicitors. He's in money trouble, and he hoped that my name would help to keep his creditors off his back.' Richard took another slug of whisky and shook his head. 'The whole thing is despicable.'

'Is he in serious money trouble?'

'Yes, I'm afraid so.' Richard frowned.

'Don't tell me any more if you don't want to,' said Fleur quickly. Richard took her hand and gave her a wan smile.

'Thank you, darling, for being so sensitive. But I don't have any secrets from you. And it's actually a relief to talk to someone about it.' He sighed. 'Lambert had been given the impression by . . . by someone . . . that Philippa was soon to come into a lot of money. And on the strength of that he began to spend well beyond his means.'

'Oh dear,' said Fleur. She wrinkled her brow. 'Is that why Philippa . . .'

'No. Philippa doesn't know about the money. But they had had a row. Philippa threatened to leave Lambert and things became rather nasty.' Richard looked at Fleur. 'Apparently you and she had a long talk about it in London.'

'Hardly a long talk,' said Fleur, frowning slightly.

'Nevertheless, she found your advice very helpful. She's desperate to see you.' Richard stroked Fleur's hair. 'I think she's beginning to see you as a mother-figure.'

'I'm not sure about that,' said Fleur, giving a little laugh.

'As for Lambert . . .' Richard shrugged. 'I've no idea whether he and Philippa will manage to patch things up, or whether he should be sent packing.'

'Sent packing,' said Fleur, with a shudder. 'He's odious.'

'And dishonest,' said Richard. 'I find it hard to believe now that he didn't marry Philippa for her money in the first place.'

'Is she rich, then?' said Fleur casually.

'She will be,' said Richard. 'When she turns thirty.' He took another swig of whisky. 'The irony is, I only signed the papers this morning.'

For a moment, Fleur was very still, then she looked up and said lightly, 'What papers?'

'This morning I signed a very large amount of money over into trust for Antony and Philippa.' He smiled at her. 'Five million each, as a matter of fact.'

Fleur stared at Richard for a few seconds.

'Five million each,' she said slowly. 'That makes ten million.' She paused, seeming to listen to the words.

'I know it seems like a lot of money,' said Richard. 'But I wanted to give them financial independence. And I'll still be more than comfortable.'

'You've just given all that money away,' said Fleur faintly. 'To your children.'

'They don't know about it yet,' said Richard. 'But I know I can trust you to keep this to yourself.'

'Of course,' murmured Fleur. She drained her glass and looked up. 'Could you . . . do you think you could pour me another whisky, please?'

Richard rose, poured another measure of the amber liquid into Fleur's glass and walked back over towards her. Suddenly he stopped.

'Fleur, what am I waiting for?' he exclaimed. 'There's something I've been meaning to ask you for a long time. I know that tonight's been very upsetting, but maybe . . . maybe that gives me even more reason to do what I'm about to do.'

Kneeling down on the carpet, still clutching her whisky glass, Richard looked up at Fleur.

'Fleur,' he said, in a trembling voice. 'Fleur, my darling, will you marry me?'

Chapter Eighteen

Early the next morning, a white Jeep pulled up outside The Maples and hooted loudly, waking Richard. Rubbing his eyes, he padded over to the bedroom window and looked out.

'It's Antony's friends,' he said to Fleur. 'They must be leaving early for Cornwall.'

Suddenly there was a knock at the door and Antony's voice said, 'Dad? We're going!'

Richard opened the door and looked at Antony and Zara, standing on the landing. They were dressed identically, in jeans and baseball caps, and each was loaded down with a huge squashy bag.

'So,' he said. 'Off to Cornwall. You will behave yourselves, won't you?'

'Of course we will,' said Antony impatiently. 'Anyway, Xanthe's mum's going to be there.'

'I know,' said Richard. 'I spoke to her yesterday. And mentioned a few ground rules.'

'Dad! What did you say?'

'Nothing very much,' said Richard grinning. 'Just that you were to have a cold bath every morning, followed by an hour of Shakespeare . . .'

'Dad!'

'I'm sure you'll have a lovely time,' said Richard, relenting. 'And we'll see you back here on Friday.'

From outside, the Jeep hooted again.

'Right,' said Antony. He looked at Zara. 'Well, we'd better go.'

'I hope Philippa's OK,' said Zara.

'Yeah.' Antony looked up at Richard and bit his lip. 'I hope she's . . .'

'She'll be fine,' said Richard reassuringly. 'Don't worry. Now, off you go, before Xanthe starts that infernal noise again.'

He watched as they shuffled down the stairs. Zara was almost bent double under the weight of her bag, and he wondered briefly what on earth she was carrying. Then, as he heard the front door slam, he turned back to Fleur.

'That was Antony and Zara,' he said unnecessarily. 'Off to Cornwall.'

'Mmm.' Fleur turned over sleepily, rumpling the duvet around her body. Richard stared at her for a moment, then took a deep breath.

'I don't know what time you want to leave,' he said. 'I'll take you to the station. Just tell me when.'

'All right,' said Fleur. She opened her eyes. 'You don't mind, do you Richard? I just need to have some time to think.'

'Of course you do,' said Richard, forcing a cheerful note into his voice. 'I completely understand. I wouldn't expect you to rush your decision.'

He sat down on the bed and looked at her. Her arms were lying on the pillow above her head; graceful arms, like a ballerina's. Her eyes had drifted shut again, recapturing the sweet sleep of morning. Through his mind passed the possibility that she might refuse him. And with it came a stab of pain, so strong and sharp it almost frightened him.

Downstairs, Gillian was making a pot of tea. She

looked up as Richard entered the kitchen.

'I saw them go,' she said. 'That young man, Mex, was driving. I hope he's responsible.'

'I'm sure he is,' said Richard. He sat down at the kitchen table and looked around.

'The house seems awfully quiet,' he said. 'I miss the thumping music already.' Gillian smiled, and put a mug of tea in front of him.

'What's going to happen about Philippa?' she said. 'Will she come out of hospital today?'

'Yes,' said Richard. 'Unless anything's happened overnight. I'll go and pick her up this morning.'

'I'll come with you,' said Gillian. 'If that's all right.'

'Of course it's all right,' said Richard. 'I'm sure she'd love to see you.' He took a sip of tea, marshalling his thoughts, then looked up. 'There's something else I should tell you,' he said. 'Fleur's going to London for a few days.'

'I see,' said Gillian. She looked at Richard's taut, pale face. 'You're not going too?' she said hesitantly.

'No,' said Richard. 'Not this time. Fleur . . .' He rubbed his face. 'Fleur needs a little time on her own. To . . . think about things.'

'I see,' said Gillian again.

'She'll be back by Saturday,' said Richard.

'Oh well,' said Gillian cheerfully. 'That's hardly any time at all.' Richard smiled wanly and drained his mug. Gillian looked anxiously at him. 'Would Fleur like some tea, do you think?' she asked. 'I'm about to go upstairs.'

'She doesn't want tea,' said Richard, suddenly remembering. 'But she asked if I could bring her up *The Times*.'

'*The Times*,' said Gillian, looking about the kitchen. 'Here it is. I'll take it up to her if you like.' She picked up the crisp, folded newspaper and looked at it curiously. 'Fleur doesn't usually read the paper,' she said. 'I wonder what she wants it for.'

'I don't know,' said Richard, pouring himself another cup of tea. 'I didn't ask.'

By ten o'clock, Fleur was ready to leave.

'We'll drop you at the station,' said Richard, carrying her suitcase down the stairs, 'and then go on to the hospital.' He paused. 'Philippa will be upset not to see you,' he added lightly.

'It's a shame,' said Fleur. Her eyes met Richard's. 'But I really don't feel I can . . .'

'No,' said Richard hastily. 'Of course not. I shouldn't have said anything.'

'You're a sweet man,' said Fleur, and ran her hand down Richard's arm. 'And I do hope Philippa comes through this.'

'She'll be all right,' said Gillian, coming into the hall. 'We'll keep her at home for a bit; look after her properly. By the time you come back, she'll probably be right as rain.' She looked at Fleur. 'You look very smart,' she said, 'all in black.'

'Such a useful colour to wear in London,' murmured Fleur. 'It doesn't show the dirt.'

'Will you be staying with your friend Johnny?' asked Gillian. 'Could we reach you there if there was an emergency with Zara?'

'I probably won't stay there, no,' said Fleur. 'I'll probably check into a hotel.' She frowned slightly. 'I'll call you when I've arrived and leave a number.'

'Good,' said Richard. He looked uncertainly at Gillian. 'Well. I suppose we ought to get going.'

As they walked out into the drive, Fleur looked back at the house appraisingly.

'It's a welcoming house, this, isn't it?' she said suddenly. 'A friendly house.'

'Yes,' said Richard eagerly. 'Very friendly. It's . . . well, I think it's a lovely house to have as a home.' Fleur met his eye.

'Yes,' she said kindly, and opened the car door. 'Yes, Richard, I'm sure it is.'

Philippa was sitting up in bed when Richard and Gillian arrived. She watched them walking through the ward, and automatically tried to give them a bright smile. But her mouth felt awkward and her cheeks stiff. She felt as though she might never smile again; as though the freezing shame sinking through her body had caused all her natural reactions to seize up.

She hadn't thought it would be like this. She'd thought she was committing the ultimate romantic gesture; that she'd wake up to find everyone gathered round her bed, blinking back their tears and stroking her hand and promising to make her life better. Instead of which she'd woken to a series of humiliating assaults on her body, administered by nurses with civil phrases on their lips and contempt in their eyes. When she'd glimpsed her father's devastated face, something inside her had crumpled, and she'd felt like crying. Except that suddenly she couldn't cry any more. The ready fountain of tears inside her had dried up; the backdrop of romantic fantasy had fallen, and what was left was cold and dry, like a stone.

She licked her lips as her father and Gillian drew near, took a breath and carefully said, 'Hello.' Her voice sounded strange and tinny to her own ears.

'Hello darling!'

'Hello, Philippa.' Gillian smiled cheerfully at her. 'How are you doing?'

'Much better,' said Philippa carefully. She felt as

though she were speaking a foreign language.

'You can come home today,' said her father. 'The discharge papers are ready.'

'That's good,' said Philippa. From a long way away, a thought occurred to her. 'Is Fleur at home?'

'No,' said her father. 'Fleur's gone to London for a few days.'

'I see,' said Philippa. A dulled flicker of disappointment ran through her and died almost immediately. 'Is she coming back?' she asked politely.

'Yes,' said Gillian at once, before Richard could answer. 'Yes, of course she's coming back.'

In the car, very little was said. When they got home, Gillian brought bowls of chicken soup into the conservatory, and Richard sat down opposite Philippa.

'We need to talk about Lambert,' he said cautiously.

'Yes.' Philippa's voice was toneless.

'Do you . . .'

'I never want to see him again.'

Richard looked at Philippa for a long time, then glanced at Gillian.

'Right,' he said. 'Well, as long as you're sure about that.'

'I want a divorce,' said Philippa. 'Everything between Lambert and me is over.' She spooned chicken soup into her mouth. 'This is good.'

'Real chicken stock,' said Gillian. 'Don't tell me they use that in those handy cardboard cartons.'

'And you're sure you won't change your mind?' persisted Richard.

'Yes,' said Philippa calmly. 'I'm quite sure.' She felt liberated; as though she were shedding a pile of unwanted clutter. Her mind felt clean and fresh; her life was free; she could begin again.

* * *

Later that day Lambert arrived by taxi at The Maples, holding a bunch of pink carnations. Richard met him at the front door and led him into the drawing room.

'Philippa's resting upstairs,' he said. 'She doesn't want to see you.'

'That's a shame,' said Lambert. 'I brought these for her.' He put the flowers on a side table, sat down on the sofa and began to polish the face of his watch with his sleeve. 'I expect she's still a bit upset,' he added.

'She is more than a bit upset,' said Richard, trying to keep his voice steady. 'I should tell you straight away that she will be filing for divorce.'

'Divorce?' Without looking up, Lambert ran an unsteady hand through his hair. 'You're joking, aren't you?'

'I'm not joking,' said Richard. 'This is not a subject for jokes.'

Lambert raised his eyes and was taken aback at Richard's tight mouth, the hostility in his gaze. Well Lambert, he thought, you've fucked this one up, haven't you? What are you going to do now? He thought for a moment, then abruptly stood up.

'Richard, I'd like to apologize,' he said, looking at Richard as sincerely as he could. 'I don't know what came over me yesterday. Too much to drink, probably.' He risked a little smile. 'I never meant to abuse your trust, sir.'

'Lambert,' began Richard wearily.

'Philippa's a very highly strung girl,' continued Lambert. 'We've had rows before, but they've always blown over. And I'm sure this will too, if you give us a chance . . .'

'You had your chance!' spat Richard. 'You had your chance, when you stood up in church and vowed to love and cherish my daughter!' His voice increased in volume. 'Did you love her? Did you cherish her? Or did you always see her simply as a source of wealth?'

He broke off, breathing hard, and Lambert stared at him in slight panic, weighing up responses in his mind. Would Richard believe him if he declared undying love for Philippa?

'I'll be honest with you, Richard,' he said at last. 'I'm only human. And man cannot live on bread alone.'

'How dare you quote the Bible at me!' shouted Richard. 'How dare you use my daughter!'

'I didn't use her!' exclaimed Lambert. 'We've had a very happy marriage!'

'You've degraded her, you've exploited her, you've turned her from a happy girl into an emotional wreck.'

'For Christ's sake, she was always an emotional wreck!' snapped Lambert, feeling a sudden sense of injustice. 'Philippa was fucked up well before I knew her! So don't lay that on me, too.'

For a moment, Richard gazed speechlessly at him, then suddenly he turned away.

'I never want to see you again,' he said quietly. 'Your employment is hereby terminated under the terms of your contract.'

'What terms?'

'Gross misconduct,' said Richard coolly. 'Abuse of trust and forgery.'

'I'll fight it!'

'If you fight, you will certainly lose; however, it's your choice. As regards the divorce,' continued Richard, 'you will be hearing from Philippa's lawyer in due course.' He paused. 'And as for the money . . .'

There was a moment of stillness; Lambert found himself leaning forward slightly, filled with sudden hope.

'I will reimburse your debt by a total of two hundred and fifty thousand pounds. No more than that. In return, you will give me a signed guarantee that you will not attempt to make contact with Philippa except through your lawyer, and you will consider the sum to be a full and final divorce settlement.'

'Two hundred and fifty?' said Lambert. 'What about the rest of my overdraft?'

'The rest of your overdraft, Lambert,' said Richard, in a voice that shook slightly, 'is your problem.'

'Two-seventy-five,' said Lambert.

'Two hundred and fifty. Absolutely no more.'

There was a long pause.

'All right,' said Lambert eventually. 'All right, I'll take it. It's a deal.' He held out his hand, then, as Richard made no attempt to take it, dropped it again. He looked with unwilling admiration at Richard. 'You're a tough man, aren't you?'

'I asked your taxi to wait in the drive,' replied Richard. He looked at his watch. 'There's a train at three.' He felt in his pocket. 'Here's the money for your ticket.' He handed an envelope to Lambert, who hesitated, shrugged, then took it.

They walked in silence to the front door.

'I also suggest,' said Richard, opening the door, 'that you resign your membership of Greyworth. Before you find yourself asked to leave.'

'You're setting out to ruin my life!' said Lambert angrily. 'I'll be a broken man!'

'I doubt it,' said Richard. 'People like you are never broken. It's others who are broken. Those who have the misfortune to come in contact with you; those who take you into their lives; who are foolish enough to trust you.'

Lambert looked at him silently for a minute, then got

into the taxi and leaned back. The taxi driver started the engine.

'Tell me,' said Richard suddenly. 'Did you ever really care for Philippa? Or was it all a sham?' Lambert screwed up his face thoughtfully.

'Sometimes I quite fancied her,' he said. 'If she dolled herself up a bit.'

'I see,' said Richard. He took a deep breath. 'Please leave. Immediately.'

He watched as the taxi swung round to the entrance of the drive and disappeared.

'Has he gone, then?' Richard turned, to see Gillian standing at the front door. 'I heard you talking to him,' she continued. 'For what it's worth, I thought you were marvellous.'

'Hardly marvellous,' said Richard. He rubbed his face wearily. 'You know, he wasn't even sorry for the way he'd behaved.'

'There's no point expecting people like that to be sorry,' said Gillian surprisingly. 'You just have to get them out of your life as quickly as you can and forget about them. You mustn't brood.'

'I'm sure you're right,' said Richard. 'But at the moment I can't help brooding. I feel very bitter.' He shook his head soberly, and walked slowly back towards the house. 'How is Philippa?'

'Oh, fine,' said Gillian, taking a few steps forward to meet him. 'She's going to be fine.' She put a hand on his arm and for a few moments they were both silent.

'I miss Fleur,' said Richard. 'I miss Fleur.' He sighed. 'She only left this morning, and already I miss her.'

'So do I,' said Gillian. She squeezed his arm comfortingly. 'But she'll be back soon. Perhaps she'll phone tonight.'

'She won't phone,' said Richard. He swallowed. 'I asked Fleur to marry me last night. That's why she went to London. She wanted to think about it.'

'I see,' said Gillian.

'Now I wish I hadn't said anything,' said Richard. He raised his head. 'Gillian, what if she says no?'

'She won't say no,' said Gillian. 'I'm sure she won't say no.'

'But she might do!'

'And she might say yes,' said Gillian. 'Think about that instead. She might say yes.'

Later on that evening, when Philippa had gone to bed, and the two of them were sitting with their coffee in the drawing room, Gillian suddenly said to Richard,

'Don't put Fleur on a pedestal.'

'What?' Richard looked up at Gillian in amazement, and she blushed.

'I'm sorry,' she said. 'I shouldn't say things like that to you.'

'Nonsense,' said Richard. 'You can say whatever you like to me.' He wrinkled his brow in thought. 'But I'm not sure what you mean.'

'It doesn't matter,' said Gillian.

'It does! Gillian, we've known each other long enough to be honest.' He leaned forward and looked at her seriously. 'Tell me what you think. What do you mean by a pedestal?'

'You thought Emily was perfect,' said Gillian bluntly. 'Now you think Fleur's perfect.' Richard laughed.

'I don't think Fleur's perfect! I think . . .' He hesitated, and coloured slightly.

'You do!' said Gillian. 'You think she's perfect! But nobody's perfect.' She thought for a second. 'One day you'll discover something about Fleur that you didn't know. Or that you hadn't noticed. Just like you did with Emily.' She bit her lip. 'And it may not be a good thing. But that doesn't mean Fleur isn't a good person.' Richard stared at her.

'Gillian, is there something you're trying to tell me? Something about Fleur?'

'No!' said Gillian. 'Don't be silly.' She gazed earnestly at Richard. 'It's just that I don't want to see you disappointed again. And if you start off with realistic expectations then maybe—' She cleared her throat awkwardly. 'Maybe you've got a better chance of happiness.'

'You're saying I'm an idealist,' said Richard slowly.

'Well, yes. I suppose I am.' Gillian frowned with embarrassment. 'But then, what do I know about it?' She put her coffee cup down with a clatter and stood up. 'It's been a long day.'

'You're right,' exclaimed Richard suddenly. 'Gillian, you understand me completely.'

'I've known you a long time,' said Gillian.

'But we've never spoken to each other like this before! You've never given me advice before!'

'I didn't feel it was appropriate,' said Gillian, flushing. Richard gazed at her as she made her way to the door.

'I wish you had.'

'Things were different then. Everything was different.'

'Before Fleur.' Gillian nodded, smiling slightly.

'Exactly.'

By Friday, Fleur still had not telephoned. Gillian and Richard paced the house like two nervous dogs while outside the sky hung above them in a grey, humid mass. Mid-morning it began to rain; a few minutes later the white Jeep pulled up in the drive, discharging Antony and Zara in a flurry of shrieks and giggles.

'Tell us all about it!' exclaimed Richard, longing for a diversion from his thoughts. 'Did you have a good time?'

'Excellent,' said Zara. 'Even though Xanthe Forrester has approximately one brain cell.'

'We went on this walk,' said Antony, 'and got completely lost . . .' He caught Zara's eye and they both dissolved into giggles.

'And we drank cider,' said Zara, when she'd recovered herself.

'You drank cider,' retorted Antony. 'The rest of us drank beer.' He began to laugh again. 'Zara, do your Cornish accent!'

'I can't.'

'Yes you can!'

'I don't have context,' said Zara. 'I need context.'

Richard met Gillian's eye.

'Well, it all sounds lovely,' he said. 'I think I'll be having a chat with Mrs Forrester a bit later on.'

'Where's Fleur?' said Zara, dropping her bag to the floor with a thump.

'Gone to London for a few days,' said Richard lightly. 'But she should be back tomorrow.'

'London?' said Zara sharply. 'What's she doing in London?'

'Oh, nothing much. I'm not really sure, to be honest.'

'She didn't tell you?'

'Not in so many words.' Richard smiled at her. 'Now, how about some hot chocolate.'

'OK,' said Zara distractedly. 'Just let me have a look at something.'

Without looking back, she hurried up the stairs, along the corridor and into Fleur's room. There she paused, took a deep breath and, with a thudding heart, pulled opened the wardrobe doors.

All Fleur's black suits were gone.

'Oh no,' said Zara aloud. 'Oh no, please.' A pain hit her in the chest like a hammer blow. 'Please, no.' Her legs began to shake, and she sank down onto the floor.

'No, please,' she muttered, burying her head in her hands. 'Please don't. Please don't. Not this time. Fleur, please don't. Please.'

By supper, the tension in the house had risen to screaming pitch. Zara sat staring at her plate, eating nothing; Richard tried to hide his nerves with a series of jokes at which nobody laughed; Gillian clattered plates briskly and snapped at Antony when he dropped a spoon on the floor. Philippa ate three mouthfuls, then announced she would finish the rest in her room.

Afterwards, the others sat in the drawing room, watching a film on television which they had all seen before. When it finished, no-one spoke; no-one made a move for bed. The next programme began, and everyone's eyes remained transfixed by the screen. We don't want to leave each other, thought Zara. We don't want to go to bed; we don't want to be on our own. When Antony yawned, and began to shift his legs in his chair, she felt a throb of panic.

'I'm off to bed,' he said eventually. 'Good night everyone.'

'Me too,' said Zara, and followed him out of the room.

On the stairs, she pulled him close.

'Let me sleep in your bed tonight,' she whispered.

'What, swap?' said Antony, puzzled.

'No,' said Zara fiercely. 'With you. I just want . . .' She swallowed. 'I just don't want to be on my own, all right?'

'Well, OK,' said Antony slowly. 'OK!' His eyes began to gleam. 'But what if someone finds out?'

'Don't worry,' said Zara. 'No-one'll come near us.'

Chapter Nineteen

'Zara! Zara!' A voice kept hissing in Zara's ear, kept hissing and hissing. Eventually she thought she might tell it to go away and pester someone else. She rubbed her eyes sleepily, opened them, and gasped.

'You may well gasp!' Fleur was standing next to the bed, dressed smartly in a red suit which Zara didn't recognize, looking down at her with a mixture of triumph and anger on her face. 'Just what do you think you're doing?'

Zara gaped at her through the dim light of the curtained room. Suddenly she became aware that she was lying in bed next to Antony; that his bare arm was lying across her chest.

'It's not what it looks like, OK?' she said quickly.

'Darling, you're in bed with a fifteen-year-old boy. Don't start pretending you stumbled into it by mistake.'

'It wasn't by mistake! But it wasn't, I mean, he wasn't . . .'

'I haven't got time for this,' interrupted Fleur. 'Get up, and get dressed. We're going.' Zara stared blankly at her, and an ominous pounding began in her chest.

'What do you mean, going?' she faltered.

'Leaving, darling. There's a car waiting for us downstairs. I met a very nice man this week. He's called Ernest. We're going to join him at his villa.'

'We can't leave,' interrupted Zara. 'I won't!'

'Don't be silly, Zara.' A note of impatience crept into Fleur's voice. 'We are leaving, and that's final.'

'I'll scream!' said Zara. 'I'll wake everyone up!'

'And they'll all come running,' said Fleur. 'And then they'll discover exactly what you and young Master Favour have been up to. How will that look to his father?'

'We weren't up to anything!' hissed Zara. 'We weren't *sleeping* together! We were just . . . sleeping together.'

'I find that very hard to believe,' said Fleur. 'Now, get up!'

The duvet heaved, and Antony's head appeared from beneath it. He peered blearily at Fleur and as he saw who it was his cheeks turned white.

'Fleur!' he faltered. 'Oh my God! I'm sorry! We didn't mean . . .' He glanced fearfully at Zara, then back at Fleur. 'Honestly . . .'

'Ssh,' said Fleur. 'You don't want your father coming in here, do you?'

'Don't tell Dad,' begged Antony. 'He won't understand.'

'Well, if you don't want your father to find out about this, I suggest you keep very quiet,' said Fleur. She looked at Zara. 'And I suggest you come with me right away.'

'I'm not leaving,' said Zara desperately.

'You'd better go,' said Antony worriedly. 'Any minute now, Dad's going to hear something and come in.'

'Sensible boy,' said Fleur. 'Come on, Zara.'

'See you later,' said Antony, snuggling back down into his duvet.

'See you later,' whispered Zara. She touched his head gently. 'See you . . .' But tears had begun to pour down her cheeks, and she couldn't continue.

The car was waiting discreetly around the corner from The Maples. It was a large navy blue Rolls-Royce, with leather seats and a uniformed driver who leapt out as soon as he saw Fleur and Zara approaching and opened the door.

'I can't go,' said Zara, stopping. 'I can't leave. I want to live here.'

'No you don't,' said Fleur.

'I do! It's lovely here! And I love Richard, and Gillian, and Antony . . .'

'We'll soon we'll be in a villa in the Algarve,' snapped Fleur. 'Doing terribly exciting things; meeting interesting people. And the life we led here will seem very dull.'

'It won't!' Zara kicked the side of the Rolls-Royce, and the driver flinched minutely.

'Don't do that!' Fleur pushed Zara angrily into the car. 'Sit down and behave yourself.'

'Why do we have to go? Give me one reason!'

'You know exactly what the reasons are, darling.'

'Give me one!' shouted Zara, and she stared at Fleur, waiting for a confrontation; for a slap, even. But Fleur was staring out of the car window and her face was trembling slightly, and she didn't seem to have a reply.

By eight o'clock, they had looked everywhere.

'I've checked the garden,' said Gillian, coming into the kitchen. 'No sign of her there.' She glanced again at Antony. 'You're sure she didn't say anything to you?'

'Nothing,' muttered Antony, without meeting her eye. 'I don't know what's happened. I haven't seen her since last night.'

'So unlike Zara,' said Richard. He frowned. 'Ah well, I expect she'll turn up.'

'You don't think we should call the police?' said Gillian.

'I think that's overdoing it,' said Richard. 'After all, it's only eight in the morning. She might have gone for an early morning walk. She'll probably arrive home any moment. Eh, Antony?'

'Yeah,' said Antony, and looked away.

Half an hour later, Gillian came running into the kitchen.

'There's a car coming into the drive!' she said. 'Perhaps it's someone with Zara!'

'There,' said Richard, smiling at her. 'I knew we were panicking over nothing.' He got up. 'Antony, why don't you make some fresh coffee? And have some breakfast! You look as though you hardly slept last night.'

'I did sleep,' said Antony at once. 'I slept really well, actually.'

'Good,' said Richard, giving him a curious look. 'Well, you make the coffee, and I'll go and see if this is Zara.'

'It's not Zara,' said Gillian, coming back into the kitchen. 'It's Fleur's friend, Johnny. And a strange man.'

'Richard loves you,' said Zara accusingly. 'You know he does.' Fleur said nothing. They had stopped at the first small town they reached, and were now waiting in the car outside the bank until it opened. In Fleur's hand, ready for use, was Richard's Gold Card.

'He wants to marry you,' persisted Zara. 'You could be really happy with him.'

'Darling, you say that every time.'

'This time it's true! This time it's different!' Zara frowned. 'You're different. Fleur, you've changed.'

'Nonsense,' said Fleur tartly.

'Johnny thinks so too. He said he thought you were ready to settle down.'

'Settle down!' mocked Fleur. 'Settle down and become a wife! Be "comfortable".'

'What's wrong with comfortable?' cried Zara. 'It's better than uncomfortable, isn't it? You liked it there! I could tell!' She peered at her mother. 'Fleur, why are we leaving?'

'Oh, darling.' Fleur turned round, and to her shock, Zara saw that her eyes were glistening slightly. 'I couldn't become a boring little Surrey woman, could I?'

'You wouldn't be a boring little Surrey woman! You'd be yourself!'

'Myself! What's that?'

'I don't know,' said Zara helplessly. 'It's whatever Richard thinks you are.'

Fleur snorted.

'Richard thinks I'm a devoted loving creature who doesn't give a fig about money.' Her hands clenched tightly around his Gold Card. 'If I married him, darling, I'd end up divorcing him.'

'Maybe you wouldn't!'

'I would, poppet. I wouldn't be able to help myself.' Fleur examined her nails. 'I know myself pretty well,' she said. 'And Richard deserves better than me.'

'He doesn't want better!' said Zara. 'He wants you!'

'You know nothing about it,' said Fleur sharply, and she turned towards the window. 'Come on,' she murmured to herself. 'Let's just get the money and get a move on.'

Hal Winters was a tall, narrow-shouldered man with a suntanned face and metal-framed spectacles. He sat next to Johnny at the kitchen table drinking coffee in great gulps, while Richard, Gillian and Antony stared at him in silence.

'Forgive us,' said Richard at last. 'This has been a bit of a shock. First Zara going missing and now . . .'

'I can understand you folks being a bit surprised,' said Hal Winters. He spoke slowly, with a rich Midwestern accent which made Antony grin in delight. 'Fleur telling you I was dead, and all.'

'Actually, now I think about it, I'm not sure she said exactly that,' said Richard, frowning. 'Did she?'

'Some sort of misunderstanding, obviously,' said Gillian briskly. 'What a shame she isn't here.'

'Hear, hear,' said Johnny, giving Richard a beady look. 'And Zara missing, too. What a strange coincidence.'

'Zara was here last night,' said Richard, wrinkling his brow. 'I've no idea what can have happened.'

'I fly back out to the States this afternoon,' said Hal Winters. He looked miserably from one face to the other. 'If I've missed my little girl . . .'

'I'm sure she'll be here soon,' said Gillian.

'My wife, Beth-Ann, was asking me last night about it,' said Hal Winters disconsolately. He rubbed his face. 'When I first told her I'd had—' He hesitated. 'Well, when I told her there might be another child – she was real upset with me. Just about cried her eyes out. But, you know, she came round to the idea. Now she's all for me bringing Zara home to meet the family. But I can't bring her with me if she isn't here, now can I?'

There was a pause.

'More coffee?' said Richard desperately.

'I guess that would be nice,' said Hal Winters.

'I'll go and phone the police,' said Gillian. 'I think we've waited long enough.'

*   *   *

'At last!' said Fleur. She sat up, and the fabric of her jacket rustled against the soft leather of the seat. 'Look! The bank's opening its doors.'

'So how much are you going to take?' said Zara, unwrapping a piece of gum.

'I haven't quite decided,' said Fleur.

'Ten thousand? Twenty thousand?'

'I don't know!' said Fleur impatiently.

'You could be happy with Richard,' cried Zara. 'But you trade all that for, like, twenty crappy thousand dollars.'

'Pounds.'

'Jesus,' said Zara. 'Like it matters! Like it means anything! It just goes into the bank and sits there. I mean, you do all this, just so every month you can look at a bunch of numbers and feel safe.'

'Money is safety, darling.'

'People are safety!' said Zara. 'Money gets spent! But people stick around.'

'No they don't,' said Fleur scornfully. 'People don't stick around.'

'They do!' said Zara. 'It's only you that doesn't stick around! You never give anyone a chance!'

'Darling, you're a child; you don't know what you're talking about,' said Fleur. Her voice shook slightly, and she flicked the Gold Card against her red-lacquered nails.

'OK, so I'm a kid,' said Zara. 'So I don't have a point of view.' She looked out of the window. 'The bank's open. So, go on then. Get the money. Throw Richard into the trash. Throw away the nicest man in the world.' She pressed an electronic button, and the window slowly purred downwards. 'Go on!' she yelled. 'Hurry up, what are you waiting for? Go and ruin his life! Ruin all our lives!'

'Shut up!' shouted Fleur. 'Just shut up! I need to think.' She lifted a shaking hand and pressed it to her brow. 'I just need to think!'

'So, Hal,' said Gillian politely. 'You work in pharmaceuticals?'

'Pain relief's my game,' said Hal Winters, brightening slightly. 'I represent a company which manufactures a high-quality analgesic in pill form, currently the number two seller in the United States.'

'Goodness,' said Gillian.

'Do you suffer from headaches at all, ma'am?'

'Well,' said Gillian. 'I suppose I do occasionally.' Hal Winters felt in his pocket and produced a small, unmarked blister pack of tablets.

'You won't find a more effective product than this,' he said. 'See, what it does, it gets to the *root* of the pain. The *core* of the pain, if you will.' He closed his eyes and gestured to the back of his neck. 'A tension headache generally starts right here,' he said. 'And then it spreads.' He opened his eyes. 'Well, what you want to do is catch it before it starts spreading. And that's what this little beauty does.'

'I see,' said Gillian faintly.

'Hal, every time you tell me about headaches, I feel one coming on,' complained Johnny. 'Is that how you manage to sell so many of your pills?'

'I've spoken to the police,' said Richard, coming into the kitchen. 'I can't say they were very helpful.'

'Dad,' said Antony quietly. 'Dad, I need to talk to you.'

'What is it?'

'Not here,' said Antony. He swallowed. 'Let's go outside.'

They walked through the hall, out of the front door

– left open, in case Zara had lost her key – and into the drive. It had rained overnight; the air was fresh and damp. Antony headed for a wooden bench which was out of earshot of the house. He wiped it clean and sat down on it.

'So,' said Richard, sitting down beside him and giving Antony a curious look. 'What's this all about?'

'It's about Zara,' said Antony.

'Antony! Do you know where she is?'

'No!' said Antony. 'I've no idea! But . . .' He reddened. 'Something happened this morning.'

'This morning?'

'Well, last night, really.'

'Antony, I don't like the sound of this.'

'It's nothing bad!' said Antony. 'Well, not really. It just sounds a bit bad.' He took a deep breath. 'Zara was lonely last night. She wanted to sleep with me. I mean, just . . . you know. Share my bed. For company.'

He gazed pleadingly at Richard, who exhaled sharply.

'I see,' he said quietly. 'Well, now this all begins to make more sense.'

'We didn't do anything! Honest! You must believe me! But Fleur . . .' Richard glanced up sharply.

'Fleur?'

'She found us. In bed together. She was . . .' Antony licked his lips nervously. 'She was pretty mad.'

'Fleur was here?'

'It was really early this morning. She came in, and saw us, and just dragged Zara away.'

'I bet she did!' exclaimed Richard angrily. 'Antony, how could you?'

'I didn't do anything!'

'Have you no judgement whatsoever?'

'I didn't think . . . I didn't realize . . .' Antony gazed

at his father. 'Dad, I'm so sorry.' His voice cracked. 'Honestly, we weren't . . . it wasn't . . .' Richard relented.

'I believe you,' he said. 'But you must understand how it will have looked to Fleur. She left her daughter in our charge. She trusted us.' He rested his head in his hands. 'I'm surprised she didn't come to me,' he said slowly.

'She just kind of dashed off,' said Antony. He bit his lip. 'Do you think she'll come back?'

'I don't know,' said Richard. He swallowed. 'I very much want to think she will. But she may decide . . . she may have decided . . .' He broke off, unable to continue.

'It's all my fault if she doesn't!' cried Antony. 'Fleur won't come back, and Zara won't meet her dad! God, I've ruined everything!'

'No you haven't,' said Richard. 'Don't be silly. There's a lot more to this than you know about.'

For a while the two of them sat in silence, each wrapped up in his own thoughts.

'You really loved Fleur, didn't you,' said Antony suddenly.

'Yes,' said Richard. 'I did.' He looked hard at Antony. 'I still do.'

'Where do you think she's gone?'

'I've no idea.' Richard stretched his legs out, then abruptly stood up. 'We must go and tell Mr Winters about this.'

'Dad! I can't!'

'You're going to have to. It's not fair on him.' Richard looked sternly at Antony. 'He seems a very decent and honourable man, and we owe him the truth.'

'But he'll kill me!'

'That I doubt.' A smile came to Richard's lips, in

spite of himself. 'We don't live in the age of the shot-gun wedding any more, you know.'

'Shotgun wedding?' Antony stared at him, aghast. 'But we didn't even . . .'

'I know you didn't. I'm joking!' Richard shook his head. 'You youngsters grow up too quickly,' he said. 'It may be fun, to drink and smoke and sleep in each other's beds. But these things bring their problems too, you know.' Antony shrugged awkwardly. 'I mean, look at you,' continued Richard. 'You're only fifteen. And Zara's only just fourteen!' Antony looked up.

'Actually Dad,' he said, 'there's something else I should tell you. About Zara's age. And about . . . other things.'

'What about Zara's age?'

'About her birthday. Remember? The birthday she had a few weeks ago.'

'Of course I remember!' said Richard impatiently. 'What about it?'

'Well,' said Antony, shuffling his feet awkwardly. 'It's a bit difficult to explain. The thing is . . .'

'Hang on,' said Richard suddenly. 'What's . . .' His voice was incredulous. 'What's that?'

Creeping down the drive, like something out of a dream, was a huge, shiny, navy blue Rolls-Royce. It purred to a halt outside the house, and then stopped.

Slowly, glancing at one another uncertainly, Richard and Antony began to approach it.

'Have they got the right house?' said Antony. 'Do you think it's a movie star?' Richard said nothing. His mouth was taut, his neck rigid with hope and nerves.

From the front seat appeared a uniformed driver. Ignoring Richard and Antony, he walked round the car to the passenger door nearest the house, and opened it.

'Look!' said Antony, giving a squeak of excitement. 'They're getting out!'

A leg appeared. A long, pale leg, followed by a red-sleeved arm.

'It's . . .' Antony glanced at his father. 'I don't believe it!'

'Fleur,' said Richard in as calm a voice as he could muster.

She turned at the sound of his voice, hesitated, then took a few steps forward and looked at him, her mouth trembling slightly. For a moment neither said anything.

'I came back, you see,' said Fleur eventually, in a quivering voice.

'Yes, I see,' said Richard. 'You came back. Have you . . .' He glanced at the Rolls-Royce. 'Have you an answer for me?'

'Yes, I have.' Fleur lifted her chin. 'Richard, I'm not going to marry you.'

A dart of pain ran through Richard's chest; dimly he heard Antony's disappointed gasp.

'I see,' he heard himself saying. 'Well, it's very good of you to let me know.'

'I won't marry you,' said Fleur fiercely. 'But I'll . . . I'll stick around for a bit.' Her eyes suddenly glistened. 'I'll stick around, if you'll let me.'

Richard stared at her speechlessly. Slowly the pain in his chest ebbed away; slowly the tension of the last week began to disappear. A cautious, hopeful happiness began to rise through his body.

'I'd like that,' he managed. 'I'd like you to stick around.'

He took a few steps forward, until he was near enough to grasp Fleur's hands, to bring them up to his face and rub his cheeks against her pale, soft skin. 'I thought you'd gone!' he said. Suddenly he felt close to tears; almost angry. 'I really thought you'd gone for good!' Fleur looked at him honestly.

'I nearly did,' she said.

'So what happened? Why did you decide—'

'Richard, don't ask,' interrupted Fleur. She lifted a finger and placed it on his lips. 'Don't ask questions unless you're sure you want to know the answer. Because the answer . . .' Her eyelashes fluttered and she looked away. 'The answer may not be what you want to hear.'

Richard gazed at her face for a few moments.

'Gillian said something very similar to me,' he said at last.

'Gillian,' said Fleur, 'is a wise woman.'

'Where's Zara?' said Antony, bored with obscure adult talk. He looked around. 'Zara?'

'Zara, sweetie,' said Fleur impatiently. 'Get out of the car.'

Slowly, cautiously, Zara climbed out of the Rolls-Royce. She stood still for a moment like a hostile cat, looking around as though suddenly unsure of her surroundings. Antony was reminded of the first time he'd seen her.

'OK,' she said, catching his eye. 'Well, we're back.' She scuffed her foot on the ground. 'You know. If you want us.'

'Of course we want you!' said Antony. 'Don't we, Dad?'

'Of course we do,' said Richard.

He gently let go of Fleur's hands and went over to Zara.

'Come on, Zara,' he said kindly. 'There's someone inside who very much wants to meet you.'

'Who?' said Fleur at once.

'I think you know who, Fleur,' said Richard, looking straight at her.

For a moment they gazed challengingly at each other. Then, as if in acquiescence, Fleur gave a tiny shrug. Richard nodded, a satisfied expression on his face, and turned back to Zara.

'Come on,' he said. 'Come on little Zara. We've had our turn. It's your turn now.' And putting his arm tenderly round Zara's narrow, bony shoulders, he led her slowly into the house.

THE END